The Golden Ball
and Other Stories

Center Point
Large Print

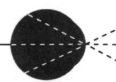

**This Large Print Book carries the
Seal of Approval of N.A.V.H.**

Agatha Christie

The
Golden Ball
and Other Stories

CENTER POINT LARGE PRINT
THORNDIKE, MAINE

The text of this Large Print edition is unabridged. In other aspects, this book may vary from the original edition. Printed in the United States of America on permanent paper. Set in 16-point Times New Roman type.

ISBN: 978-1-62899-159-8

Library of Congress Cataloging-in-Publication Data

Christie, Agatha, 1890–1976.
[Short stories. Selections]
The Golden Ball and other stories / Agatha Christie. — Center Point large print edition.
pages cm
Summary: A collection of short stories where the answers are as unexpected as they are satisfying—Provided by publisher.
ISBN 978-1-62899-159-8 (library binding : alk. paper)
1. Detective and mystery stories, English. 2. Large type books. I. Title.
PR6005.H66G64 2014
823′.914—dc23
                                                    2014015598

Contents

The Golden Ball
and Other Stories

One

THE LISTERDALE MYSTERY

*"The Listerdale Mystery" was first
published as "The Benevolent Butler" in
Grand Magazine, December 1925.*

• • •

Mrs. St. Vincent was adding up figures. Once or twice she sighed, and her hand stole to her aching forehead. She had always disliked arithmetic. It was unfortunate that nowadays her life should seem to be composed entirely of one particular kind of sum, the ceaseless adding together of small necessary items of expenditure making a total that never failed to surprise and alarm her.

Surely it couldn't come to *that!* She went back over the figures. She had made a trifling error in the pence, but otherwise the figures were correct.

Mrs. St. Vincent sighed again. Her headache by now was very bad indeed. She looked up as the door opened and her daughter Barbara came into the room. Barbara St. Vincent was a very pretty girl, she had her mother's delicate features, and the same proud turn of the head, but her eyes were dark instead of blue, and she had a different mouth, a sulky red mouth not without attraction.

"Oh! Mother," she cried. "Still juggling with those horrid old accounts? Throw them all into the fire."

"We must know where we are," said Mrs. St. Vincent uncertainly.

The girl shrugged her shoulders.

"We're always in the same boat," she said drily. "Damned hard up. Down to the last penny as usual."

Mrs. St. Vincent sighed.

"I wish—" she began, and then stopped.

"I must find something to do," said Barbara in hard tones. "And find it quickly. After all, I have taken that shorthand and typing course. So have about one million other girls from all I can see! 'What experience?' 'None, but—' 'Oh! thank you, good morning. We'll let you know.' But they never do! I must find some other kind of a job— *any* job."

"Not yet, dear," pleaded her mother. "Wait a little longer."

Barbara went to the window and stood looking out with unseeing eyes that took no note of the dingy line of houses opposite.

"Sometimes," she said slowly, "I'm sorry Cousin Amy took me with her to Egypt last winter. Oh! I know I had fun—about the only fun I've ever had or am likely to have in my life. I *did* enjoy myself—enjoyed myself thoroughly. But it was very unsettling. I mean—coming back to *this*."

She swept a hand round the room. Mrs. St. Vincent followed it with her eyes and winced. The room was typical of cheap furnished lodgings. A dusty aspidistra, showily ornamental furniture, a gaudy wallpaper faded in patches. There were signs that the personality of the tenants had struggled with that of the landlady; one or two pieces of good china, much cracked and mended, so that their saleable value was *nil,* a piece of embroidery thrown over the back of the sofa, a water colour sketch of a young girl in the fashion of twenty years ago; near enough still to Mrs. St. Vincent not to be mistaken.

"It wouldn't matter," continued Barbara, "if we'd never known anything else. But to think of Ansteys—"

She broke off, not trusting herself to speak of that dearly loved home which had belonged to the St. Vincent family for centuries and which was now in the hands of strangers.

"If only father—hadn't speculated—and borrowed—"

"My dear," said Mrs. St. Vincent, "your father was never, in any sense of the word, a businessman."

She said it with a graceful kind of finality, and Barbara came over and gave her an aimless sort of kiss, as she murmured, "Poor old Mums. I won't say anything."

Mrs. St. Vincent took up her pen again, and bent

over her desk. Barbara went back to the window. Presently the girl said:

"Mother. I heard from—from Jim Masterton this morning. He wants to come over and see me."

Mrs. St. Vincent laid down her pen and looked up sharply.

"Here?" she exclaimed.

"Well, we can't ask him to dinner at the Ritz very well," sneered Barbara.

Her mother looked unhappy. Again she looked round the room with innate distaste.

"You're right," said Barbara. "It's a disgusting place. Genteel poverty! Sounds all right—a white-washed cottage, in the country, shabby chintzes of good design, bowls of roses, crown Derby tea service that you wash up yourself. That's what it's like in books. In real life, with a son starting on the bottom rung of office life, it means London. Frowsy landladies, dirty children on the stairs, fellow lodgers who always seem to be half-castes, haddocks for breakfasts that aren't quite—quite and so on."

"If only—" began Mrs. St. Vincent. "But, really, I'm beginning to be afraid we can't afford even this room much longer."

"That means a bed-sitting room horror! for you and me," said Barbara. "And a cupboard under the tiles for Rupert. And when Jim comes to call, I'll receive him in that dreadful room

12

downstairs with tabbies all round the walls knitting, and staring at us, and coughing that dreadful kind of gulping cough they have!"

There was a pause.

"Barbara," said Mrs. St. Vincent at last. "Do you—I mean—would you—?"

She stopped, flushing a little.

"You needn't be delicate, Mother," said Barbara. "Nobody is nowadays. Marry Jim, I suppose you mean? I would like a shot if he asked me. But I'm so awfully afraid he won't."

"Oh, Barbara, dear."

"Well, it's one thing seeing me out there with Cousin Amy, moving (as they say in novelettes) in the best society. He *did* take a fancy to me. Now he'll come here and see me in *this!* And he's a funny creature, you know, fastidious and old-fashioned. I—I rather like him for that. It reminds me of Ansteys and the village—everything a hundred years behind the times, but so—so—oh! I don't know—so fragrant. Like lavender!"

She laughed, half-ashamed of her eagerness. Mrs. St. Vincent spoke with a kind of earnest simplicity.

"I should like you to marry Jim Masterton," she said. "He is—one of us. He is very well off, also, but that I don't mind about so much."

"I do," said Barbara. "I'm sick of being hard up."

"But, Barbara, it isn't—"

"Only for that? No. I do really. I—oh! Mother, can't you *see* I do?"

Mrs. St. Vincent looked very unhappy.

"I wish he could see you in your proper setting, darling," she said wistfully.

"Oh, well!" said Barbara. "Why worry? We might as well try and be cheerful about things. Sorry I've had such a grouch. Cheer up, darling."

She bent over her mother, kissed her forehead lightly, and went out. Mrs. St. Vincent, relinquishing all attempts at finance, sat down on the uncomfortable sofa. Her thoughts ran round in circles like squirrels in a cage.

"One may say what one likes, appearances *do* put a man off. Not later—not if they were really engaged. He'd know then what a sweet, dear girl she is. But it's so easy for young people to take the tone of their surroundings. Rupert, now, he's quite different from what he used to be. Not that I want my children to be stuck up. That's not it a bit. But I should hate it if Rupert got engaged to that dreadful girl in the tobacconist's. I daresay she may be a very nice girl, really. But she's not our kind. It's all so difficult. Poor little Babs. If I could do anything—anything. But where's the money to come from? We've sold everything to give Rupert his start. We really can't even afford this."

To distract herself Mrs. St. Vincent picked up the *Morning Post*, and glanced down the advertise-

14

ments on the front page. Most of them she knew by heart. People who wanted capital, people who had capital and were anxious to dispose of it on note of hand alone, people who wanted to buy teeth (she always wondered why), people who wanted to sell furs and gowns and who had optimistic ideas on the subject of price.

Suddenly she stiffened to attention. Again and again she read the printed words.

"To gentle people only. Small house in Westminster, exquisitely furnished, offered to those who would really care for it. Rent purely nominal. No agents."

A very ordinary advertisement. She had read many the same or—well, nearly the same. Nominal rent, that was where the trap lay.

Yet, since she was restless and anxious to escape from her thoughts she put on her hat straight away, and took a convenient bus to the address given in the advertisement.

It proved to be that of a firm of house agents. Not a new bustling firm—a rather decrepit, old-fashioned place. Rather timidly she produced the advertisement, which she had torn out, and asked for particulars.

The white-haired old gentleman who was attending to her stroked his chin thoughtfully.

"Perfectly. Yes, perfectly, madam. That house, the house mentioned in the advertisement is No. 7 Cheviot Place. You would like an order?"

"I should like to know the rent first?" said Mrs. St. Vincent.

"Ah! the rent. The exact figure is not settled, but I can assure you that it is purely nominal."

"Ideas of what is purely nominal can vary," said Mrs. St. Vincent.

The old gentleman permitted himself to chuckle a little.

"Yes, that's an old trick—an old trick. But you can take my word for it, it isn't so in this case. Two or three guineas a week, perhaps, not more."

Mrs. St. Vincent decided to have the order. Not, of course, that there was any real likelihood of her being able to afford the place. But, after all, she might just *see* it. There must be some grave disadvantage attaching to it, to be offered at such a price.

But her heart gave a little throb as she looked up at the outside of 7 Cheviot Place. A gem of a house. Queen Anne, and in perfect condition! A butler answered the door, he had grey hair and little side whiskers, and the meditative calm of an archbishop. A kindly archbishop, Mrs. St. Vincent thought.

He accepted the order with a benevolent air.

"Certainly, madam. I will show you over. The house is ready for occupation."

He went before her, opening doors, announcing rooms.

"The drawing room, the white study, a powder closet through here, madam."

It was perfect—a dream. The furniture all of the period, each piece with signs of wear, but polished with loving care. The loose rugs were of beautiful dim old colours. In each room were bowls of fresh flowers. The back of the house looked over the Green Park. The whole place radiated an old-world charm.

The tears came into Mrs. St. Vincent's eyes, and she fought them back with difficulty. So had Ansteys looked—Ansteys. . . .

She wondered whether the butler had noticed her emotion. If so, he was too much the perfectly trained servant to show it. She liked these old servants, one felt safe with them, at ease. They were like friends.

"It is a beautiful house," she said softly. "Very beautiful. I am glad to have seen it."

"Is it for yourself alone, madam?"

"For myself and my son and daughter. But I'm afraid—"

She broke off. She wanted it so dreadfully—so dreadfully.

She felt instinctively that the butler understood. He did not look at her, as he said in a detached impersonal way:

"I happen to be aware, madam, that the owner requires above all, suitable tenants. The rent is of no importance to him. He wants the house to be tenanted by someone who will really care for and appreciate it."

"I should appreciate it," said Mrs. St. Vincent in a low voice.

She turned to go.

"Thank you for showing me over," she said courteously.

"Not at all, madam."

He stood in the doorway, very correct and upright as she walked away down the street. She thought to herself: "He knows. He's sorry for me. He's one of the old lot too. He'd like *me* to have it—not a labour member, or a button manufacturer! We're dying out, our sort, but we band together."

In the end she decided not to go back to the agents What was the good? She could afford the rent—but there were servants to be considered. There would have to be servants in a house like that.

The next morning a letter lay by her plate. It was from the house agents. It offered her the tenancy of 7 Cheviot Place for six months at two guineas a week, and went on: "You have, I presume, taken into consideration the fact that the servants are remaining at the landlord's expense? It is really a unique offer."

It was. So startled was she by it, that she read the letter out. A fire of questions followed and she described her visit of yesterday.

"Secretive little Mums!" cried Barbara. "Is it really so lovely?"

Rupert cleared his throat, and began a judicial cross-questioning.

"There's something behind all this. It's fishy if you ask me. Decidedly fishy."

"So's my egg," said Barbara wrinkling her nose. "Ugh! Why should there be something behind it? That's just like you, Rupert, always making mysteries out of nothing. It's those dreadful detective stories you're always reading."

"The rent's a joke," said Rupert. "In the city," he added importantly, "one gets wise to all sorts of queer things. I tell you, there's something very fishy about this business."

"Nonsense," said Barbara. "House belongs to a man with lots of money, he's fond of it, and he wants it lived in by decent people whilst he's away. Something of that kind. Money's probably no object to him."

"What did you say the address was?" asked Rupert of his mother.

"Seven Cheviot Place."

"Whew!" He pushed back his chair. "I say, this is exciting. That's the house Lord Listerdale disappeared from."

"Are you sure?" asked Mrs. St. Vincent doubtfully.

"Positive. He's got a lot of other houses all over London, but this is the one he lived in. He walked out of it one evening saying he was going to his club, and nobody ever saw him again. Supposed to have done a bunk to East Africa or somewhere like that, but nobody knows why. Depend upon it, he was murdered in that house. You say there's a lot of panelling?"

"Ye-es," said Mrs. St. Vincent faintly: "but—"

Rupert gave her no time. He went on with immense enthusiasm.

"Panelling! There you are. Sure to be a secret recess somewhere. Body's been stuffed in there and has been there ever since. Perhaps it was embalmed first."

"Rupert, dear, don't talk nonsense," said his mother.

"Don't be a double-dyed idiot," said Barbara. "You've been taking that peroxide blonde to the pictures too much."

Rupert rose with dignity—such dignity as his lanky and awkward age allowed, and delivered a final ultimatum.

"You take that house, Mums. *I'll* ferret out the mystery. You see if I don't."

Rupert departed hurriedly, in fear of being late at the office.

The eyes of the two women met.

"Could we, Mother?" murmured Barbara tremulously. "Oh! if we could."

"The servants," said Mrs. St. Vincent pathetically, "would *eat,* you know. I mean, of course, one would want them to—but that's the drawback. One can so easily—just do without things—when it's only oneself."

She looked piteously at Barbara, and the girl nodded.

"We must think it over," said the mother.

But in reality her mind was made up. She had seen the sparkle in the girl's eyes. She thought to herself: "Jim Masterton *must* see her in proper surroundings. This is a chance—a wonderful chance. I must take it."

She sat down and wrote to the agents accepting their offer.

"Quentin, where did the lilies come from? I really can't buy expensive flowers."

"They were sent up from King's Cheviot, madam. It has always been the custom here."

The butler withdrew. Mrs. St. Vincent heaved a sigh of relief. What would she do without Quentin? He made everything so *easy.* She thought to herself, "It's too good to last. I shall wake up soon, I know I shall, and find it's been all a dream. I'm so *happy* here—two months already, and it's passed like a flash."

Life indeed had been astonishingly pleasant. Quentin, the butler, had displayed himself the autocrat of 7 Cheviot Place. "If you will leave everything to me, madam," he had said respect-fully. "You will find it the best way."

Each week, he brought her the housekeeping books, their totals astonishingly low. There were only two other servants, a cook and a housemaid. They were pleasant in manner, and efficient in their duties, but it was Quentin who ran the house. Game and poultry appeared on the table sometimes, causing Mrs. St. Vincent solicitude. Quentin reassured her. Sent up from Lord Listerdale's country seat, King's Cheviot, or from his Yorkshire moor. "It has always been the custom, madam."

Privately Mrs. St. Vincent doubted whether the absent Lord Listerdale would agree with those words. She was inclined to suspect Quentin of usurping his master's authority. It was clear that he had taken a fancy to them, and that in his eyes nothing was too good for them.

Her curiosity aroused by Rupert's declaration, Mrs. St. Vincent had make a tentative reference to Lord Listerdale when she next interviewed the house agent. The white-haired old gentleman had responded immediately.

Yes, Lord Listerdale was in East Africa, had been there for the last eighteen months.

"Our client is rather an eccentric man," he had said, smiling broadly. "He left London in a most unconventional manner, as you may perhaps remember? Not a word to anyone. The news-papers got hold of it. There were actually inquiries on foot at Scotland Yard. Luckily news was received from Lord Listerdale himself from East Africa. He invested his cousin, Colonel Carfax, with power of attorney. It is the latter who conducts all Lord Listerdale's affairs. Yes, rather eccentric, I fear. He has always been a great traveller in the wilds—it is quite on the cards that he may not return for years to England, though he is getting on in years."

"Surely he is not so very old," said Mrs. St. Vincent, with a sudden memory of a bluff, bearded face, rather like an Elizabethan sailor, which she had once noticed in an illustrated magazine.

"Middle-aged," said the white-haired gentleman. "Fifty-three, according to Debrett."

This conversation Mrs. St. Vincent had retailed to Rupert with the intention of rebuking that young gentleman.

Rupert, however, was undismayed.

"It looks fishier than ever to me," he had declared. "Who's this Colonel Carfax? Probably comes into the title if anything happens to Listerdale. The letter from East Africa was probably forged. In three years, or whatever it is, this Carfax will presume death, and take the title. Meantime, he's got all the handling of the estate. Very fishy, I call it."

He had condescended graciously to approve the house. In his leisure moments he was inclined to tap the panelling and make elaborate measurements for the possible location of a secret room, but little by little his interest in the mystery of Lord Listerdale abated. He was also less enthusiastic on the subject of the tobacconist's daughter. Atmosphere tells.

To Barbara the house had brought great satisfaction. Jim Masterton had come home, and was a frequent visitor. He and Mrs. St. Vincent got on splendidly together, and he said something to Barbara one day that startled her.

"This house is a wonderful setting for your mother, you know."

"For *Mother?*"

"Yes. It was made for her! She belongs to it in an extraordinary way. You know there's something queer about this house altogether, something uncanny and haunting."

"Don't get like Rupert," Barbara implored him. "He is convinced that the wicked Colonel Carfax murdered Lord Listerdale and hid his body under the floor."

Masterton laughed.

"I admire Rupert's detective zeal. No, I didn't mean anything of *that* kind. But there's something in the air, some atmosphere that one doesn't quite understand."

They had been three months in Cheviot Place when Barbara came to her mother with a radiant face.

"Jim and I—we're engaged. Yes—last night. Oh, Mother! It all seems like a fairy tale come true."

"Oh, my dear! I'm so glad—so glad."

Mother and daughter clasped each other close.

"You know Jim's almost as much in love with you as he is with me," said Barbara at last, with a mischievous laugh.

Mrs. St. Vincent blushed very prettily.

"He is," persisted the girl. "You thought this house would make such a beautiful setting for me, and all the time it's really a setting for *you*. Rupert and I don't quite belong here. You do."

"Don't talk nonsense, darling."

"It's not nonsense. There's a flavour of enchanted castle about it, with you as an enchanted princess and Quentin as—as—oh! a benevolent magician."

Mrs. St. Vincent laughed and admitted the last item.

Rupert received the news of his sister's engagement very calmly.

"I thought there was something of the kind in the wind," he observed sapiently.

He and his mother were dining alone together; Barbara was out with Jim.

Quentin placed the port in front of him, and withdrew noiselessly.

"That's a rum old bird," said Rupert, nodding towards the closed door. "There's something odd about him, you know, something—"

"Not fishy?" interrupted Mrs. St. Vincent, with a faint smile.

"Why, Mother, how did you know what I was going to say?" demanded Rupert in all seriousness.

"It's rather a word of yours, darling. You think everything is fishy. I suppose you have an idea that it was Quentin who did away with Lord Listerdale and put him under the floor?"

"Behind the panelling," corrected Rupert. "You always get things a little bit wrong, Mother. No, I've inquired about that. Quentin was down at King's Cheviot at the time."

Mrs. St. Vincent smiled at him, as she rose from table and went up to the drawing room. In some ways Rupert was a long time growing up.

Yet a sudden wonder swept over her for the first time as to Lord Listerdale's reasons for leaving England so abruptly. There must be something behind it, to account for that sudden decision. She was still thinking the matter over when Quentin came in with the coffee tray, and she spoke out impulsively.

"You have been with Lord Listerdale a long time, haven't you, Quentin?"

"Yes, madam; since I was a lad of twenty-one. That was in the late Lord's time. I started as third footman."

"You must know Lord Listerdale very well. What kind of a man is he?"

The butler turned the tray a little, so that she could help herself to sugar more conveniently, as he replied in even unemotional tones:

"Lord Listerdale was a very selfish gentleman, madam: with no consideration for others."

He removed the tray and bore it from the room. Mrs. St. Vincent sat with her coffee cup in her hand, and a puzzled frown on her face. Something struck her as odd in the speech apart from the views it expressed. In another minute it flashed home to her.

Quentin had used the word *"was"* not "is." But then, he must think—must believe—She pulled herself up. She was as bad as Rupert! But a very definite uneasiness assailed her. Afterwards she dated her first suspicions from that moment.

With Barbara's happiness and future assured, she had time to think her own thoughts, and against her will, they began to centre round the mystery of Lord Listerdale. What was the real story? Whatever it was Quentin knew something about it. Those had been odd words of his—"a very selfish gentleman—no consideration for others." What lay behind them? He had spoken as a judge might speak, detachedly and impartially.

Was Quentin involved in Lord Listerdale's disappearance? Had he taken an active part in any tragedy there might have been? After all, ridiculous as Rupert's assumption had seemed at the time, that single letter with its power of attorney coming from East Africa was—well, open to suspicion.

But try as she would, she could not believe any

real evil of Quentin. Quentin, she told herself over and over again, was *good*—she used the word as simply as a child might have done. Quentin was *good*. But he knew something!

She never spoke with him again of his master. The subject was apparently forgotten. Rupert and Barbara had other things to think of, and there were no further discussions.

It was towards the end of August that her vague surmises crystallized into realities. Rupert had gone for a fortnight's holiday with a friend who had a motorcycle and trailer. It was some ten days after his departure that Mrs. St. Vincent was startled to see him rush into the room where she sat writing.

"Rupert!" she exclaimed.

"I know, Mother. You didn't expect to see me for another three days. But something's happened. Anderson—my pal, you know—didn't much care where he went, so I suggested having a look in at King's Cheviot—"

"King's Cheviot? But why—?"

"You know perfectly well, Mother, that I've always scented something fishy about things here. Well, I had a look at the old place—it's let, you know—nothing there. Not that I actually expected to find anything—I was just nosing round, so to speak."

Yes, she thought. Rupert was very like a dog at this moment. Hunting in circles for something vague and undefined, led by instinct, busy and happy.

"It was when we were passing through a village about eight or nine miles away that it happened—that I saw him, I mean."

"Saw whom?"

"Quentin—just going into a little cottage. Something fishy here, I said to myself, and we stopped the bus, and I went back. I rapped on the door and he himself opened it."

"But I don't understand. Quentin hasn't been away—"

"I'm coming to that, Mother. If you'd only listen, and not interrupt. It was Quentin, and it wasn't Quentin, if you know what I mean."

Mrs. St. Vincent clearly did not know, so he elucidated matters further.

"It was Quentin all right, but it wasn't *our* Quentin. It was the real man."

"Rupert!"

"You listen. I was taken in myself at first, and said: 'It is Quentin, isn't it?' And the old Johnny said: 'Quite right, sir, that is my name. What can I do for you?' And then I saw that it wasn't our man, though it was precious like him, voice and all. I asked a few questions, and it all came out. The old chap hadn't an idea of anything fishy being on. He'd been butler to Lord Listerdale all right, and was retired on a pension and given this cottage just about the time that Lord Listerdale was supposed to have gone off to Africa. You see where that leads us. This man's an impostor—he's playing the part of Quentin for purposes of his own. My theory is that he came up to town that evening, pretending to be the butler from King's Cheviot, got an interview with Lord Listerdale, killed him and hid his body behind the panelling. It's an old house, there's sure to be a secret recess—"

"Oh, don't let's go into all that again," interrupted Mrs. St. Vincent wildly. "I can't bear it. Why should he—that's what I want to know— why? *If* he did such a thing—which I don't believe for one minute, mind you—what was the *reason* for it all?"

"You're right," said Rupert. "Motive—that's important. Now I've made inquiries. Lord Listerdale had a lot of house property In the last two days I've discovered that practically every one of these houses of his has been let in the last eighteen months to people like ourselves for a merely nominal rent—*and with the proviso that the servants should remain.* And in every case Quentin himself—the man calling himself Quentin, I mean—has been there for part of the time as butler. That looks as though there were something—jewels, or papers—secreted in one of Lord Listerdale's houses, and the gang doesn't know which. I'm assuming a gang, but of course this fellow Quentin may be in it single-handed. There's a—"

Mrs. St. Vincent interrupted him with a certain amount of determination:

"Rupert! Do stop talking for one minute. You're making my head spin. Anyway, what you are saying is nonsense—about gangs and hidden papers."

"There's another theory," admitted Rupert. "This Quentin may be someone that Lord Listerdale has injured. The real butler told me a long story about a man called Samuel Lowe—an under-gardener he was, and about the same height and build as Quentin himself. He'd got a grudge against Listerdale—"

Mrs. St. Vincent started.

"With no consideration for others." The words came back to her mind in their passionless, measured accents. Inadequate words, but what might they not stand for?

In her absorption she hardly listened to Rupert. He made a rapid explanation of something that she did not take in, and went hurriedly from the room.

Then she woke up. Where had Rupert gone? What was he going to do? She had not caught his last words. Perhaps he was going for the police. In that case. . . .

She rose abruptly and rang the bell. With his usual promptness, Quentin answered it.

"You rang, madam?"

"Yes. Come in, please, and shut the door."

The butler obeyed, and Mrs. St. Vincent was silent a moment whilst she studied him with earnest eyes.

She thought: "He's been kind to me—nobody knows how kind. The children wouldn't understand. This wild story of Rupert's may be all nonsense—on the other hand, there may—yes, there may—be something in it. Why should one judge? One can't *know*. The rights and wrongs of it, I mean . . . And I'd stake my life—yes, I would!—on his being a good man."

Flushed and tremulous, she spoke.

"Quentin, Mr. Rupert has just got back. He has been down to King's Cheviot—to a village near there—"

She stopped, noticing the quick start he was not able to conceal.

"He has—seen someone," she went on in measured accents.

She thought to herself: "There—he's warned. At any rate, he's warned."

After that first quick start, Quentin had resumed his unruffled demeanour, but his eyes were fixed on her face, watchful and keen, with something in them she had not seen there before. They were, for the first time, the eyes of a man and not of a servant.

He hesitated for a minute, then said in a voice which also had subtly changed:

"Why do you tell me this, Mrs. St. Vincent?"

Before she could answer, the door flew open and Rupert strode into the room. With him was a dignified middle-aged man with little side whiskers and the air of a benevolent archbishop. *Quentin!*

"Here he is," said Rupert. "The real Quentin. I had him outside in the taxi. Now, Quentin, look at this man and tell me—is he Samuel Lowe?"

It was for Rupert a triumphant moment. But it was short-lived, almost at once he scented something wrong. For while the real Quentin was looking abashed and highly uncomfortable the second Quentin was smiling, a broad smile of undisguised enjoyment.

He slapped his embarrassed duplicate on the back.

"It's all right, Quentin. Got to let the cat out of the bag some time, I suppose. You can tell 'em who I am."

The dignified stranger drew himself up.

"This, sir," he announced, in a reproachful tone, "is my master, Lord Listerdale, sir."

The next minute beheld many things. First, the complete collapse of the cocksure Rupert. Before he knew what was happening, his mouth still open from the shock of the discovery, he found himself being gently manoeuvred towards the door, a friendly voice that was, and yet was not, familiar in his ear.

"It's quite all right, my boy. No bones broken.

But I want a word with your mother. Very good work of yours, to ferret me out like this."

He was outside on the landing gazing at the shut door. The real Quentin was standing by his side, a gentle stream of explanation flowing from his lips. Inside the room Lord Listerdale was confronting Mrs. St. Vincent.

"Let me explain—if I can! I've been a selfish devil all my life—the fact came home to me one day. I thought I'd try a little altruism for a change, and being a fantastic kind of fool, I started my career fantastically. I'd sent subscriptions to odd things, but I felt the need of doing something— well, something *personal.* I've been sorry always for the class that can't beg, that must suffer in silence—poor gentlefolk. I have a lot of house property. I conceived the idea of leasing these houses to people who—well, needed and appreciated them. Young couples with their way to make, widows with sons and daughters starting in the world. Quentin has been more than butler to me, he's a friend. With his consent and assistance I borrowed his personality. I've always had a talent for acting. The idea came to me on my way to the club one night, and I went straight off to talk it over with Quentin. When I found they were making a fuss about my disappearance, I arranged that a letter should come from me in East Africa. In it, I gave full instructions to my cousin, Maurice Carfax. And—well, that's the long and short of it."

He broke off rather lamely, with an appealing glance at Mrs. St. Vincent. She stood very straight, and her eyes met his steadily.

"It was a kind plan," she said. "A very unusual one, and one that does you credit. I am—most grateful. But—of course, you understand that we cannot stay?"

"I expected that," he said. "Your pride won't let you accept what you'd probably style 'charity.'"

"Isn't that what it is?" she asked steadily.

"No," he answered. "Because I ask something in exchange."

"Something?"

"Everything." His voice rang out, the voice of one accustomed to dominate.

"When I was twenty-three," he went on, "I married the girl I loved. She died a year later. Since then I have been very lonely. I have wished very much I could find a certain lady—the lady of my dreams. . . ."

"Am I that?" she asked, very low. "I am so old—so faded."

He laughed.

"Old? You are younger than either of your children. Now I am old, if you like."

But her laugh rang out in turn. A soft ripple of amusement.

"You? You are a boy still. A boy who loves to dress up."

She held out her hands and he caught them in his.

Two

The Girl in the Train

"The Girl in the Train"
was first published in *Grand Magazine*,
February 1924.

• • •

"And that's that!" observed George Rowland ruefully, as he gazed up at the imposing smoke-grimed façade of the building he had just quitted.

It might be said to represent very aptly the power of Money—and Money, in the person of William Rowland, uncle to the aforementioned George, had just spoken its mind very freely. In the course of a brief ten minutes, from being the apple of his uncle's eye, the heir to his wealth, and a young man with a promising business career in front of him, George had suddenly become one of the vast army of the unemployed.

"And in these clothes they won't even give me the dole," reflected Mr. Rowland gloomily, "and as for writing poems and selling them at the door at twopence (or 'what you care to give, lydy') I simply haven't got the brains."

It was true that George embodied a veritable triumph of the tailor's art. He was exquisitely and beautifully arrayed. Solomon and the lilies of the field were simply not in it with George. But man cannot live by clothes alone—unless he has had some considerable training in the art—and Mr. Rowland was painfully aware of the fact.

"And all because of that rotten show last night," he reflected sadly.

The rotten show last night had been a Covent Garden Ball. Mr. Rowland had returned from it at a somewhat late—or rather early—hour—as a matter of fact, he could not strictly say that he remembered returning at all. Rogers, his uncle's butler, was a helpful fellow, and could doubtless give more details on the matter. A splitting head, a cup of strong tea, and an arrival at the office at five minutes to twelve instead of half-past nine had precipitated the catastrophe. Mr. Rowland, senior, who for twenty-four years had condoned and paid up as a tactful relative should, had suddenly abandoned these tactics and revealed himself in a totally new light. The inconsequence of George's replies (the young man's head was still opening and shutting like some mediaeval instrument of the Inquisition) had displeased him still further. William Rowland was nothing if not thorough. He cast his nephew adrift upon the world in a few short succinct words, and then settled down to his interrupted survey of some oilfields in Peru.

George Rowland shook the dust of his uncle's

office from off his feet, and stepped out into the City of London. George was a practical fellow. A good lunch, he considered, was essential to a review of the situation. He had it. Then he retraced his steps to the family mansion. Rogers opened the door. His well-trained face expressed no surprise at seeing George at this unusual hour.

"Good afternoon, Rogers. Just pack up my things for me, will you? I'm leaving here."

"Yes, sir. Just for a short visit, sir?"

"For good, Rogers. I am going to the colonies this afternoon."

"Indeed, sir?"

"Yes. That is, if there is a suitable boat. Do you know anything about the boats, Rogers?"

"Which colony were you thinking of visiting, sir?"

"I'm not particular. Any of 'em will do. Let's say Australia. What do you think of the idea, Rogers?"

Rogers coughed discreetly.

"Well, sir, I've certainly heard it said that there's room out there for anyone who really wants to work."

Mr. Rowland gazed at him with interest and admiration.

"Very neatly put, Rogers. Just what I was thinking myself. I shan't go to Australia—not today, at any rate. Fetch me an *A.B.C.*, will you? We will select something nearer at hand."

Rogers brought the required volume. George opened it at random and turned the pages with a rapid hand.

"Perth—too far away—Putney Bridge—too near at hand. Ramsgate? I think not. Reigate also leaves me cold. Why—what an extraordinary thing! There's actually a place called Rowland's Castle. Ever heard of it, Rogers?"

"I fancy, sir, that you go there from Waterloo."

"What an extraordinary fellow you are, Rogers. You know everything. Well, well, Rowland's Castle! I wonder what sort of a place it is."

"Not much of a place, I should say, sir."

"All the better; there'll be less competition. These quiet little country hamlets have a lot of the old feudal spirit knocking about. The last of the original Rowlands ought to meet with instant appreciation. I shouldn't wonder if they elected me mayor in a week."

He shut up the *A.B.C.* with a bang.

"The die is cast. Pack me a small suitcase, will you, Rogers? Also my compliments to the cook, and will she oblige me with the loan of the cat. Dick Whittington, you know. When you set out to become a Lord Mayor, a cat is essential."

"I'm sorry, sir, but the cat is not available at the present moment."

"How is that?"

"A family of eight, sir. Arrived this morning."

"You don't say so. I thought its name was Peter."

"So it is, sir. A great surprise to all of us."

"A case of careless christening and the deceitful sex, eh? Well, well, I shall have to go catless. Pack up those things at once, will you?"

"Very good, sir."

Rogers hesitated, then advanced a little farther into the room.

"You'll excuse the liberty, sir, but if I was you, I shouldn't take too much notice of anything Mr. Rowland said this morning. He was at one of those city dinners last night, and—"

"Say no more," said George. "I understand."

"And being inclined to gout—"

"I know, I know. Rather a strenuous evening for you, Rogers, with two of us, eh? But I've set my heart on distinguishing myself at Rowland's Castle—the cradle of my historic race—that would go well in a speech, wouldn't it? A wire to me there, or a discreet advertisement in the morning papers, will recall me at any time if a fricassée of veal is in preparation. And now—to Waterloo!—as Wellington said on the eve of the historic battle."

Waterloo Station was not at its brightest and best that afternoon. Mr. Rowland eventually discovered a train that would take him to his destination, but it was an undistinguished train, an unimposing train—a train that nobody seemed anxious to travel by. Mr. Rowland had a first-class carriage to himself, up in the front of the train. A fog was descending in an indeterminate way over the metropolis, now it lifted, now it descended. The platform was deserted, and only the asthmatic breathing of the engine broke the silence.

And then, all of a sudden, things began to happen with bewildering rapidity.

A girl happened first. She wrenched open the door and jumped in, rousing Mr. Rowland from something perilously near a nap, exclaiming as she did so: "Oh! hide me—oh! please hide me."

George was essentially a man of action—his not to reason why, his but to do and die, etc. There is only one place to hide in a railway carriage—under the seat. In seven seconds the girl was bestowed there, and George's suitcase, negligently standing on end, covered her retreat. None too soon. An infuriated face appeared at the carriage window.

"My niece! You have her here. I want my niece."

George, a little breathless, was reclining in the corner, deep in the sporting column of the evening paper, one-thirty edition. He laid it aside with the air of a man recalling himself from far away.

"I beg your pardon, sir?" he said politely.

"My niece—what have you done with her?"

Acting on the policy that attack is always better than defence, George leaped into action.

"What the devil do you mean?" he cried, with a very creditable imitation of his own uncle's manner.

The other paused a minute, taken aback by this

sudden fierceness. He was a fat man, still panting a little as though he had run some way. His hair was cut *en brosse*, and he had a moustache of the Hohenzollern persuasion. His accents were decidedly guttural, and the stiffness of his carriage denoted that he was more at home in uniform than out of it. George had the true-born Briton's prejudice against foreigners—and an especial distaste for German-looking foreigners.

"What the devil do you mean, sir?" he repeated angrily.

"She came in here," said the other. "I saw her. What have you done with her?"

George flung aside the paper and thrust his head and shoulders through the window.

"So that's it, is it?" he roared. "Blackmail. But you've tried it on the wrong person. I read all about you in the *Daily Mail* this morning. Here, guard, guard!"

Already attracted from afar by the altercation, that functionary came hurrying up.

"Here, guard," said Mr. Rowland, with that air of authority which the lower classes so adore. "This fellow is annoying me. I'll give him in charge for attempted blackmail if necessary. Pretends I've got his niece hidden in here. There's a regular gang of these forcigners trying this sort of thing on. It ought to be stopped. Take him away, will you? Here's my card if you want it."

The guard looked from one to the other. His

mind was soon made up. His training led him to despise foreigners, and to respect and admire well-dressed gentlemen who travelled first class.

He laid his hand on the shoulder of the intruder.

"Here," he said, "you come out of this."

At this crisis the stranger's English failed him, and he plunged into passionate profanity in his native tongue.

"That's enough of that," said the guard. "Stand away, will you? She's due out."

Flags were waved and whistles were blown. With an unwilling jerk the train drew out of the station.

George remained at his observation post until they were clear of the platform. Then he drew in his head, and picking up the suitcase tossed it into the rack.

"It's quite all right. You can come out," he said reassuringly.

The girl crawled out.

"Oh!" she gasped. "How can I thank you?"

"That's quite all right. It's been a pleasure, I assure you," returned George nonchalantly.

He smiled at her reassuringly. There was a slightly puzzled look in her eyes. She seemed to be missing something to which she was accustomed. At that moment, she caught sight of herself in the narrow glass opposite, and gave a heartfelt gasp.

Whether the carriage cleaners do, or do not,

sweep under the seats every day is doubtful. Appearances were against their doing so, but it may be that every particle of dirt and smoke finds its way there like a homing bird. George had hardly had time to take in the girl's appearance, so sudden had been her arrival, and so brief the space of time before she crawled into hiding, but it was certainly a trim and well-dressed young woman who had disappeared under the seat. Now her little red hat was crushed and dented, and her face was disfigured with long streaks of dirt.

"Oh!" said the girl.

She fumbled for her bag. George, with the tact of a true gentleman, looked fixedly out of the window and admired the streets of London south of the Thames.

"How can I thank you?" said the girl again.

Taking this as a hint that conversation might now be resumed, George withdrew his gaze, and made another polite disclaimer, but this time with a good deal of added warmth in his manner.

The girl was absolutely lovely! Never before, George told himself, had he seen such a lovely girl. The *empressement* of his manner became even more marked.

"I think it was simply splendid of you," said the girl with enthusiasm.

"Not at all. Easiest thing in the world. Only too pleased been of use," mumbled George.

"Splendid," she reiterated emphatically.

It is undoubtedly pleasant to have the loveliest girl you have even seen gazing into your eyes and telling you how splendid you are. George enjoyed it as much as anyone could.

Then there came a rather difficult silence. It seemed to dawn upon the girl that further explanation might be expected. She flushed a little.

"The awkward part of it is," she said nervously, "that I'm afraid I can't explain."

She looked at him with a piteous air of uncertainty.

"You can't explain?"

"No."

"How perfectly splendid!" said Mr. Rowland with enthusiasm.

"I beg your pardon?"

"I said, How perfectly splendid. Just like one of those books that keep you up all night. The heroine always says 'I can't explain' in the first chapter. She explains in the last, of course, and there's never any real reason why she shouldn't have done so in the beginning—except that it would spoil the story. I can't tell you how pleased I am to be mixed up in a real mystery—I didn't know there were such things. I hope it's got something to do with secret documents of immense importance, and the Balkan express. I dote upon the Balkan express."

The girl stared at him with wide, suspicious eyes.

"What makes you say the Balkan express?" she asked sharply.

"I hope I haven't been indiscreet," George hastened to put in. "Your uncle travelled by it, perhaps."

"My uncle—" She paused, then began again. "My uncle—"

"Quite so," said George sympathetically. "I've got an uncle myself. Nobody should be held responsible for their uncles. Nature's little throwbacks—that's how I look at it."

The girl began to laugh suddenly. When she spoke George was aware of the slight foreign inflection in her voice. At first he had taken her to be English.

"What a refreshing and unusual person you are, Mr.—"

"Rowland. George to my friends."

"My name is Elizabeth—"

She stopped abruptly.

"I like the name of Elizabeth," said George, to cover her momentary confusion. "They don't call you Bessie, or anything horrible like that, I hope?"

She shook her head.

"Well," said George, "now that we know each other, we'd better get down to business. If you'll stand up, Elizabeth, I'll brush down the back of your coat."

She stood up obediently, and George was as good as his word.

46

"Thank you, Mr. Rowland."

"George. George to my friends, remember. And you can't come into my nice empty carriage, roll under the seat, induce me to tell lies to your uncle, and then refuse to be friends, can you?"

"Thank you, George."

"That's better."

"Do I look quite all right now?" asked Elizabeth, trying to see over her left shoulder.

"You look—oh! you look—you look all right," said George, curbing himself sternly.

"It was all so sudden, you see," explained the girl.

"It must have been."

"He saw us in the taxi, and then at the station I just bolted in here knowing he was close behind me. Where is this train going to, by the way?"

"Rowland's Castle," said George firmly.

The girl looked puzzled.

"Rowland's Castle?"

"Not at once, of course. Only after a good deal of stopping and slow going. But I confidently expect to be there before midnight. The old South-Western was a very reliable line—slow but sure—and I'm sure the Southern Railway is keeping up the old traditions."

"I don't know that I want to go to Rowland's Castle," said Elizabeth doubtfully.

"You hurt me. It's a delightful spot."

"Have you ever been there?"

"Not exactly. But there are lots of other places you can go to, if you don't fancy Rowland's Castle. There's Woking, and Weybridge, and Wimbledon. The train is sure to stop at one or other of them."

"I see," said the girl. "Yes, I can get out there, and perhaps motor back to London. That would be the best plan, I think."

Even as she spoke, the train began to slow up. Mr. Rowland gazed at her with appealing eyes.

"If I can do anything—"

"No, indeed. You've done a lot already."

There was a pause, then the girl broke out suddenly:

"I—I wish I could explain. I—"

"For heaven's sake don't do that! It would spoil everything. But look here, isn't there anything that I could do? Carry the secret papers to Vienna—or something of that kind? There always are secret papers. Do give me a chance."

The train had stopped. Elizabeth jumped quickly out on to the platform. She turned and spoke to him through the window.

"Are you in earnest? Would you really do something for us—for me?"

"I'd do anything in the world for you, Elizabeth."

"Even if I could give you no reasons?"

"Rotten things, reasons!"

"Even if it were—dangerous?"

48

"The more danger, the better."

She hesitated a minute then seemed to make up her mind.

"Lean out of the window. Look down the platform as though you weren't really looking." Mr. Rowland endeavoured to comply with this somewhat difficult recommendation. "Do you see that man getting in—with a small dark beard— light overcoat? Follow him, see what he does and where he goes."

"Is that all?" asked Mr. Rowland. "What do I—?"

She interrupted him.

"Further instructions will be sent to you. Watch him—and guard this." She thrust a small sealed packet into his hand. "Guard it with your life. It's the key to everything."

The train went on. Mr. Rowland remained staring out of the window, watching Elizabeth's tall, graceful figure threading its way down the platform. In his hand he clutched the small sealed packet.

The rest of his journey was both monotonous and uneventful. The train was a slow one. It stopped everywhere. At every station, George's head shot out of the window, in case his quarry should alight. Occasionally he strolled up and down the platform when the wait promised to be a long one, and reassured himself that the man was still there.

49

The eventual destination of the train was Portsmouth, and it was there that the black-bearded traveller alighted. He made his way to a small second-class hotel where he booked a room. Mr. Rowland also booked a room.

The rooms were in the same corridor, two doors from each other. The arrangement seemed satisfactory to George. He was a complete novice in the art of shadowing, but was anxious to acquit himself well, and justify Elizabeth's trust in him.

At dinner George was given a table not far from that of his quarry. The room was not full, and the majority of the diners George put down as commercial travellers, quiet respectable men who ate their food with appetite. Only one man attracted his special notice, a small man with ginger hair and moustache and a suggestion of horsiness in his apparel. He seemed to be interested in George also, and suggested a drink and a game of billiards when the meal had come to a close. But George had just espied the black-bearded man putting on his hat and overcoat, and declined politely. In another minute he was out in the street, gaining fresh insight into the difficult art of shadowing. The chase was a long and a weary one—and in the end it seemed to lead nowhere. After twisting and turning through the streets of Portsmouth for about four miles, the man returned to the hotel, George hard upon his heels. A faint doubt assailed the latter. Was it possible that the man was aware of his presence? As he debated this point, standing in the hall, the outer door was pushed open, and the little ginger man entered. Evidently he, too, had been out for a stroll.

George was suddenly aware that the beauteous damsel in the office was addressing him.

"Mr. Rowland, isn't it? Two gentlemen have called to see you. Two foreign gentlemen. They are in the little room at the end of the passage."

Somewhat astonished, George sought the room in question. Two men who were sitting there, rose to their feet and bowed punctiliously.

"Mr. Rowland? I have no doubt, sir, that you can guess our identity."

George gazed from one to the other of them. The spokesman was the elder of the two, a grey-haired, pompous gentleman who spoke excellent English. The other was a tall, somewhat pimply young man, with a blond Teutonic cast of countenance which was not rendered more attractive by the fierce scowl which he wore at the present moment.

Somewhat relieved to find that neither of his visitors was the old gentleman he had encountered at Waterloo, George assumed his most debonair manner.

"Pray sit down, gentlemen. I'm delighted to make your acquaintance. How about a drink?"

The elder man held up a protesting hand.

"Thank you, Lord Rowland—not for us. We have but a few brief moments—just time for you to answer a question."

"It's very kind of you to elect me to the peerage," said George. "I'm sorry you won't have a drink. And what is this momentous question?"

"Lord Rowland, you left London in company with a certain lady. You arrived here alone. Where is the lady?"

George rose to his feet.

"I fail to understand the question," he said coldly, speaking as much like the hero of a novel as he could. "I have the honour to wish you good evening, gentlemen."

"But you do understand it. You understand it perfectly," cried the younger man, breaking out suddenly. "What have you done with Alexa?"

"Be calm, sir," murmured the other. "I beg of you to be calm."

"I can assure you," said George, "that I know no lady of that name. There is some mistake."

The older man was eyeing him keenly.

"That can hardly be," he said drily. "I took the liberty of examining the hotel register. You entered yourself as Mr. G. Rowland of Rowland's Castle."

George was forced to blush.

"A—a little joke of mine," he explained feebly

"A somewhat poor subterfuge. Come, let us not beat about the bush. Where is Her Highness?"

"If you mean Elizabeth—"

With a howl of rage the young man flung himself forward again.

"Insolent pig-dog! To speak of her thus."

"I am referring," said the other slowly, "as you very well know, to the Grand Duchess Anastasia Sophia Alexandra Marie Helena Olga Elizabeth of Catonia."

"Oh!" said Mr. Rowland helplessly.

He tried to recall all that he had ever known of Catonia. It was, as far as he remembered, a small Balkan kingdom, and he seemed to remember something about a revolution having occurred there. He rallied himself with an effort.

"Evidently we mean the same person," he said cheerfully, "only *I* call her Elizabeth."

"You will give me satisfaction for that," snarled the younger man. "We will fight."

"Fight?"

"A duel."

"I never fight duels," said Mr. Rowland firmly.

"Why not?" demanded the other unpleasantly.

"I'm too afraid of getting hurt."

"Aha! is that so? Then I will at least pull your nose for you."

The younger man advanced fiercely. Exactly what happened was difficult to see, but he described a sudden semicircle in the air and fell to the ground with a heavy thud. He picked himself up in a dazed manner. Mr. Rowland was smiling pleasantly.

"As I was saying," he remarked, "I'm always afraid of getting hurt. That's why I thought it well to learn jujitsu."

There was a pause. The two foreigners looked doubtfully at this amiable looking young man, as though they suddenly realized that some dangerous quality lurked behind the pleasant nonchalance of his manner. The younger Teuton was white with passion.

"You will repent this," he hissed.

The older man retained his dignity.

"That is your last word, Lord Rowland? You refuse to tell us Her Highness's whereabouts?"

"I am unaware of them myself."

"You can hardly expect me to believe that."

"I am afraid you are of an unbelieving nature, sir."

The other merely shook his head, and murmuring: "This is not the end. You will hear from us again," the two men took their leave.

George passed his hand over his brow. Events were proceeding at a bewildering rate. He was evidently mixed up in a first-class European scandal.

"It might even mean another war," said George hopefully, as he hunted round to see what had become of the man with the black beard.

To his great relief, he discovered him sitting in a corner of the commercial room. George sat down in another corner. In about three minutes the black-bearded man got up and went up to bed. George followed and saw him go into his room and close the door. George heaved a sigh of relief.

"I need a night's rest," he murmured. "Need it badly."

Then a dire thought struck him. Supposing the black-bearded man had realized that George was on his trail? Supposing that he should slip away during the night whilst George himself was sleeping thc sleep of the just? A few minutes' reflection suggested to Mr. Rowland a way of dealing with his difficulty. He unravelled one of his socks till he got a good length of neutral-coloured wool, then creeping quietly out of his room, he pasted one end of the wool to the farther side of the stranger's door with stamp paper, carrying the wool across it and along to his own room. There he hung the end with a small silver bell—a relic of last night's entertainment. He surveyed these arrangements with a good deal of satisfaction. Should the black-bearded man attempt to leave his room George would be instantly warned by the ringing of the bell.

This matter disposed of, George lost no time in seeking his couch. The small packet he placed carefully under his pillow. As he did so, he fell into a momentary brown study. His thoughts could have been translated thus:

"Anastasia Sophia Marie Alexandra Olga

Elizabeth. Hang it all, I've missed out one. I wonder now—"

He was unable to go to sleep immediately, being tantalized with his failure to grasp the situation. What was it all about? What was the connection between the escaping Grand Duchess, the sealed packet and the black-bearded man? What was the Grand Duchess escaping from? Were the foreigners aware that the sealed packet was in his possession? What was it likely to contain?

Pondering these matters, with an irritated sense that he was no nearer the solution, Mr. Rowland fell asleep.

He was awakened by the faint jangle of a bell. Not one of those men who awake to instant action, it took him just a minute and a half to realize the situation. Then he jumped up, thrust on some slippers, and, opening the door with the utmost caution, slipped out into the corridor. A faint moving patch of shadow at the far end of the passage showed him the direction taken by his quarry. Moving as noiselessly as possible, Mr. Rowland followed the trail. He was just in time to see the black-bearded man disappear into a bathroom. That was puzzling, particularly so as there was a bathroom just opposite his own room. Moving up close to the door, which was ajar, George peered through the crack. The man was on his knees by the side of the bath, doing something to the skirting board immediately behind it. He remained there for about five minutes, then he rose to his feet, and George beat a prudent retreat. Safe in the shadow of his own door, he watched the other pass and regain his own room.

"Good," said George to himself. "The mystery of the bathroom will be investigated tomorrow morning."

He got into bed and slipped his hand under the pillow to assure himself that the precious packet was still there. In another minute, he was scattering the bedclothes in a panic. The packet was gone!

It was a sadly chastened George who sat consuming eggs and bacon the following morning. He had failed Elizabeth. He had allowed the precious packet she had entrusted to his charge to be taken from him, and the "Mystery of the Bathroom" was miserably inadequate. Yes, undoubtedly George had made a mutt of himself.

After breakfast he strolled upstairs again. A chambermaid was standing in the passage looking perplexed.

"Anything wrong, my dear?" said George kindly.

"It's the gentleman here, sir. He asked to be called at half-past eight, and I can't get any answer and the door's locked."

"You don't say so," said George.

An uneasy feeling rose in his own breast. He

hurried into his room. Whatever plans he was forming were instantly brushed aside by a most unexpected sight. There on the dressing table was the little packet which had been stolen from him the night before!

George picked it up and examined it. Yes, it was undoubtedly the same. But the seals had been broken. After a minute's hesitation, he unwrapped it. If other people had seen its contents there was no reason why he should not see them also. Besides, it was possible that the contents had been abstracted. The unwound paper revealed a small cardboard box, such as jewellers use. George opened it. Inside, nestling on a bed of cotton wool, was a plain gold wedding ring.

He picked it up and examined it. There was no inscription inside—nothing whatever to make it out from any other wedding ring. George dropped his head into his hands with a groan.

"Lunacy," he murmured. "That's what it is. Stark staring lunacy. There's no sense anywhere."

Suddenly he remembered the chambermaid's statement, and at the same time he observed that there was a broad parapet outside the window. It was not a feat he would ordinarily have attempted, but he was so aflame with curiosity and anger that he was in the mood to make light of difficulties. He sprang upon the window sill. A few seconds later he was peering in at the window of the room occupied by the black-bearded man. The window was open and the room was empty. A little further along was a fire escape. It was clear how the quarry had taken his departure.

George jumped in through the window. The missing man's effects were still scattered about. There might be some clue amongst them to shed light on George's perplexities. He began to hunt about, starting with the contents of a battered kit bag.

It was a sound that arrested his search—a very slight sound, but a sound indubitably in the room. George's glance leapt to the big wardrobe. He sprang up and wrenched open the door. As he did so, a man jumped out from it and went rolling over the floor locked in George's embrace. He was no mean antagonist. All George's special tricks availed very little. They fell apart at length in sheer exhaustion, and for the first time George saw who his adversary was. It was the little man with the ginger moustache.

"Who the devil are you?" demanded George.

For answer the other drew out a card and handed it to him. George read it aloud.

"Detective-Inspector Jarrold, Scotland Yard."

"That's right, sir. And you'd do well to tell me all you know about this business."

"I would, would I?" said George thoughtfully. "Do you know, Inspector, I believe you're right. Shall we adjourn to a more cheerful spot?"

In a quiet corner of the bar George unfolded his

soul. Inspector Jarrold listened sympathetically.

"Very puzzling, as you say, sir," he remarked when George had finished. "There's a lot as I can't make head or tail of myself, but there's one or two points I can clear up for you. I was here after Mardenberg (your black-bearded friend) and your turning up and watching him the way you did made me suspicious. I couldn't place you. I slipped into your room last night when you were out of it, and it was I who sneaked the little packet from under your pillow. When I opened it and found it wasn't what I was after, I took the first opportunity of returning it to your room."

"That makes things a little clearer certainly," said George thoughtfully. "I seem to have made rather an ass of myself all through."

"I wouldn't say that, sir. You did uncommon well for a beginner. You say you visited the bathroom this morning and took away what was concealed behind the skirting board?"

"Yes. But it's only a rotten love letter," said George gloomily. "Dash it all, I didn't mean to go nosing out the poor fellow's private life."

"Would you mind letting me see it, sir?"

George took a folded letter from his pocket and passed it to the inspector. The latter unfolded it.

"As you say, sir. But I rather fancy that if you drew lines from one dotted *i* to another, you'd get a different result. Why, bless you, sir, this is a plan of the Portsmouth harbour defences."

"What?"

"Yes. We've had our eye on the gentleman for some time. But he was too sharp for us. Got a woman to do most of the dirty work."

"A woman?" said George, in a faint voice. "What was her name?"

"She goes by a good many, sir. Most usually known as Betty Brighteyes. A remarkably good-looking young woman she is."

"Betty—Brighteyes," said George. "Thank you, Inspector."

"Excuse me, sir, but you're not looking well."

"I'm not well. I'm very ill. In fact, I think I'd better take the first train back to town."

The Inspector looked at his watch.

"That will be a slow train, I'm afraid, sir. Better wait for the express."

"It doesn't matter," said George gloomily. "No train could be slower than the one I came down by yesterday."

Seated once more in a first-class carriage, George leisurely perused the day's news. Suddenly he sat bolt upright and stared at the sheet in front of him.

"A romantic wedding took place yesterday in London when Lord Roland Gaigh, second son of the Marquis of Axminster, was married to the Grand Duchess Anastasia of Catonia. The ceremony was kept a profound secret. The Grand Duchess has been living in Paris with her uncle since the upheaval in Catonia. She met Lord Roland when he was secretary to the British Embassy in Catonia and their attachment dates from that time."

"Well, I'm—"

Mr. Rowland could not think of anything strong enough to express his feelings. He continued to stare into space. The train stopped at a small station and a lady got in. She sat down opposite him.

"Good morning, George," she said sweetly.

"Good heavens!" cried George. "Elizabeth!"

She smiled at him. She was, if possible, lovelier than ever.

"Look here," cried George, clutching his head. "For God's sake tell me. Are you the Grand Duchess Anastasia, or are you Betty Brighteyes?"

She stared at him.

"I'm not either. I'm Elizabeth Gaigh. I can tell you all about it now. And I've got to apologize too. You see, Roland (that's my brother) has always been in love with Alexa—"

"Meaning the Grand Duchess?"

"Yes, that's what the family call her. Well, as I say, Roland was always in love with her, and she with him. And then the revolution came, and Alexa was in Paris, and they were just going to fix it up when old Stürm, the chancellor, came along and insisted on carrying off Alexa and forcing her to marry Prince Karl, her cousin, a horrid pimply person—"

"I fancy I've met him," said George.

"Whom she simply hates. And old Prince Usric, her uncle, forbade her to see Roland again. So she ran away to England, and I came up to town and met her, and we wired to Roland who was in Scotland. And just at the very last minute, when we were driving to the Registry Office in a taxi, whom should we meet in another taxi face to face, but old Prince Usric. Of course he followed us, and we were at our wits' end what to do because he'd have made the most fearful scene, and, anyway, he is her guardian. Then I had the brilliant idea of changing places. You can practically see nothing of a girl nowadays but the tip of her nose. I put on Alexa's red hat and brown wrap coat, and she put on my grey. Then we told the taxi to go to Waterloo, and I skipped out there and hurried into the station. Old Osric followed the red hat all right, without a thought for the other occupant of the taxi sitting huddled up inside, but of course it wouldn't do for him to see my face. So I just bolted into your carriage and threw myself on your mercy."

"I've got that all right," said George. "It's the rest of it."

"I know. That's what I've got to apologize about. I hope you won't be awfully cross. You see, you looked so keen on its being a real mystery— like in books, that I really couldn't resist the temptation. I picked out a rather sinister looking man on the platform and told you to follow him. And then I thrust the parcel on you."

"Containing a wedding ring."

"Yes. Alexa and I bought that, because Roland wasn't due to arrive from Scotland until just before the wedding. And of course I knew that by the time I got to London they wouldn't want it— they would have had to use a curtain ring or something."

"I see," said George. "It's like all these things— so simple when you know! Allow me, Elizabeth."

He stripped off her left glove, and uttered a sigh of relief at the sight of the bare third finger.

"That's all right," he remarked. "That ring won't be wasted after all."

"Oh!" cried Elizabeth; "but I don't know anthing about you "

"You know how nice I am," said George. "By the way, it has just occurred to me, you are the Lady Elizabeth Gaigh, of course."

"Oh! George, are you a snob?"

"As a matter of fact, I am, rather. My best dream was one where King George borrowed half a crown from me to see him over the weekend. But I was thinking of my uncle—the one from whom I am estranged. He's a frightful snob. When he knows I'm going to marry you, and that we'll have a title in the family, he'll make me a partner at once!"

"Oh! George, is he very rich?"

"Elizabeth, are you mercenary?"

"Very. I adore spending money. But I was thinking of Father. Five daughters, full of beauty and blue blood. He's just yearning for a rich son-in-law."

"H'm," said George. "It will be one of those marriages made in Heaven and approved on earth. Shall we live at Rowland's Castle? They'd be sure to make me Lord Mayor with you for a wife. Oh! Elizabeth, darling, it's probably contravening the company's by-laws, but I simply must kiss you!"

Three

THE MANHOOD
OF EDWARD ROBINSON

"The Manhood of Edward Robinson" was
first published as "The Day of His
Dreams" in *Grand Magazine*, December
1924.

• • •

"With a swing of his mighty arms, Bill
lifted her right off her feet, crushing her to
his breast. With a deep sigh she yielded her
lips in such a kiss as he had never dreamed
of—"

With a sigh, Mr. Edward Robinson put down
When Love is King and stared out of the window
of the underground train. They were running
through Stamford Brook. Edward Robinson was
thinking about Bill. Bill was the real hundred per
cent he-man beloved of lady novelists. Edward
envied him his muscles, his rugged good looks
and his terrific passions. He picked up the book
again and read the description of the proud
Marchesa Bianca (she who had yielded her lips).
So ravishing was her beauty, the intoxication of

her was so great, that strong men went down before her like ninepins, faint and helpless with love.

"Of course," said Edward to himself, "it's all bosh, this sort of stuff. All bosh, it is. And yet, I wonder—"

His eyes looked wistful. Was there such a thing as a world of romance and adventure somewhere? Were there women whose beauty intoxicated? Was there such a thing as love that devoured one like a flame?

"This is real life, this is," said Edward. "I've got to go on the same just like all the other chaps."

On the whole, he supposed, he ought to consider himself a lucky young man. He had an excellent berth—a clerkship in a flourishing concern. He had good health, no one dependent upon him, and he was engaged to Maud.

But the mere thought of Maud brought a shadow over his face. Though he would never have admitted it, he was afraid of Maud. He loved her—yes—he still remembered the thrill with which he had admired the back of her white neck rising out of the cheap four and elevenpenny blouse on the first occasion they had met. He had sat behind her at the cinema, and the friend he was with had known her and had introduced them. No doubt about it, Maud was very superior. She was good looking and clever and very ladylike, and she was always right about everything. The kind of girl, everyone said, who would make such an excellent wife.

Edward wondered whether the Marchesa Bianca would have made an excellent wife. Somehow, he doubted it. He couldn't picture the voluptuous Bianca, with her red lips and her swaying form, tamely sewing on buttons, say, for the virile Bill. No, Bianca was Romance, and this was real life. He and Maud would be very happy together. She had so much common sense. . . .

But all the same, he wished that she wasn't quite so—well, sharp in manner. So prone to "jump upon him."

It was, of course, her prudence and her common sense which made her do so. Maud was very sensible. And, as a rule, Edward was very sensible too, but sometimes—He had wanted to get married this Christmas, for instance. Maud had pointed out how much more prudent it would be to wait a while—a year or two, perhaps. His salary was not large. He had wanted to give her an expensive ring—she had been horror stricken, and had forced him to take it back and exchange it for a cheaper one. Her qualities were all excellent qualities, but sometimes Edward wished that she had more faults and less virtues. It was her virtues that drove him to desperate deeds.

For instance—

A blush of guilt overspread his face. He had got to tell her—and tell her soon. His secret guilt was already making him behave strangely. Tomorrow was the first of three days holiday, Christmas Eve, Christmas Day and Boxing Day. She had suggested that he should come round and spend the day with her people, and in a clumsy foolish manner, a manner that could not fail to arouse her suspicions, he had managed to get out of it—had told a long, lying story about a pal of his in the country with whom he had promised to spend the day.

And there was no pal in the country. There was only his guilty secret.

Three months ago, Edward Robinson, in company with a few hundred thousand other young men, had gone in for a competition in one of the weekly papers. Twelve girls' names had to be arranged in order of popularity. Edward had had a brilliant idea. His own preference was sure to be wrong—he had noticed that in several similar competitions. He wrote down the twelve names arranged in his own order of merit, then he wrote them down again this time placing one from the top and one from the bottom of the list alternately.

When the result was announced, Edward had got eight right out of the twelve, and was awarded the first prize of £500. This result, which might easily be ascribed to luck, Edward persisted in regarding as the direct outcome of his "system." He was inordinately proud of himself.

The next thing was, what to do with the £500? He knew very well what Maud would say. Invest it. A nice little nest egg for the future. And, of course, Maud would be quite right, he knew that. But to win money as the result of a competition is an entirely different feeling from anything else in the world.

Had the money been left to him as a legacy, Edward would have invested it religiously in Conversion Loan or Savings Certificates as a matter of course. But money that one has achieved by a mere stroke of the pen, by a lucky and unbelievable chance, comes under the same heading as a child's sixpence—"for your very own—to spend as you like."

And in a certain rich shop which he passed daily on his way to the office, was the unbelievable dream, a small two-seater car, with a long shining nose, and the price clearly displayed on it—£465.

"If I were rich," Edward had said to it, day after day. "If I were rich, I'd have you."

And now he was—if not rich—at least possessed of a lump sum of money sufficient to realize his dream. That car, that shining alluring piece of loveliness, was his if he cared to pay the price.

He had meant to tell Maud about the money. Once he had told her, he would have secured himself against temptation. In face of Maud's horror and disapproval, he would never have the courage to persist in his madness. But, as it chanced, it was Maud herself who clinched the matter. He had taken her to the cinema—and to the best seats in the house. She had pointed out to him, kindly but firmly, the criminal folly of his behaviour—wasting good money—three and sixpence against two and fourpence, when one saw just as well from the latter places.

Edward took her reproaches in sullen silence. Maud felt contentedly that she was making an impression. Edward could not be allowed to continue in these extravagant ways. She loved Edward, but she realized that he was weak—hers the task of being ever at hand to influence him in the way he should go. She observed his wormlike demeanour with satisfaction.

Edward was indeed wormlike. Like worms, he turned. He remained crushed by her words, but it was at that precise minute that he made up his mind to buy the car.

"Damn it," said Edward to himself. "For once in my life, I'll do what I like. Maud can go hang!"

And the very next morning he had walked into that palace of plate glass, with its lordly inmates in their glory of gleaming enamel and shimmering metal, and with an insouciance that surprised himself, he bought the car. It was the easiest thing in the world, buying a car!

It had been his for four days now. He had gone about, outwardly calm, but inwardly bathed in

71

ecstasy. And to Maud he had as yet breathed no word. For four days, in his luncheon hour, he had received instruction in the handling of the lovely creature. He was an apt pupil.

Tomorrow, Christmas Eve, he was to take her out into the country. He had lied to Maud, and he would lie again if need be. He was enslaved body and soul by his new possession. It stood to him for Romance, for Adventure, for all the things that he had longed for and had never had. Tomorrow, he and his mistress would take the road together. They would rush through the keen cold air, leaving the throb and fret of London far behind— out into the wide clear spaces. . . .

At this moment, Edward, though he did not know it, was very near to being a poet.

Tomorrow—

He looked down at the book in his hand—*When Love is King.* He laughed and stuffed it into his pocket. The car, and the red lips of the Marchesa Bianca, and the amazing prowess of Bill seemed all mixed up together. Tomorrow—

The weather, usually a sorry jade to those who count upon her, was kindly disposed towards Edward. She gave him the day of his dreams, a day of glittering frost, and pale-blue sky, and a primrose-yellow sun.

So, in a mood of high adventure, of daredevil wickedness, Edward drove out of London. There was trouble at Hyde Park Corner, and a sad *contretemps* at Putney Bridge, there was much protesting of gears, and a frequent jarring of brakes, and much abuse was freely showered upon Edward by the drivers of other vehicles. But for a novice he did not acquit himself so badly, and presently he came out on to one of those fair wide roads that are the joy of the motorist. There was little congestion on this particular road today. Edward drove on and on, drunk with his mastery over this creature of the gleaming sides, speeding through the cold white world with the elation of a god.

It was a delirious day. He stopped for lunch at an old-fashioned inn, and again later for tea. Then reluctantly he turned homewards—back again to London, to Maud, to the inevitable explanation, recriminations. . . .

He shook off the thought with a sigh. Let tomorrow look after itself. He still had today. And what could be more fascinating than this? Rushing through the darkness with the head-lights searching out the way in front. Why, this was the best of all!

He judged that he had no time to stop anywhere for dinner. This driving through the darkness was a ticklish business. It was going to take longer to get back to London than he had thought. It was just eight o'clock when he passed through Hindhead and came out upon the rim of the Devil's Punch Bowl. There was moonlight, and the snow that had fallen two days ago was still unmelted.

He stopped the car and stood staring. What did it matter if he didn't get back to London until midnight? What did it matter if he never got back? He wasn't going to tear himself away from this at once.

He got out of the car, and approached the edge. There was a path winding down temptingly near him. Edward yielded to the spell. For the next half hour he wandered deliriously in a snowbound world. Never had he imagined anything quite like this. And it was his, his very own, given to him by his shining mistress who waited for him faithfully on the road above.

He climbed up again, got into the car and drove off, still a little dizzy from that discovery of sheer beauty which comes to the most prosaic men once in a while.

Then, with a sigh, he came to himself, and thrust his hand into the pocket of the car where he had stuffed an additional muffler earlier in the day.

But the muffler was no longer there. The pocket was empty. No, not completely empty—there was something scratchy and hard—like pebbles.

Edward thrust his hand deep down. In another minute he was staring like a man bereft of his senses. The object that he held in his hand, dangling from his fingers, with the moonlight striking a hundred fires from it, was a diamond necklace.

Edward stared and stared. But there was no doubting possible. A diamond necklace worth probably thousands of pounds (for the stones were large ones) had been casually reposing in the side-pocket of the car.

But who had put it there? It had certainly not been there when he started from town. Someone must have come along when he was walking about in the snow, and deliberately thrust it in. But why? Why choose *his* car? Had the owner of the necklace made a mistake? Or was it—could it possibly be *a stolen* necklace?

And then, as all these thoughts went whirling through his brain, Edward suddenly stiffened and went cold all over. *This was not his car.*

It was very like it, yes. It was the same brilliant shade of scarlet—red as the Marchesa Bianca's lips—it had the same long and gleaming nose, but by a thousand small signs, Edward realized that it was not his car. Its shining newness was scarred here and there, it bore signs, faint but unmistakeable, of wear and tear. In that case. . . .

Edward, without more ado, made haste to turn the car. Turning was not his strong point. With the car in reverse, he invariably lost his head and twisted the wheel the wrong way. Also, he frequently became entangled between the accelerator and the foot brake with disastrous results. In the end, however, he succeeded, and straight away the car began purring up the hill again.

Edward remembered that there had been another car standing some little distance away. He had not noticed it particularly at the time. He had returned from his walk by a different path from that by which he had gone down into the hollow. This second path had brought him out on the road immediately behind, as he had thought, his own car. It must really have been the other one.

In about ten minutes he was once more at the spot where he had halted. But there was now no car at all by the roadside. Whoever had owned this car must now have gone off in Edward's—he also, perhaps, misled by the resemblance.

Edward took out the diamond necklace from his pocket and let it run through his fingers perplexedly.

What to do next? Run on to the nearest police station? Explain the circumstances, hand over the necklace, and give the number of his own car.

By the by, what was the number of his car? Edward thought and thought, but for the life of him he couldn't remember. He felt a cold sinking sensation. He was going to look the most utter fool at the police station. There was an eight in it, that was all that he could remember. Of course, it didn't really matter—at least . . . He looked uncomfortably at the diamonds. Supposing they should think—oh, but they wouldn't—and yet again they might—that he had stolen the car and the diamonds? Because, after all, when one came to think of it, would anyone in their senses thrust a valuable diamond necklace carelessly into the open pocket of a car?

Edward got out and went round to the back of the motor. Its number was XR10061. Beyond the fact that that was certainly not the number of his car, it conveyed nothing to him. Then he set to work systematically to search all the pockets. In the one where he had found the diamonds he made a discovery—a small scrap of paper with some words pencilled on it. By the light of the headlights, Edward read them easily enough.

"Meet me, Greane, corner of Salter's Lane, ten o'clock."

He remembered the name Greane. He had seen it on a signpost earlier in the day. In a minute, his mind was made up. He would go to this village, Greane, find Salter's Lane, meet the person who had written the note, and explain the circumstances. That would be much better than looking a fool in the local police station.

He started off almost happily. After all, this was an adventure. This was the sort of thing that didn't happen every day. The diamond necklace made it exciting and mysterious.

He had some little difficulty in finding Greane, and still more difficulty in finding Salter's Lane, but after knocking up two cottages, he succeeded.

Still, it was a few minutes after the appointed hour when he drove cautiously along a narrow road, keeping a sharp lookout on the left-hand side where he had been told Salter's Lane branched off.

He came upon it quite suddenly round a bend, and even as he drew up, a figure came forward out of the darkness.

"At last!" a girl's voice cried. "What an age you've been, Gerald!"

As she spoke, the girl stepped right into the glare of the headlights, and Edward caught his breath. She was the most glorious creature he had ever seen.

She was quite young, with hair black as night, and wonderful scarlet lips. The heavy cloak that she wore swung open, and Edward saw that she was in full evening dress—a kind of flame-coloured sheath, outlining her perfect body. Round her neck was a row of exquisite pearls.

Suddenly the girl started.

"Why," she cried; "it isn't Gerald."

"No," said Edward hastily. "I must explain." He took the diamond necklace from his pocket and held it out to her. "My name is Edward—"

He got no further, for the girl clapped her hands and broke in:

"Edward, of course! I am so glad. But that idiot Jimmy told me over the phone that he was sending Gerald along with the car. It's awfully sporting of you to come. I've been dying to meet you. Remember I haven't seen you since I was six years old. I see you've got the necklace all right. Shove it in your pocket again. The village policeman might come along and see it. Brrr, it's cold as ice waiting here! Let me get in."

As though in a dream Edward opened the door, and she sprang lightly in beside him. Her furs swept his cheek, and an elusive scent, like that of violets after rain, assailed his nostrils.

He had no plan, no definite thought even. In a minute, without conscious volition, he had yielded himself to the adventure. She had called him Edward—what matter if he were the wrong Edward? She would find him out soon enough. In the meantime, let the game go on. He let in the clutch and they glided off.

Presently the girl laughed. Her laugh was just as wonderful as the rest of her.

"It's easy to see you don't know much about cars. I suppose they don't have them out there?"

"I wonder where 'out there' is?" thought Edward. Aloud he said, "Not much."

"Better let me drive," said the girl. "It's tricky work finding your way round these lanes until we get on the main road again."

He relinquished his place to her gladly. Presently they were humming through the night at a pace and with a recklessness that secretly appalled Edward. She turned her head towards him.

"I like pace. Do you? You know—you're not a

bit like Gerald. No one would ever take you to be brothers. You're not a bit like what I imagined, either."

"I suppose," said Edward, "that I'm so completely ordinary. Is that it?"

"Not ordinary—different. I can't make you out. How's poor old Jimmy? Very fed up, I suppose?"

"Oh, Jimmy's all right," said Edward.

"It's easy enough to say that—but it's rough luck on him having a sprained ankle. Did he tell you the whole story?"

"Not a word. I'm completely in the dark. I wish you'd enlighten me."

"Oh, the thing worked like a dream. Jimmy went in at the front door, togged up in his girl's clothes. I gave him a minute or two, and then shinned up to the window. Agnes Larella's maid was there laying out Agnes's dress and jewels, and all the rest. Then there was a great yell downstairs, and the squib went off, and everyone shouted fire. The maid dashed out, and I hopped in, helped myself to the necklace, and was out and down in a flash, and out of the place by the back way across the Punch Bowl. I shoved the necklace and the notice where to pick me up in the pocket of the car in passing. Then I joined Louise at the hotel, having shed my snow boots of course. Perfect alibi for me. She'd no idea I'd been out at all."

"And what about Jimmy?"

"Well, you know more about that than I do."

"He didn't tell me anything," said Edward easily.

"Well, in the general rag, he caught his foot in his skirt and managed to sprain it. They had to carry him to the car, and the Larellas' chauffeur drove him home. Just fancy if the chauffeur had happened to put his hand in the pocket!"

Edward laughed with her, but his mind was busy. He understood the position more or less now. The name of Larella was vaguely familiar to him—it was a name that spelt wealth. This girl, and an unknown man called Jimmy, had conspired together to steal the necklace, and had succeeded. Owing to his sprained ankle and the presence of the Larellas' chauffeur Jimmy had not been able to look in the pocket of the car before telephoning to the girl—probably had had no wish to do so. But it was almost certain that the other unknown "Gerald" would do so at any early opportunity. And in it, he would find Edward's muffler!

"Good going," said the girl.

A tram flashed past them, they were on the outskirts of London. They flashed in and out of the traffic. Edward's heart stood in his mouth. She was a wonderful driver, this girl, but she took risks!

Quarter of an hour later they drew up before an imposing house in a frigid square.

"We can shed some of our clothing here," said the girl, "before we go on to Ritson's."

"Ritson's?" queried Edward. He mentioned the famous nightclub almost reverently.

"Yes, didn't Gerald tell you?"

"He did not," said Edward grimly. "What about my clothes?"

She frowned.

"Didn't they tell you *anything?* We'll rig you up somehow. We've got to carry this through."

A stately butler opened the door and stood aside to let them enter.

"Mr. Gerald Champneys rang up, your ladyship. He was very anxious to speak to you, but he wouldn't leave a message."

"I bet he was anxious to speak to her," said Edward to himself. "At any rate, I know my full name now. Edward Champneys. But who is she? Your ladyship, they called her. What does she want to steal a necklace for? Bridge debts?"

In the *feuilletons* which he occasionally read, the beautiful and titled heroine was always driven desperate by bridge debts.

Edward was led away by the stately butler, and delivered over to a smooth-mannered valet. A quarter of an hour later he rejoined his hostess in the hall, exquisitely attired in evening clothes made in Savile Row which fitted him to a nicety.

Heavens! What a night!

They drove in the car to the famous Ritson's. In common with everyone else Edward had read scandalous paragraphs concerning Ritson's.

Anyone who was anyone turned up at Ritson's sooner or later. Edward's only fear was that someone who knew the real Edward Champneys might turn up. He consoled himself by the reflection that the real man had evidently been out of England for some years.

Sitting at a little table against the wall, they sipped cocktails. Cocktails! To the simple Edward they represented the quintessence of the fast life. The girl, wrapped in a wonderful embroidered shawl, sipped nonchalantly. Suddenly she dropped the shawl from her shoulders and rose.

"Let's dance."

Now the one thing that Edward could do to perfection was to dance. When he and Maud took the floor together at the Palais de Danse, lesser lights stood still and watched in admiration.

"I nearly forgot," said the girl suddenly. "The necklace?"

She held out her hand. Edward, completely bewildered, drew it from his pocket and gave it to her. To his utter amazement, she coolly clasped it round her neck. Then she smiled up at him intoxicatingly.

"Now," she said softly, "we'll dance."

They danced. And in all Ritson's nothing more perfect could be seen.

Then, as at length they returned to their table, an old gentleman with a would-be rakish air accosted Edward's companion.

"Ah! Lady Noreen, always dancing! Yes, yes. Is Captain Folliot here tonight?"

"Jimmy's taken a toss—racked his ankle."

"You don't say so? How did that happen?"

"No details as yet."

She laughed and passed on.

Edward followed, his brain in a whirl. He knew now. Lady Noreen Eliot, the famous Lady Noreen herself, perhaps the most talked of girl in England. Celebrated for her beauty, for her daring—the leader of that set known as the Bright Young People. Her engagement to Captain James Folliot, V.C., of the Household Cavalry, had been recently announced.

But the necklace? He still couldn't understand the necklace. He must risk giving himself away, but know he must.

As they sat down again, he pointed to it.

"Why that, Noreen?" he said. "Tell me why?"

She smiled dreamily, her eyes far away, the spell of the dance still holding her.

"It's difficult for you to understand, I suppose. One gets so tired of the same thing—always the same thing. Treasure hunts were all very well for a while, but one gets used to everything. 'Burglaries' were my idea. Fifty pounds entrance fee, and lots to be drawn. This is the third. Jimmy and I drew Agnes Larella. You know the rules? Burglary to be carried out within three days and the loot to be worn for at least an hour in a public place, or you forfeit your stake and a hundred-pound fine. It's rough luck on Jimmy spraining his ankle, but we'll scoop the pool all right."

"I see," said Edward, drawing a deep breath. "I see."

Noreen rose suddenly, pulling her shawl round her.

"Drive me somewhere in the car. Down to the docks. Somewhere horrible and exciting. Wait a minute—" She reached up and unclasped the diamonds from her neck. "You'd better take these again. I don't want to be murdered for them."

They went out of Ritson's together. The car stood in a small bystreet, narrow and dark. As they turned the corner towards it, another car drew up to the curb, and a young man sprang out.

"Thank the Lord, Noreen, I've got hold of you at last," he cried. "There's the devil to pay. That ass Jimmy got off with the wrong car. God knows where those diamonds are at this minute. We're in the devil of a mess."

Lady Noreen stared at him.

"What do you mean? We've got the diamonds—at least Edward has."

"Edward?"

"Yes." She made a slight gesture to indicate the figure by her side.

"It's I who am in the devil of a mess," thought Edward. "Ten to one this is brother Gerald."

The young man stared at him.

"What do you mean?" he said slowly. "Edward's in Scotland."

"Oh!" cried the girl. She stared at Edward. "Oh!"

Her colour came and went.

"So you," she said, in a low voice, "are the real thing?"

It took Edward just one minute to grasp the situation. There was awe in the girl's eyes—was it, could it be—admiration? Should he explain? Nothing so tame! He would play up to the end.

He bowed ceremoniously.

"I have to thank you, Lady Noreen," he said, in the best highwayman manner, "for a most delightful evening."

One quick look he cast at the car from which the other had just alighted. A scarlet car with a shining bonnet. His car!

"And I will wish you good evening."

One quick spring and he was inside, his foot on the clutch. The car started forward. Gerald stood paralysed, but the girl was quicker. As the car slid past she leapt for it, alighting on the running board.

The car swerved, shot blindly round the corner and pulled up. Noreen, still panting from her spring, laid her hand on Edward's arm.

"You must give it me—oh, you must give it me. I've got to return it to Agnes Larella. Be a sport—we've had a good evening together—

we've danced—we've been—pals. Won't you give it to me? To *me?*"

A woman who intoxicated you with her beauty. There were such women then. . . .

Also, Edward was only too anxious to get rid of the necklace. It was a heaven-sent opportunity for a *beau geste.*

He took it from his pocket and dropped it into her outstretched hand.

"We've been—pals," he said.

"Ah!" Her eyes smouldered—lit up.

Then surprisingly she bent her head to him. For a moment he held her, her lips against his. . . .

Then she jumped off. The scarlet car sped forward with a great leap.

Romance!

Adventure!

At twelve o'clock on Christmas Day, Edward Robinson strode into the tiny drawing room of a house in Clapham with the customary greeting of "Merry Christmas."

Maud, who was rearranging a piece of holly, greeted him coldly.

"Have a good day in the country with that friend of yours?" she inquired.

"Look here," said Edward. "That was a lie I told you. I won a competition—£500, and I bought a car with it. I didn't tell you because I knew you'd kick up a row about it. That's the first thing. I've bought the car and there's nothing more to be said about it. The second thing is this—I'm not going to hang about for years. My prospects are quite good enough and I mean to marry you next month. See?"

"Oh!" said Maud faintly.

Was this—could this be—*Edward* speaking in this masterful fashion?

"Will you?" said Edward. "Yes or no?"

She gazed at him, fascinated. There was awe and admiration in her eyes, and the sight of that look was intoxicating to Edward. Gone was that patient motherliness which had roused him to exasperation.

So had the Lady Noreen looked at him last night. But the Lady Noreen had receded far away, right into the region of Romance, side by side with the Marchesa Bianca. This was the Real Thing. This was his woman.

"Yes or no?" he repeated, and drew a step nearer.

"Ye—ye-es," faltered Maud. "But, oh, Edward, what has happened to you? You're quite different today."

"Yes," said Edward. "For twenty-four hours I've been a man instead of a worm—and, by God, it pays!"

He caught her in his arms almost as Bill the superman might have done.

"Do you love me, Maud? Tell me, do you love me?"

"Oh, Edward!" breathed Maud. "I adore you. . . ."

88

Four

JANE IN SEARCH OF A JOB

"Jane in Search of a Job"
was first published in *Grand Magazine*,
August 1924.

• • •

Jane Cleveland rustled the pages of the *Daily Leader* and sighed. A deep sigh that came from the innermost recesses of her being. She looked with distaste at the marble-topped table, the poached egg on toast which reposed on it, and the small pot of tea. Not because she was not hungry. That was far from being the case. Jane was extremely hungry. At that moment she felt like consuming a pound and a half of well-cooked beefsteak, with chip potatoes, and possibly French beans. The whole washed down with some more exciting vintage than tea.

But young women whose exchequers are in a parlous condition cannot be choosers. Jane was lucky to be able to order a poached egg and a pot of tea. It seemed unlikely that she would be able to do so tomorrow. That is unless—

She turned once more to the advertisement columns of the *Daily Leader.* To put it plainly,

Jane was out of a job, and the position was becoming acute. Already the genteel lady who presided over the shabby boardinghouse was looking askance at this particular young woman.

"And yet," said Jane to herself, throwing up her chin indignantly, which was a habit of hers, "and yet I'm intelligent and good-looking and well educated. What more does anyone want?"

According to the *Daily Leader*, they seemed to want shorthand typists of vast experience, managers for business houses with a little capital to invest, ladies to share in the profits of poultry farming (here again a little capital was required), and innumerable cooks, housemaids and parlour-maids—particularly parlourmaids.

"I wouldn't mind being a parlourmaid," said Jane to herself. "But there again, no one would take me without experience. I could go somewhere, I dare say, as a Willing Young Girl—but they don't pay willing young girls anything to speak of."

She sighed again, propped the paper up in front of her, and attacked the poached egg with all the vigour of healthy youth.

When the last mouthful had been despatched, she turned the paper, and studied the Agony and Personal column whilst she drank her tea. The Agony column was always the last hope.

Had she but possessed a couple of thousand pounds, the thing would have been easy enough.

There were at least seven unique opportunities—all yielding not less than three thousand a year. Jane's lip curled a little.

"If I had two thousand pounds," she murmured, "it wouldn't be easy to separate me from it."

She cast her eyes rapidly down to the bottom of the column and ascended with the ease born of long practice.

There was the lady who gave such wonderful prices for cast-off clothing. "Ladies' wardrobes inspected at their own dwellings." There were gentlemen who bought anything—but principally teeth. There were ladies of title going abroad who would dispose of their furs at a ridiculous figure. There was the distressed clergyman and the hard-working widow, and the disabled officer, all needing sums varying from fifty pounds to two thousand. And then suddenly Jane came to an abrupt halt. She put down her teacup and read the advertisement through again.

"There's a catch in it, of course," she murmured. "There always is a catch in these sort of things. I shall have to be careful. But still—"

The advertisement which so intrigued Jane Cleveland ran as follows:

If a young lady of twenty-five to thirty years of age, eyes dark blue, very fair hair, black lashes and brows, straight nose, slim figure, height five feet seven inches, good mimic and able to speak French, will call at 7 Endersleigh Street, between 5 and 6 p.m., she will hear of something to her advantage.

"Guileless Gwendolen, or why girls go wrong," murmured Jane. "I shall certainly have to be careful. But there are too many specifications, really, for that sort of thing. I wonder now . . . Let us overhaul the catalogue."

She proceeded to do so.

"Twenty-five to thirty—I'm twenty-six. Eyes dark blue, that's right. Hair very fair—black lashes and brows—all OK. Straight nose? Ye-es—straight enough, anyway. It doesn't hook or turn up. And I've got a slim figure—slim even for nowadays. I'm only five feet six inches—but I could wear high heels. I *am* a good mimic—nothing wonderful, but I can copy people's voices, and I speak French like an angel or a Frenchwoman. In fact, I'm absolutely the goods. They ought to tumble over themselves with delight when I turn up. Jane Cleveland, go in and win."

Resolutely Jane tore out the advertisement and placed it in her handbag. Then she demanded her bill, with a new briskness in her voice.

At ten minutes to five Jane was reconnoitring in the neighbourhood of Endersleigh Street. Endersleigh Street itself is a small street sandwiched between two larger streets in the neighbourhood of Oxford Circus. It is drab, but respectable.

No. 7 seemed in no way different from the neighbouring houses. It was composed like they were of offices. But looking up at it, it dawned upon Jane for the first time that she was not the only blue-eyed, fair-haired, straight-nosed, slim-figured girl of between twenty-five and thirty years of age. London was evidently full of such girls, and forty or fifty of them at least were grouped outside No. 7 Endersleigh Street.

"Competition," said Jane. "I'd better join the queue quickly."

She did so, just as three more girls turned the corner of the street. Others followed them. Jane amused herself by taking stock of her immediate neighbours. In each case she managed to find something wrong—fair eyelashes instead of dark, eyes more grey than blue, fair hair that owed its fairness to art and not to Nature, interesting variations in noses, and figures that only an all-embracing charity could have described as slim. Jane's spirits rose.

"I believe I've got as good an all-round chance as anyone," she murmured to herself. "I wonder what it's all about? A beauty chorus, I hope."

The queue was moving slowly but steadily forward. Presently a second stream of girls began, issuing from inside the house. Some of them tossed their heads, some of them smirked.

"Rejected," said Jane, with glee. "I hope to goodness they won't be full up before I get in."

And still the queue of girls moved forwards. There were anxious glances in tiny mirrors, and a frenzied powdering of noses. Lipsticks were brandished freely.

"I wish I had a smarter hat," said Jane to herself sadly.

At last it was her turn. Inside the door of the house was a glass door at one side, with the legend, Messrs. Cuthbertsons, inscribed on it. It was through this glass door that the applicants were passing one by one. Jane's turn came. She drew a deep breath and entered.

Inside was an outer office, obviously intended for clerks. At the end was another glass door. Jane was directed to pass through this, and did so. She found herself in a smaller room. There was a big desk in it, and behind the desk was a keen-eyed man of middle age with a thick rather foreign-looking moustache. His glance swept over Jane, then he pointed to a door on the left.

"Wait in there, please," he said crisply.

Jane obeyed. The apartment she entered was already occupied. Five girls sat there, all very upright and all glaring at each other. It was clear to Jane that she had been included amongst the likely candidates, and her spirits rose. Neverthe-less, she was forced to admit that these five girls were equally eligible with herself as far as the terms of the advertisement went.

The time passed. Streams of girls were evidently passing through the inner office. Most of them were dismissed through another door giving on the corridor, but every now and then a recruit arrived to swell the select assembly. At half-past six there were fourteen girls assembled there.

Jane heard a murmur of voices from the inner office, and then the foreign-looking gentleman, whom she had nicknamed in her mind "the Colonel" owing to the military character of his moustache, appeared in the doorway.

"I will see you ladies one at a time, if you please," he announced. "In the order in which you arrived, please."

Jane was, of course, the sixth on the list. Twenty minutes elapsed before she was called in. "The Colonel" was standing with his hands behind his back. He put her through a rapid catechism, tested her knowledge of French, and measured her height.

"It is possible, mademoiselle," he said in French, "that you may suit. I do not know. But it is possible."

"What is this post, if I may ask?" said Jane bluntly.

He shrugged his shoulders.

"That I cannot tell you as yet. If you are chosen—then you shall know."

"This seems very mysterious," objected Jane. "I couldn't possibly take up anything without knowing all about it. Is it connected with the stage, may I ask?"

"The stage? Indeed, no."

"Oh!" said Jane, rather taken aback.

He was looking at her keenly.

"You have intelligence, yes? And discretion?"

"I've quantities of intelligence and discretion," said Jane calmly. "What about the pay?"

"The pay will amount to two thousand pounds—for a fortnight's work."

"Oh!" said Jane faintly.

She was too taken aback by the munificence of the sum named to recover all at once.

The Colonel resumed speaking.

"One other young lady I have already selected. You and she are equally suitable. There may be others I have not yet seen. I will give you instruction as to your further proceedings. You know Harridge's Hotel?"

Jane gasped. Who in England did not know Harridge's Hotel? That famous hostelry situated modestly in a bystreet of Mayfair, where notabilities and royalties arrived and departed as a matter of course. Only this morning Jane had read of the arrival of the Grand Duchess Pauline of Ostrova. She had come over to open a big bazaar in aid of Russian refugees, and was, of course, staying at Harridge's.

"Yes," said Jane, in answer to the Colonel's question.

"Very good. Go there. Ask for Count Streptitch. Send up your card—you have a card?"

Jane produced one. The Colonel took it from her and inscribed in the corner a minute P. He handed the card back to her.

"That ensures that the count will see you. He will understand that you come from me. The final decision lies with him—and another. If he considers you suitable, he will explain matters to you, and you can accept or decline his proposal. Is that satisfactory?"

"Perfectly satisfactory," said Jane.

"So far," she murmured to herself as she emerged into the street, "I can't see the catch. And yet, there must be one. There's no such thing as money for nothing. It must be crime! There's nothing else left."

Her spirits rose. In moderation Jane did not object to crime. The papers had been full lately of the exploits of various girl bandits. Jane had seriously thought of becoming one if all else failed.

She entered the exclusive portals of Harridge's with slight trepidation. More than ever, she wished that she had a new hat.

But she walked bravely up to the bureau and produced her card, and asked for Count Streptitch without a shade of hesitation in her manner. She fancied that the clerk looked at her rather curiously. He took the card, however, and gave it to a small page boy with some low-voiced instructions which Jane did not catch. Presently the page returned, and Jane was invited to accompany him. They went up in the lift and along a corridor to some big double doors where the page knocked. A moment later Jane found herself in a big room, facing a tall thin man with a fair beard, who was holding her card in a languid white hand.

"Miss Jane Cleveland," he read slowly. "I am Count Streptitch."

His lips parted suddenly in what was presumably intended to be a smile, disclosing two rows of white even teeth. But no effect of merriment was obtained.

"I understand that you applied in answer to our advertisement," continued the count. "The good Colonel Kranin sent you on here."

"He *was* a colonel," thought Jane, pleased with her perspicacity, but she merely bowed her head.

"You will pardon me if I ask you a few questions?"

He did not wait for a reply, but proceeded to put Jane through a catechism very similar to that of Colonel Kranin. Her replies seemed to satisfy him. He nodded his head once or twice.

"I will ask you now, mademoiselle, to walk to the door and back again slowly."

"Perhaps they want me to be a mannequin," thought Jane, as she complied. "But they wouldn't pay two thousand pounds to a mannequin. Still, I suppose I'd better not ask questions yet awhile."

Count Streptitch was frowning. He tapped on the table with his white fingers. Suddenly he rose, and opening the door of an adjoining room, he spoke to someone inside.

He returned to his seat, and a short middle-aged lady came through the door, closing it behind her. She was plump and extremely ugly, but had nevertheless the air of being a person of importance.

"Well, Anna Michaelovna," said the count. "What do you think of her?"

The lady looked Jane up and down much as though the girl had been a waxwork at a show. She made no pretence of any greeting.

"She might do," she said at length. "Of actual likeness in the real sense of the word, there is very little. But the figure and the colouring are very good, better than any of the others. What do you think of it, Feodor Alexandrovitch?"

"I agree with you, Anna Michaelovna."

"Does she speak French?"

"Her French is excellent."

Jane felt more and more of a dummy. Neither of these strange people appeared to remember that she was a human being.

"But will she be discreet?" asked the lady, frowning heavily at the girl.

"This is the Princess Poporensky," said Count Streptitch to Jane in French. "She asks whether you can be discreet?"

Jane addressed her reply to the princess.

"Until I have had the position explained to me, I can hardly make promises."

"It is just what she says there, the little one," remarked the lady. "I think she is intelligent, Feodor Alexandrovitch—more intelligent than the others. Tell me, little one, have you also courage?"

"I don't know," said Jane, puzzled. "I don't particularly like being hurt, but I can bear it."

"Ah! that is not what I mean. You do not mind danger, no?"

"Oh!" said Jane. "Danger! That's all right. I like danger."

"And you are poor? You would like to earn much money?"

"Try me," said Jane with something approaching enthusiasm.

Count Streptitch and Princess Poporensky exchanged glances. Then, simultaneously, they nodded.

"Shall I explain matters, Anna Michaelovna?" the former asked.

The princess shook her head.

"Her Highness wishes to do that herself."

"It is unnecessary—and unwise."

"Nevertheless those are her commands. I was to bring the girl in as soon as you had done with her."

Streptitch shrugged his shoulders. Clearly he was not pleased. Equally clearly he had no intention of disobeying the edict. He turned to Jane.

"The Princess Poporensky will present you to Her Highness the Grand Duchess Pauline. Do not be alarmed."

Jane was not in the least alarmed. She was delighted at the idea of being presented to a real live grand duchess. There was nothing of the Socialist about Jane. For the moment she had even ceased to worry about her hat.

The Princess Poporensky led the way, waddling along with a gait that she managed to invest with a certain dignity in spite of adverse circumstances. They passed through the adjoining room, which was a kind of antechamber, and the princess knocked upon a door in the farther wall. A voice from inside replied and the princess opened the door and passed in, Jane close upon her heels.

"Let me present to you, madame," said the princess in a solemn voice, "Miss Jane Cleveland."

A young woman who had been sitting in a big armchair at the other end of the room jumped up and ran forward. She stared fixedly at Jane for a minute or two, and then laughed merrily.

"But this is splendid, Anna," she replied. "I never imagined we should succeed so well. Come, let us see ourselves side by side."

Taking Jane's arm, she drew the girl across the room, pausing before a full-length mirror which hung on the wall.

"You see?" she cried delightedly. "It is a perfect match!"

Already, with her first glance at the Grand Duchess Pauline, Jane had begun to understand. The Grand Duchess was a young woman perhaps a year or two older than Jane. She had the same shade of fair hair, and the same slim figure. She was, perhaps, a shade taller. Now that they stood side by side, the likeness was very apparent. Detail for detail, the colouring was almost exactly the same.

The Grand Duchess clapped her hands. She seemed an extremely cheerful young woman.

"Nothing could be better," she declared. "You must congratulate Feodor Alexandrovitch for me, Anna. He has indeed done well."

"As yet, madame," murmured the princess, in a low voice, "this young woman does not know what is required of her."

"True," said the Grand Duchess, becoming somewhat calmer in manner. "I forgot. Well, I will enlighten her. Leave us together, Anna Michaelovna."

"But, madame—"

"Leave us alone, I say."

She stamped her foot angrily. With considerable reluctance Anna Michaelovna left the room. The

Grand Duchess sat down and motioned to Jane to do the same.

"They are tiresome, these old women," remarked Pauline. "But one has to have them. Anna Michaelovna is better than most. Now then, Miss—ah, yes, Miss Jane Cleveland. I like the name. I like you too. You are sympathetic. I can tell at once if people are sympathetic."

"That's very clever of you, ma'am," said Jane, speaking for the first time.

"I am clever," said Pauline calmly. "Come now, I will explain things to you. Not that there is much to explain. You know the history of Ostrova. Practically all of my family are dead—massacred by the Communists. I am, perhaps, the last of my line. I am a woman, I cannot sit upon the throne. You think they would let me be. But no, wherever I go attempts are made to assassinate me. Absurd, is it not? These vodka-soaked brutes never have any sense of proportion."

"I see," said Jane, feeling that something was required of her.

"For the most part I live in retirement—where I can take precautions, but now and then I have to take part in public ceremonies. While I am here, for instance, I have to attend several semipublic functions. Also in Paris on my way back. I have an estate in Hungary, you know. The sport there is magnificent."

"Is it really?" said Jane.

"Superb. I adore sport. Also—I ought not to tell you this, but I shall because your face is so sympathetic—there are plans being made there— very quietly, you understand. Altogether it is very important that I should not be assassinated during the next two weeks."

"But surely the police—" began Jane.

"The police? Oh, yes, they are very good, I believe. And we too—we have our spies. It is possible that I shall be forewarned when the attempt is to take place. But then, again, I might not."

She shrugged her shoulders.

"I begin to understand," said Jane slowly. "You want me to take your place?"

"Only on certain occasions," said the Grand Duchess eagerly. "You must be somewhere at hand, you understand? I may require you twice, three times, four times in the next fortnight. Each time it will be upon the occasion of some public function. Naturally in intimacy of any kind, you could not represent me."

"Of course not," agreed Jane.

"You will do very well indeed. It was clever of Feodor Alexandrovitch to think of an advertise-ment, was it not?"

"Supposing," said Jane, "that I get assassinated?"

The Grand Duchess shrugged her shoulders.

"There is the risk, of course, but according to our own secret information, they want to kidnap me, not kill me outright. But I will be quite honest—it is always possible that they might throw a bomb."

"I see," said Jane.

She tried to imitate the light-hearted manner of Pauline. She wanted very much to come to the question of money, but did not quite see how best to introduce the subject. But Pauline saved her the trouble.

"We will pay you well, of course," she said carelessly. "I cannot remember now exactly how much Feodor Alexandrovitch suggested. We were speaking in francs or kronen."

"Colonel Kranin," said Jane, "said something about two thousand pounds."

"That was it," said Pauline, brightening. "I remember now. It is enough, I hope? Or would you rather have three thousand?"

"Well," said Jane, "if it's all the same to you, I'd rather have three thousand."

"You are businesslike, I see," said the Grand Duchess kindly. "I wish I was. But I have no idea of money at all. What I want I have to have, that is all."

It seemed to Jane a simple but admirable attitude of mind.

"And of course, as you say, there is danger," Pauline continued thoughtfully. "Although you do not look to me as though you minded danger. I do not myself. I hope you do not think that it is because I am a coward that I want you to take my place? You see, it is most important for Ostrova that I should marry and have at least two sons. After that, it does not matter what happens to me."

"I see," said Jane.

"And you accept?"

"Yes," said Jane resolutely. "I accept."

Pauline clapped her hands vehemently several times. Princess Poporensky appeared immediately.

"I have told her all, Anna," announced the Grand Duchess. "She will do what we want, and she is to have three thousand pounds. Tell Feodor to make a note of it. She is really very like me, is she not? I think she is better looking, though."

The princess waddled out of the room, and returned with Count Streptitch.

"We have arranged everything, Feodor Alexandrovitch," the Grand Duchess said.

He bowed.

"Can she play her part, I wonder?" he queried, eyeing Jane doubtfully.

"I'll show you," said the girl suddenly. "You permit, ma'am?" she said to the Grand Duchess.

The latter nodded delightedly.

Jane stood up.

"But this is splendid, Anna," she said. "I never imagined we should succeed so well. Come, let us see ourselves, side by side."

And, as Pauline had done, she drew the other girl to the glass.

"You see? A perfect match!"

Words, manner and gesture, it was an excellent imitation of Pauline's greeting. The princess nodded her head, and uttered a grunt of approbation.

"It is good, that," she declared. "It would deceive most people."

"You are very clever," said Pauline appreciatively. "I could not imitate anyone else to save my life."

Jane believed her. It had already struck her that Pauline was a young woman who was very much herself.

"Anna will arrange details with you," said the Grand Duchess. "Take her into my bedroom, Anna, and try some of my clothes on her."

She nodded a gracious farewell, and Jane was convoyed away by the Princess Poporensky.

"This is what Her Highness will wear to open the bazaar," explained the old lady, holding up a daring creation of white and black. "This is in three days' time. It may be necessary for you to take her place there. We do not know. We have not yet received information."

At Anna's bidding, Jane slipped off her own shabby garments, and tried on the frock. It fitted her perfectly. The other nodded approvingly.

"It is almost perfect—just a shade long on you, because you are an inch or so shorter than Her Highness."

"That is easily remedied," said Jane quickly. "The Grand Duchess wears low-heeled shoes, I noticed. If I wear the same kind of shoes, but with high heels, it will adjust things nicely."

Anna Michaelovna showed her the shoes that the Grand Duchess usually wore with the dress. Lizard skin with a strap across. Jane memorized them, and arranged to get a pair just like them, but with different heels.

"It would be well," said Anna Michaelovna, "for you to have a dress of distinctive colour and material quite unlike Her Highness's. Then in case it becomes necessary for you to change places at a moment's notice, the substitution is less likely to be noticed."

Jane thought a minute.

"What about a flame-red marocain? And I might, perhaps, have plain glass pince-nez. That alters the appearance very much."

Both suggestions were approved, and they went into further details.

Jane left the hotel with banknotes for a hundred pounds in her purse, and instructions to purchase the necessary outfit and engage rooms at the Blitz Hotel as Miss Montresor of New York.

On the second day after this, Count Streptitch called upon her there.

"A transformation indeed," he said, as he bowed.

Jane made him a mock bow in return. She was enjoying the new clothes and the luxury of her life very much.

"All this is very nice," she sighed. "But I suppose that your visit means I must get busy and earn my money."

"That is so. We have received information. It seems possible that an attempt will be made to kidnap Her Highness on the way home from the bazaar. That is to take place, as you know, at Orion House, which is about ten miles out of London. Her Highness will be forced to attend the bazaar in person, as the Countess of Anchester, who is promoting it, knows her personally. But the following is the plan I have concocted."

Jane listened attentively as he outlined it to her.

She asked a few questions, and finally declared that she understood perfectly the part that she had to play.

The next day dawned bright and clear—a perfect day for one of the great events of the London Season, the bazaar at Orion House, promoted by the Countess of Anchester in aid of Ostrovian refugees in this country.

Having regard to the uncertainty of the English climate, the bazaar itself took place within the spacious rooms of Orion House, which has been for five hundred years in the possession of the Earls of Anchester. Various collections had been loaned, and a charming idea was the gift by a hundred society women of one pearl each taken from their own necklaces, each pearl to be sold by auction on the second day. There were also numerous sideshows and attractions in the grounds.

Jane was there early in the rôle of Miss Montresor. She wore a dress of flame-coloured marocain, and a small red cloche hat. On her feet were high-heeled lizard-skin shoes.

The arrival of the Grand Duchess Pauline was a great event. She was escorted to the platform and duly presented with a bouquet of roses by a small child. She made a short but charming speech and declared the bazaar open. Count Streptitch and Princess Poporensky were in attendance upon her.

She wore the dress that Jane had seen, white with a bold design of black, and her hat was a small cloche of black with a profusion of white ospreys hanging over the brim and a tiny lace veil coming halfway down the face. Jane smiled to herself.

The Grand Duchess went round the bazaar, visiting every stall, making a few purchases, and being uniformly gracious. Then she prepared to depart.

Jane was prompt to take up her cue. She requested a word with the Princess Poporensky and asked to be presented to the Grand Duchess.

"Ah, yes!" said Pauline, in a clear voice. "Miss Montresor, I remember the name. She is an American journalist, I believe. She has done much for our cause. I should be glad to give her a short interview for her paper. Is there anywhere where we could be undisturbed?"

A small anteroom was immediately placed at the Grand Duchess's disposal, and Count Streptitch was despatched to bring in Miss Montresor. As soon as he had done so, and withdrawn again, the Princess Poporensky remaining in attendance, a rapid exchange of garments took place.

Three minutes later, the door opened and the Grand Duchess emerged, her bouquet of roses held up to her face.

Bowing graciously, and uttering a few words of farewell to Lady Anchester in French, she passed out and entered her car which was waiting. Princess Poporensky took her place beside her, and the car drove off.

"Well," said Jane, "that's that. I wonder how Miss Montresor's getting on."

"No one will notice her. She can slip out quietly."

"That's true," said Jane. "I did it nicely, didn't I?"

"You acted your part with great distinction."

"Why isn't the count with us?"

"He was forced to remain. Someone must watch over the safety of Her Highness."

"I hope nobody's going to throw bombs," said Jane apprehensively. "Hi! we're turning off the main road. Why's that?"

Gathering speed, the car was shooting down a side road.

Jane jumped up and put her head out of the

111

window, remonstrating with the driver. He only laughed and increased his speed. Jane sank back into her seat again.

"Your spies were right," she said, with a laugh. "We're for it all right. I suppose the longer I keep it up, the safer it is for the Grand Duchess. At all events we must give her time to return to London safely."

At the prospect of danger, Jane's spirits rose. She had not relished the prospect of a bomb, but this type of adventure appealed to her sporting instincts.

Suddenly, with a grinding of brakes, the car pulled up in its own length. A man jumped on the step. In his hand was a revolver.

"Put your hands up," he snarled.

The Princess Poporensky's hands rose swiftly, but Jane merely looked at him disdainfully, and kept her hands on her lap.

"Ask him the meaning of this outrage," she said in French to her companion.

But before the latter had time to say a word, the man broke in. He poured out a torrent of words in some foreign language.

Not understanding a single thing, Jane merely shrugged her shoulders and said nothing. The chauffeur had got down from his seat and joined the other man.

"Will the illustrious lady be pleased to descend?" he asked, with a grin.

Raising the flowers to her face again, Jane stepped out of the car. The Princess Poporensky followed her.

"Will the illustrious lady come this way?"

Jane took no notice of the man's mock insolent manner, but of her own accord she walked towards a low-built, rambling house which stood about a hundred yards away from where the car had stopped. The road had been a cul-de-sac ending in the gateway and drive which led to this apparently untenanted building.

The man, still brandishing his pistol, came close behind the two women. As they passed up the steps, he brushed past them and flung open a door on the left. It was an empty room, into which a table and two chairs had evidently been brought.

Jane passed in and sat down. Anna Michaelovna followed her. The man banged the door and turned the key.

Jane walked to the window and looked out.

"I could jump out, of course," she remarked. "But I shouldn't get far. No, we'll just have to stay here for the present and make the best of it. I wonder if they'll bring us anything to eat?"

About half an hour later her question was answered.

A big bowl of steaming soup was brought in and placed on the table in front of her. Also two pieces of dry bread.

"No luxury for aristocrats evidently," remarked

Jane cheerily as the door was shut and locked again. "Will you start, or shall I?"

The Princess Poporensky waved the mere idea of food aside with horror.

"How could I eat? Who knows what danger my mistress might not be in?"

"She's all right," said Jane. "It's myself I'm worrying about. You know these people won't be at all pleased when they find they have got hold of the wrong person. In fact, they may be very unpleasant. I shall keep up the haughty Grand Duchess stunt as long as I can, and do a bunk if the opportunity offers."

The Princess Poporensky offered no reply.

Jane, who was hungry, drank up all the soup. It had a curious taste, but was hot and savoury.

Afterwards she felt rather sleepy. The Princess Poporensky seemed to be weeping quietly. Jane arranged herself on her uncomfortable chair in the least uncomfortable way, and allowed her head to droop.

She slept.

Jane awoke with a start. She had an idea that she had been a very long time asleep. Her head felt heavy and uncomfortable.

And then suddenly she saw something that jerked her faculties wide awake again.

She was wearing the flame-coloured marocain frock.

She sat up and looked around her. Yes, she was still in the room in the empty house. Everything was exactly as it had been when she went to sleep, except for two facts. The first was that the Princess Poporensky was no longer sitting on the other chair. The second was her own inexplicable change of costume.

"I can't have dreamt it," said Jane. "Because if I'd dreamt it, I shouldn't be here."

She looked across at the window and registered a second significant fact. When she had gone to sleep the sun had been pouring through the window. Now the house threw a sharp shadow on the sunlit drive.

"The house faces west," she reflected. "It was afternoon when I went to sleep. Therefore it must be tomorrow morning now. Therefore that soup was drugged. Therefore—oh, I don't know. It all seems mad."

She got up and went to the door. It was unlocked. She explored the house. It was silent and empty.

Jane put her hand to her aching head and tried to think.

And then she caught sight of a torn newspaper lying by the front door. It had glaring headlines which caught her eye.

"American Girl Bandit in England," she read. "The Girl in the Red Dress. Sensational Holdup at Orion House Bazaar."

Jane staggered out into the sunlight. Sitting on the steps she read, her eyes growing bigger and bigger. The facts were short and succinct.

Just after the departure of the Grand Duchess Pauline, three men and a girl in a red dress had produced revolvers and successfully held up the crowd. They had annexed the hundred pearls and made a getaway in a fast racing car. Up to now, they had not been traced.

In the stop press (it was a late evening paper) were a few words to the effect that the "girl bandit in the red dress" had been staying at the Blitz as a Miss Montresor of New York.

"I'm dished," said Jane. "Absolutely dished. I always knew there was a catch in it."

And then she started. A strange sound had smote the air. The voice of a man, uttering one word at frequent intervals.

"Damn," it said. "Damn." And yet again, "Damn!"

Jane thrilled to the sound. It expressed so exactly her own feelings. She ran down the steps. By the corner of them lay a young man. He was endeavouring to raise his head from the ground. His face struck Jane as one of the nicest faces she had ever seen. It was freckled and slightly quizzical in expression.

"Damn my head," said the young man. "Damn it. I—"

He broke off and stared at Jane.

"I must be dreaming," he said faintly.

"That's what I said," said Jane. "But we're not. What's the matter with your head?"

"Somebody hit me on it. Fortunately it's a thick one."

He pulled himself into a sitting position, and made a wry face.

"My brain will begin to function shortly, I expect. I'm still in the same old spot, I see."

"How did you get here?" asked Jane curiously.

"That's a long story. By the way, you're not the Grand Duchess What's-her-name, are you?"

"I'm not. I'm plain Jane Cleveland."

"You're not plain anyway," said the young man, looking at her with frank admiration.

Jane blushed.

"I ought to get you some water or something, oughtn't I?" she asked uncertainly.

"I believe it is customary," agreed the young man. "All the same, I'd rather have whisky if you can find it."

Jane was unable to find any whisky. The young man took a deep draught of water, and announced himself better.

"Shall I relate my adventures, or will you relate yours?" he asked.

"You first."

"There's nothing much to mine. I happened to notice that the Grand Duchess went into that room with low-heeled shoes on and came out with high-heeled ones. It struck me as rather odd. I don't like things to be odd.

"I followed the car on my motor bicycle, I saw you taken into the house. About ten minutes later a big racing car came tearing up. A girl in red got out and three men. She had low-heeled shoes on, all right. They went into the house. Presently low heels came out dressed in black and white, and went off in the first car, with an old pussy and a tall man with a fair beard. The others went off in the racing car. I thought they'd all gone, and was just trying to get in at that window and rescue you when someone hit me on the head from behind. That's all. Now for your turn."

Jane related her adventures.

"And it's awfully lucky for me that you did follow," she ended. "Do you see what an awful hole I should have been in otherwise? The Grand Duchess would have had a perfect alibi. She left the bazaar before the holdup began, and arrived in London in her car. Would anybody ever have believed my fantastic improbable story?"

"Not on your life," said the young man with conviction.

They had been so absorbed in their respective narratives that they had been quite oblivious of their surroundings. They looked up now with a slight start to see a tall sad-faced man leaning against the house. He nodded at them.

"Very interesting," he commented.

"Who are you?" demanded Jane.

The sad-faced man's eyes twinkled a little.

"Detective-Inspector Farrell," he said gently. "I've been very interested in hearing your story and this young lady's. We might have found a little difficulty in believing hers, but for one or two things."

"For instance?"

"Well, you see, we heard this morning that the real Grand Duchess had eloped with a chauffeur in Paris."

Jane gasped.

"And then we knew that this American 'girl bandit' had come to this country, and we expected a coup of some kind. We'll have laid hands on them very soon, I can promise you that. Excuse me a minute, will you?"

He ran up the steps into the house.

"Well!" said Jane. She put a lot of force into the expression.

"I think it was awfully clever of you to notice those shoes," she said suddenly.

"Not at all," said the young man. "I was brought up in the boot trade. My father's a sort of boot king. He wanted me to go into the trade—marry and settle down. All that sort of thing. Nobody in particular—just the principle of the thing. But I wanted to be an artist." He sighed.

"I'm so sorry," said Jane kindly.

"I've been trying for six years. There's no

blinking it. I'm a rotten painter. I've a good mind to chuck it and go home like the prodigal son. There's a good billet waiting for me."

"A job is the great thing," agreed Jane wistfully. "Do you think you could get me one trying on boots somewhere?"

"I could give you a better one than that—if you'd take it."

"Oh, what?"

"Never mind now. I'll tell you later. You know, until yesterday I never saw a girl I felt I could marry."

"Yesterday?"

"At the bazaar. And then I saw her—the one and only Her!"

He looked very hard at Jane.

"How beautiful the delphiniums are," said Jane hurriedly, with very pink cheeks.

"They're lupins," said the young man.

"It doesn't matter," said Jane.

"Not a bit," he agreed. And he drew a little nearer.

Five

A Fruitful Sunday

"A Fruitful Sunday" was first published
in the *Daily Mail*, 11 August 1928.

• • •

"Well, really, I call this too delightful," said
Miss Dorothy Pratt for the fourth time. "How I
wish the old cat could see me now. She and her
Janes!"

The "old cat" thus scathingly alluded to was
Miss Pratt's highly estimable employer, Mrs.
Mackenzie Jones, who had strong views upon the
Christian names suitable for parlourmaids and
had repudiated Dorothy in favour of Miss Pratt's
despised second name of Jane.

Miss Pratt's companion did not reply at once—
for the best of reasons. When you have just
purchased a Baby Austin, fourth hand, for the sum
of twenty pounds, and are taking it out for the
second time only, your whole attention is
necessarily focused on the difficult task of using
both hands and feet as the emergencies of the
moment dictate.

"Er—ah!" said Mr. Edward Palgrove and
negotiated a crisis with a horrible grinding sound

that would have set a true motorist's teeth on edge.

"Well, you don't talk to a girl much," complained Dorothy.

Mr. Palgrove was saved from having to respond as at that moment he was roundly and soundly cursed by the driver of a motor omnibus.

"Well, of all the impudence," said Miss Pratt, tossing her head.

"I only wish *he* had this foot brake," said her swain bitterly.

"Is there anything wrong with it?"

"You can put your foot on it till kingdom comes," said Mr. Palgrove. "But nothing happens."

"Oh, well, Ted, you can't expect everything for twenty pounds. After all, here we are, in a real car, on Sunday afternoon going out of town the same as everybody else."

More grinding and crashing sounds.

"Ah," said Ted, flushed with triumph. "That was a better change."

"You do drive something beautiful," said Dorothy admiringly.

Emboldened by feminine appreciation, Mr. Palgrove attempted a dash across Hammersmith Broadway, and was severely spoken to by a policeman.

"Well, I never," said Dorothy, as they proceeded towards Hammersmith Bridge in a chastened fashion. "I don't know what the police are coming to. You'd think they'd be a bit more civil spoken seeing the way they've been shown up lately."

"Anyway, I didn't want to go along this road," said Edward sadly. "I wanted to go down the Great West Road and do a bust."

"And be caught in a trap as likely as not," said Dorothy. "That's what happened to the master the other day. Five pounds and costs."

"The police aren't so dusty after all," said Edward generously. "They pitch into the rich all right. No favour. It makes me mad to think of these swells who can walk into a place and buy a couple of Rolls-Royces without turning a hair. There's no sense in it. I'm as good as they are."

"And the jewellery," said Dorothy, sighing. "Those shops in Bond Street. Diamonds and pearls and I don't know what! And me with a string of Woolworth pearls."

She brooded sadly upon the subject. Edward was able once more to give his full attention to his driving. They managed to get through Richmond without mishap. The altercation with the policeman had shaken Edward's nerve. He now took the line of least resistance, following blindly behind any car in front whenever a choice of thoroughfares presented itself.

In this way he presently found himself following a shady country lane which many an experienced motorist would have given his soul to find.

"Rather clever turning off the way I did," said Edward, taking all the credit to himself.

"Sweetly pretty, I call it," said Miss Pratt. "And I do declare, there's a man with fruit to sell."

Sure enough, at a convenient corner, was a small wicker table with baskets of fruit on it, and the legend eat more fruit displayed on a banner.

"How much?" said Edward apprehensively when frenzied pulling of the hand brake had produced the desired result.

"Lovely strawberries," said the man in charge.

He was an unprepossessing-looking individual with a leer.

"Just the thing for the lady. Ripe fruit, fresh picked. Cherries too. Genuine English. Have a basket of cherries, lady?"

"They do look nice ones," said Dorothy.

"Lovely, that's what they are," said the man hoarsely. "Bring you luck, lady, that basket will." He at last condescended to reply to Edward. "Two shillings, sir, and dirt cheap. You'd say so if you knew what was inside the basket."

"They look awfully nice," said Dorothy.

Edward sighed and paid over two shillings. His mind was obsessed by calculation. Tea later, petrol—this Sunday motoring business wasn't what you'd call *cheap*. That was the worst of taking girls out! They always wanted everything they saw.

"Thank you, sir," said the unprepossessing-looking one. "You've got more than your money's worth in that basket of cherries."

Edward shoved his foot savagely down and the Baby Austin leaped at the cherry vendor after the manner of an infuriated Alsatian.

"Sorry," said Edward. "I forgot she was in gear."

"You ought to be careful, dear," said Dorothy. "You might have hurt him."

Edward did not reply. Another half mile brought them to an ideal spot by the banks of a stream. The Austin was left by the side of the road and Edward and Dorothy sat affectionately upon the river bank and munched cherries. A Sunday paper lay unheeded at their feet.

"What's the news?" said Edward at last, stretching himself flat on his back and tilting his hat to shade his eyes.

Dorothy glanced over the headlines.

"The Woeful Wife. Extraordinary story. Twenty-eight people drowned last week. Reported death of Airman. Startling Jewel Robbery. Ruby Necklace worth fifty thousand pounds missing. Oh, Ted! Fifty thousand pounds. Just fancy!" She went on reading. "The necklace is composed of twenty-one stones set in platinum and was sent by registered post from Paris. On arrival, the packet was found to contain a few pebbles and the jewels were missing."

"Pinched in the post," said Edward. "The posts in France are awful, I believe."

"I'd like to see a necklace like that," said Dorothy. "All glowing like blood—pigeon's

125

blood, that's what they call the colour. I wonder what it would feel like to have a thing like that hanging round your neck."

"Well, *you're* never likely to know, my girl," said Edward facetiously.

Dorothy tossed her head.

"Why not, I should like to know. It's amazing the way girls can get on in the world. I might go on the stage."

"Girls that behave themselves don't get anywhere," said Edward discouragingly.

Dorothy opened her mouth to reply, checked herself, and murmured, "Pass me the cherries.

"I've been eating more than you have," she remarked. "I'll divide up what's left and—why, whatever's this at the bottom of the basket?"

She drew it out as she spoke—a long glittering chain of blood-red stones.

They both stared at it in amazement.

"In the basket, did you say?" said Edward at last.

Dorothy nodded.

"Right at the bottom—under the fruit."

Again they stared at each other.

"How did it get there, do you think?"

"I can't imagine. It's odd, Ted, just after reading that bit in the paper—about the rubies."

Edward laughed.

"You don't imagine you're holding fifty thousand pounds in your hand, do you?"

"I just said it was odd. Rubies set in platinum. Platinum is that sort of dull silvery stuff—like this. Don't they sparkle and aren't they a lovely colour? I wonder how many of them there are?" She counted. "I say, Ted, there are twenty-one exactly."

"No!"

"Yes. The same number as the paper said. Oh, Ted, you don't think—"

"It could be." But he spoke irresolutely. "There's some sort of way you can tell—scratching them on glass."

"That's diamonds. But you know, Ted, that was a very odd-looking man—the man with the fruit—a nasty-looking man. And he was funny about it—said we'd got more than our money's worth in the basket."

"Yes, but look here, Dorothy, what would he want to hand us over fifty thousand pounds for?"

Miss Pratt shook her head, discouraged.

"It doesn't seem to make sense," she admitted. "Unless the police were after him."

"The police?" Edward paled slightly.

"Yes. It goes on to say in the paper—'the police have a clue.'"

Cold shivers ran down Edward's spine.

"I don't like this, Dorothy. Supposing the police get after *us*."

Dorothy stared at him with her mouth open.

"But we haven't done anything, Ted. We found it in the basket."

"And that'll sound a silly sort of story to tell! It isn't likely."

"It isn't very," admitted Dorothy. "Oh, Ted, do you really think it is it? It's like a fairy story!"

"I don't think it sounds like a fairy story," said Edward. "It sounds to me more like the kind of story where the hero goes to Dartmoor unjustly accused for fourteen years."

But Dorothy was not listening. She had clasped the necklace round her neck and was judging the effect in a small mirror taken from her handbag.

"The same as a duchess might wear," she murmured ecstatically.

"I won't believe it," said Edward violently. "They're imitation. They *must* be imitation."

"Yes, dear," said Dorothy, still intent on her reflection in the mirror. "Very likely."

"Anything else would be too much of a—a coincidence."

"Pigeon's blood," murmured Dorothy.

"It's absurd. That's what I say. Absurd. Look here, Dorothy, are you listening to what I say, or are you not?"

Dorothy put away the mirror. She turned to him, one hand on the rubies round her neck.

"How do I look?" she asked.

Edward stared at her, his grievance forgotten. He had never seen Dorothy quite like this. There was a triumph about her, a kind of regal beauty that was completely new to him. The belief that she had jewels round her neck worth fifty thousand pounds had made of Dorothy Pratt a new woman. She looked insolently serene, a kind of Cleopatra and Semiramis and Zenobia rolled into one.

"You look—you look—stunning," said Edward humbly.

Dorothy laughed, and her laugh, too, was entirely different.

"Look here," said Edward. "We've got to do something. We must take them to a police station or something."

"Nonsense," said Dorothy. "You said yourself just now that they wouldn't believe you. You'll probably be sent to prison for stealing them."

"But—but what else can we do?"

"Keep them," said the new Dorothy Pratt.

Edward stared at her.

"Keep them? You're mad."

"We found them, didn't we? Why should we think they're valuable. We'll keep them and I shall wear them."

"And the police will pinch *you*."

Dorothy considered this for a minute or two.

"All right," she said. "We'll sell them. And you can buy a Rolls-Royce, or two Rolls-Royces, and I'll buy a diamond head-thing and some rings."

Still Edward stared. Dorothy showed impatience.

"You've got your chance now—it's up to you to

take it. We didn't steal the thing—I wouldn't hold with that. It's come to us and it's probably the only chance we'll ever have of getting all the things we want. Haven't you got any spunk at all, Edward Palgrove?"

Edward found his voice.

"Sell it, you say? That wouldn't be so jolly easy. Any jeweller would want to know where I got the blooming thing."

"You don't take it to a jeweller. Don't you ever read detective stories, Ted? You take it to a 'fence,' of course."

"And how should I know any fences? I've been brought up respectable."

"Men ought to know everything," said Dorothy. "That's what they're for."

He looked at her. She was serene and unyielding.

"I wouldn't have believed it of you," he said weakly.

"I thought you had more spirit."

There was a pause. Then Dorothy rose to her feet.

"Well," she said lightly. "We'd best be getting home."

"Wearing that thing round your neck?"

Dorothy removed the necklace, looked at it reverently and dropped it into her handbag.

"Look here," said Edward. "You give that to me."

"No."

"Yes, you do. I've been brought up honest, my girl."

"Well, you can go on being honest. You need have nothing to do with it."

"Oh, hand it over," said Edward recklessly. "I'll do it. I'll find a fence. As you say, it's the only chance we shall ever have. We came by it honest—bought it for two shillings. It's no more than what gentlemen do in antique shops every day of their life and are proud of it."

"That's it!" said Dorothy. "Oh, Edward, you're splendid!"

She handed over the necklace and he dropped it into his pocket. He felt worked up, exalted, the very devil of a fellow! In this mood he started the Austin. They were both too excited to remember tea. They drove back to London in silence. Once at a crossroads, a policeman stepped towards the car, and Edward's heart missed a beat. By a miracle, they reached home without mishap.

Edward's last words to Dorothy were imbued with the adventurous spirit.

"We'll go through with this. Fifty thousand pounds! It's worth it!"

He dreamt that night of broad arrows and Dartmoor, and rose early, haggard and unrefreshed. He had to set about finding a fence—and how to do it he had not the remotest idea!

His work at the office was slovenly and brought down upon him two sharp rebukes before lunch.

How did one find a "fence"? Whitechapel, he

fancied, was the correct neighbourhood—or was it Stepney?

On his return to the office a call came through for him on the telephone. Dorothy's voice spoke—tragic and tearful.

"Is that you, Ted? I'm using the telephone, but she may come in any minute, and I'll have to stop. Ted, you haven't done anything, have you?"

Edward replied in the negative.

"Well, look here, Ted, you mustn't. I've been lying awake all night. It's been awful. Thinking of how it says in the Bible you mustn't steal. I must have been mad yesterday—I really must. You won't do anything, will you, Ted, dear?"

Did a feeling of relief steal over Mr. Palgrove? Possibly it did—but he wasn't going to admit any such thing.

"When I say I'm going through with a thing, I go through with it," he said in a voice such as might belong to a strong superman with eyes of steel.

"Oh, but, Ted, dear, you mustn't. Oh, Lord, she's coming. Look here, Ted, she's going out to dinner tonight. I can slip out and meet you. Don't do anything till you've seen me. Eight o'clock. Wait for me round the corner." Her voice changed to a seraphic murmur. "Yes, ma'am, I think it was a wrong number. It was Bloomsbury 0234 they wanted."

As Edward left the office at six o'clock, a huge headline caught his eye.

Hurriedly he extended a penny. Safely ensconced in the Tube, having dexterously managed to gain a seat, he eagerly perused the printed sheet. He found what he sought easily enough.

A suppressed whistle escaped him.

"Well—I'm—"

And then another adjacent paragraph caught his eye. He read it through and let the paper slip to the floor unheeded.

Precisely at eight o'clock, he was waiting at the rendezvous. A breathless Dorothy, looking pale but pretty, came hurrying along to join him.

"You haven't done anything, Ted?"

"I haven't done anything." He took the ruby chain from his pocket. "You can put it on."

"But, Ted—"

"The police have got the rubies all right—and the man who pinched them. And now read this!"

He thrust a newspaper paragraph under her nose. Dorothy read:

NEW ADVERTISING STUNT

A clever new advertising dodge is being adopted by the All-English Fivepenny Fair who intend to challenge the famous Woolworths. Baskets of fruit were sold yesterday and will be on sale every

Sunday. Out of every fifty baskets, one will contain an imitation necklace in different coloured stones. These necklaces are really wonderful value for the money. Great excitement and merriment was caused by them yesterday and EAT MORE FRUIT will have a great vogue next Sunday. We congratulate the Fivepenny Fair on their resource and wish them all good luck in their campaign of Buy British Goods.

"Well—" said Dorothy.

And after a pause: "Well!"

"Yes," said Edward. "I felt the same."

A passing man thrust a paper into his hand.

"Take one, brother," he said.

"The price of a virtuous woman is far above rubies."

"There!" said Edward. "I hope that cheers you up."

"I don't know," said Dorothy doubtfully. "I don't exactly want to *look* like a good woman."

"You don't," said Edward. "That's why the man gave me that paper. With those rubies round your neck you don't look one little bit like a good woman."

Dorothy laughed.

"You're rather a dear, Ted," she said. "Come on, let's go to the pictures."

Six

THE GOLDEN BALL

"The Golden Ball" was first published as "Playing the Innocent" in the *Daily Mail*, 5 August 1929.

• • •

George Dundas stood in the City of London meditating.

All about him toilers and moneymakers surged and flowed like an enveloping tide. But George, beautifully dressed, his trousers exquisitely creased, took no heed of them. He was busy thinking what to do next.

Something had occurred! Between George and his rich uncle (Ephraim Leadbetter of the firm of Leadbetter and Gilling) there had been what is called in a lower walk of life "words." To be strictly accurate the words had been almost entirely on Mr. Leadbetter's side. They had flowed from his lips in a steady stream of bitter indignation, and the fact that they consisted almost entirely of repetition did not seem to have worried him. To say a thing once beautifully and then let it alone was not one of Mr. Leadbetter's mottos.

The theme was a simple one—the criminal folly and wickedness of a young man, who has his way to make, taking a day off in the middle of the week without even asking leave. Mr. Leadbetter, when he had said everything he could think of and several things twice, paused for breath and asked George what he meant by it.

George replied simply that he had felt he wanted a day off. A holiday, in fact.

And what, Mr. Leadbetter wanted to know, were Saturday afternoon and Sunday? To say nothing of Whitsuntide, not long past, and August Bank Holiday to come?

George said he didn't care for Saturday afternoons, Sundays or Bank Holidays. He meant a real day, when it might be possible to find some spot where half London was not assembled already.

Mr. Leadbetter then said that he had done his best by his dead sister's son—nobody could say he hadn't given him a chance. But it was plain that it was no use. And in future George could have five real days with Saturday and Sunday added to do with as he liked.

"The golden ball of opportunity has been thrown up for you, my boy," said Mr. Leadbetter in a last touch of poetical fancy. "And you have failed to grasp it."

George said it seemed to him that that was just what he *had* done, and Mr. Leadbetter dropped poetry for wrath and told him to get out.

Hence George—meditating. Would his uncle relent or would he not? Had he any secret affection for George, or merely a cold distaste?

It was just at that moment that a voice—a most unlikely voice—said, "Hallo!"

A scarlet touring car with an immense long bonnet had drawn up to the curb beside him. At the wheel was that beautiful and popular society girl, Mary Montresor. (The description is that of the illustrated papers who produced a portrait of her at least four times a month.) She was smiling at George in an accomplished manner.

"I never knew a man could look so like an island," said Mary Montresor. "Would you like to get in?"

"I should love it above all things," said George with no hesitation, and stepped in beside her.

They proceeded slowly because the traffic forbade anything else.

"I'm tired of the city," said Mary Montresor. "I came to see what it was like. I shall go back to London."

Without presuming to correct her geography, George said it was a splendid idea. They proceeded sometimes slowly, sometimes with wild bursts of speed when Mary Montresor saw a chance of cutting in. It seemed to George that she was somewhat optimistic in the latter view, but he reflected that one could only die once. He thought it best, however, to essay no conversation. He preferred his fair driver to keep strictly to the job in hand.

It was she who reopened the conversation, choosing the moment when they were doing a wild sweep round Hyde Park Corner.

"How would you like to marry me?" she inquired casually.

George gave a gasp, but that may have been due to a large bus that seemed to spell certain destruction. He prided himself on his quickness in response.

"I should love it," he replied easily.

"Well," said Mary Montresor, vaguely. "Perhaps you may some day."

They turned into the straight without accident, and at that moment George perceived large new bills at Hyde Park Corner Tube station. Sandwiched between GRAVE POLITICAL SITUATION and COLONEL IN DOCK, one said SOCIETY GIRL TO MARRY DUKE and the other DUKE OF EDGEHILL AND MISS MONTRESOR.

"What's this about the Duke of Edgehill?" demanded George sternly.

"Me and Bingo? We're engaged."

"But then—what you said just now—"

"Oh, *that,*" said Mary Montresor. "You see, I haven't made up my mind who I shall actually *marry.*"

"Then why did you get engaged to him?"

"Just to see if I could. Everybody seemed to

think it would be frightfully difficult, and it wasn't a bit!"

"Very rough luck on—er—Bingo," said George, mastering his embarrassment at calling a real live duke by a nickname.

"Not at all," said Mary Montresor. "It will be good for Bingo if anything *could* do him good—which I doubt."

George made another discovery—again aided by a convenient poster.

"Why, of course, it's cup day at Ascot. I should have thought that was the one place you were simply bound to be today."

Mary Montresor sighed.

"I wanted a holiday," she said plaintively.

"Why, so did I," said George, delighted. "And as a result my uncle has kicked me out to starve."

"Then in case we marry," said Mary, "my twenty thousand a year may come in useful?"

"It will certainly provide us with a few home comforts," said George.

"Talking of homes," said Mary, "let's go in the country and find a home we would like to live in."

It seemed a simple and charming plan. They negotiated Putney Bridge, reached the Kingston bypass and with a sigh of satisfaction Mary pressed her foot down on the accelerator. They got into the country very quickly. It was half an hour later that with a sudden exclamation Mary shot out a dramatic hand and pointed.

On the brow of a hill in front of them there nestled a house of what house agents describe (but seldom truthfully) as "old-world" charm. Imagine the description of most houses in the country really come true for once, and you get an idea of this house.

Mary drew up outside a white gate.

"We'll leave the car and go up and look at it. It's our house!"

"Decidedly, it's our house," agreed George. "But just for the moment other people seem to be living in it."

Mary dismissed the other people with a wave of her hand. They walked up the winding drive together. The house appeared even more desirable at close quarters.

"We'll go and peep in at all the windows," said Mary.

George demurred.

"Do you think the other people—?"

"I shan't consider them. It's our house—they're only living in it by a sort of accident. Besides, it's a lovely day and they're sure to be out. And if anyone does catch us, I shall say—I shall say— that I thought it was Mrs.—Mrs. Pardonstenger's house, and that I *am* so sorry I made a mistake."

"Well, that ought to be safe enough," said George reflectively.

They looked in through windows. The house was delightfully furnished. They had just got to the study when footsteps crunched on the gravel behind them and they turned to face a most irreproachable butler.

"Oh!" said Mary. And then putting on her most enchanting smile, she said, "Is Mrs. Pardonstenger in? I was looking to see if she was in the study."

"Mrs. Pardonstenger is at home, madam," said the butler. "Will you come this way, please."

They did the only thing they could. They followed him. George was calculating what the odds against this happening could possibly be. With a name like Pardonstenger he came to the conclusion it was about one in twenty thousand. His companion whispered, "Leave it to me. It will be all right."

George was only too pleased to leave it to her. The situation, he considered, called for feminine finesse.

They were shown into a drawing room. No sooner had the butler left the room than the door almost immediately reopened and a big florid lady with peroxide hair came in expectantly.

Mary Montresor made a movement towards her, then paused in well-simulated surprise.

"Why!" she exclaimed. "It *isn't* Amy! What an extraordinary thing!"

"It *is* an extraordinary thing," said a grim voice.

A man had entered behind Mrs. Pardonstenger, an enormous man with a bulldog face and a sinister frown. George thought he had never seen such an unpleasant brute. The man closed the door and stood with his back against it.

"A very extraordinary thing," he repeated sneeringly. "But I fancy we understand your little game!" He suddenly produced what seemed an outsize in revolvers. "Hands up. Hands up, I say. Frisk 'em, Bella."

George in reading detective stories had often wondered what it meant to be frisked. Now he knew. Bella (alias Mrs. P.) satisfied herself that neither he nor Mary concealed any lethal weapons on their persons.

"Thought you were mighty clever, didn't you?" sneered the man. "Coming here like this and playing the innocents. You've made a mistake this time—a bad mistake. In fact, I very much doubt whether your friends and relations will ever see you again. Ah! you would, would you?" as George made a movement. "None of your games. I'd shoot you as soon as look at you."

"Be careful, George," quavered Mary.

"I shall," said George with feeling. "Very careful."

"And now march," said the man. "Open the door, Bella. Keep your hands above your heads, you two. The lady first that's right. I'll come behind you both. Across the hall. Upstairs. . . ."

They obeyed. What else could they do? Mary mounted the stairs, her hands held high. George followed. Behind them came the huge ruffian, revolver in hand.

Mary reached the top of the staircase and turned the corner. At the same moment, without the least warning, George lunged out in a fierce backward kick. He caught the man full in the middle and he capsized backwards down the stairs. In a moment George had turned and leaped down after him, kneeling on his chest. With his right hand, he picked up the revolver which had fallen from the other's hand as he fell.

Bella gave a scream and retreated through a baize door. Mary came running down the stairs, her face as white as paper.

"George, you haven't killed him?"

The man was lying absolutely still. George bent over him.

"I don't think I've killed him," he said regretfully. "But he's certainly taken the count all right."

"Thank God." She was breathing rapidly.

"Pretty neat," said George with permissible self-admiration. "Many a lesson to be learnt from a jolly old mule. Eh, what?"

Mary pulled at his hand.

"Come away," she cried feverishly. "Come away quick."

"If we had something to tie this fellow up with," said George, intent on his own plans. "I suppose you couldn't find a bit of rope or cord anywhere?"

"No, I couldn't," said Mary. "And come away, please—please—I'm so frightened."

"You needn't be frightened," said George with manly arrogance. "*I'm* here."

"Darling George, please—for my sake. I don't want to be mixed up in this. *Please* let's go."

The exquisite way in which she breathed the words "for my sake" shook George's resolution. He allowed himself to be led forth from the house and hurried down the drive to the waiting car. Mary said faintly: "You drive. I don't feel I can." George took command of the wheel.

"But we've got to see this thing through," he said. "Heaven knows what blackguardism that nasty looking fellow is up to. I won't bring the police into it if you don't want me to—but I'll have a try on my own. I ought to be able to get on their track all right."

"No, George, I don't want you to."

"We have a first-class adventure like this, and you want me to back out of it? Not on my life."

"I'd no idea you were so bloodthirsty," said Mary tearfully.

"I'm not bloodthirsty. I didn't begin it. The damned cheek of the fellow—threatening us with an outsize revolver. By the way—why on earth didn't that revolver go off when I kicked him downstairs?"

He stopped the car and fished the revolver out of the side-pocket of the car where he had placed it. After examining it, he whistled.

"Well, I'm damned! The thing isn't loaded. If I'd known that—" He paused, wrapped in thought. "Mary, this is a very curious business."

"I know it is. That's why I'm begging you to leave it alone."

"Never," said George firmly.

Mary uttered a heartrending sigh.

"I see," she said, "that I shall have to tell you. And the worst of it is that I haven't the least idea how you'll take it."

"What do you mean—tell me?"

"You see, it's like this." She paused. "I feel girls should stick together nowadays—they should insist on knowing something about the men they meet."

"Well?" said George, utterly fogged.

"And the most important thing to a girl is how a man will behave in an emergency—has he got presence of mind—courage—quick wittedness? That's the kind of thing you can hardly ever know—until it's too late. An emergency mightn't arise until you'd been married for years. All you do know about a man is how he dances and if he's good at getting taxis on a wet night."

"Both very useful accomplishments," George pointed out.

"Yes, but one wants to feel a man is a man."

"The great wide-open spaces where men *are* men," George quoted absently.

"Exactly. But we have no wide-open spaces in

England. So one has to create a situation artificially. That's what I did."

"Do you mean—?"

"I do mean. That house, as it happens, actually *is* my house. We came to it by design—not by chance. And the man—that man that you nearly killed—"

"Yes?"

"He's Rube Wallace—the film actor. He does prizefighters, you know. The dearest and gentlest of men. I engaged him. Bella's his wife. That's why I was so terrified that you'd killed him. Of course the revolver wasn't loaded. It's a stage property. Oh, George, are you very angry?"

"Am I the first person you have—er—tried this test on?"

"Oh, no. There have been—let me see—nine and a half!"

"Who was the half?" inquired George with curiosity.

"Bingo," replied Mary coldly.

"Did any of them think of kicking like a mule?"

"No—they didn't. Some tried to bluster and some gave in at once, but they all allowed themselves to be marched upstairs and tied up, and gagged. Then, of course, I managed to work myself loose from my bonds—like in books— and I freed them and we got away—finding the house empty."

"And nobody thought of the mule trick or anything like it?"

"No."

"In that case," said George graciously, "I forgive you."

"Thank you, George," said Mary meekly.

"In fact," said George, "the only question that arises is: Where do we go now? I'm not sure if it's Lambeth Palace or Doctor's Commons, wherever that is."

"What *are* you talking about?"

"The licence. A special licence, I think, is indicated. You're too fond of getting engaged to one man and then immediately asking another one to marry you."

"I didn't ask you to marry me!"

"You did. At Hyde Park Corner. Not a place I should choose for a proposal myself, but everyone has their idiosyncrasies in these matters."

"I did nothing of the kind. I just asked, as a joke, whether you would care to marry me? It wasn't intended seriously."

"If I were to take counsel's opinion, I am sure that he would say it constituted a genuine proposal. Besides, you know you want to marry me."

"I don't."

"Not after nine-and-a-half failures? Fancy what a feeling of security it will give you to go through life with a man who can extricate you from any dangerous situation."

Mary appeared to weaken slightly at this telling argument. But she said firmly: "I wouldn't marry any man unless he went on his knees to me."

George looked at her. She was adorable. But George had other characteristics of the mule beside its kick. He said with equal firmness:

"To go on one's knees to any woman is degrading. I will not do it."

Mary said with enchanting wistfulness: "What a pity."

They drove back to London. George was stern and silent. Mary's face was hidden by the brim of her hat. As they passed Hyde Park Corner, she murmured softly:

"Couldn't you go on your knees to me?"

George said firmly: "No."

He felt he was being a superman. She admired him for his attitude. But unluckily he suspected her of mulish tendencies herself. He drew up suddenly.

"Excuse me," he said.

He jumped out of the car, retraced his steps to a fruit barrow they had just passed and returned so quickly that the policeman who was bearing down upon them to ask what they meant by it, had not had time to arrive.

George drove on, lightly tossing an apple into Mary's lap.

"Eat more fruit," he said. "Also symbolical."

"Symbolical?"

"Yes. Originally Eve gave Adam an apple. Nowadays Adam gives Eve one. See?"

"Yes," said Mary rather doubtfully.

"Where shall I drive you?" inquired George formally.

"Home, please."

He drove to Grosvenor Square. His face was absolutely impassive. He jumped out and came round to help her out. She made a last appeal.

"Darling George—couldn't you? Just to please me?"

"Never," said George.

And at that moment it happened. He slipped, tried to recover his balance and failed. He was kneeling in the mud before her. Mary gave a squeal of joy and clapped her hands.

"Darling George! Now I will marry you. You can go straight to Lambeth Palace and fix up with the Archbishop of Canterbury about it."

"I didn't mean to," said George hotly. "It was a bl—er—a banana skin." He held the offender up reproachfully.

"Never mind," said Mary. "It happened. When we quarrel and you throw it in my teeth that I proposed to you, I can retort that you had to go on your knees to me before I would marry you. And all because of that blessed banana skin! It *was* a blessed banana skin you were going to say?"

"Something of the sort," said George.

• • •

At five-thirty that afternoon, Mr. Leadbetter was informed that his nephew had called and would like to see him.

"Called to eat humble pie," said Mr. Leadbetter to himself. "I dare say I was rather hard on the lad, but it was for his own good."

And he gave orders that George should be admitted.

George came in airily.

"I want a few words with you, uncle," he said. "You did me a grave injustice this morning. I should like to know whether, at my age, you could have gone out into the street, disowned by your relatives, and between the hours of eleven-fifteen and five-thirty acquire an income of twenty thousand a year. This is what I have done!"

"You're mad, boy."

"Not mad, resourceful! I am going to marry a young, rich, beautiful society girl. One, moreover, who is throwing over a duke for my sake."

"Marrying a girl for her money? I'd not have thought it of you."

"And you'd have been right. I would never have dared to ask her if she hadn't—very fortunately—asked me. She retracted afterwards, but I made her change her mind. And do you know, uncle, how all this was done? By a judicious expenditure of twopence and a grasping of the golden ball of opportunity."

"Why the tuppence?" asked Mr. Leadbetter, financially interested.

"One banana—off a barrow. Not everyone would have thought of that banana. Where do you get a marriage licence? Is it Doctor's Commons or Lambeth Palace?"

Seven

THE RAJAH'S EMERALD

"The Rajah's Emerald" was first
published in *Red Magazine*, 30 July 1926.

• • •

With a serious effort James Bond bent his
attention once more on the little yellow book in
his hand. On its outside the book bore the simple
but pleasing legend, "Do you want your salary
increased by £300 per annum?" Its price was
one shilling. James had just finished reading two
pages of crisp paragraphs instructing him to
look his boss in the face, to cultivate a dynamic
personality, and to radiate an atmosphere of
efficiency. He had now arrived at a subtler matter,
"There is a time for frankness, there is a time for
discretion," the little yellow book informed him.
"A strong man does not always blurt out *all* he
knows." James let the little book close, and raising
his head, gazed out over a blue expanse of ocean.
A horrible suspicion assailed him, that he was *not*
a strong man. A strong man would have been in
command of the present situation, not a victim
to it. For the sixtieth time that morning James
rehearsed his wrongs.

This was his holiday. His holiday? Ha, ha! Sardonic laughter. Who had persuaded him to come to that fashionable seaside resort, Kimpton-on-Sea? Grace. Who had urged him into an expenditure of more than he could afford? Grace. And he had fallen in with the plan eagerly. She had got him here, and what was the result? Whilst he was staying in an obscure boardinghouse about a mile and a half from the seafront, Grace who should have been in a similar boardinghouse (not the same one—the proprieties of James's circle were very strict) had flagrantly deserted him, and was staying at no less than the Esplanade Hotel upon the seafront.

It seemed that she had friends there. Friends! Again James laughed sardonically. His mind went back over the last three years of his leisurely courtship of Grace. Extremely pleased she had been when he first singled her out for notice. That was before she had risen to heights of glory in the millinery salon at Messrs Bartles in the High Street. In those early days it had been James who gave himself airs, now alas! the boot was on the other leg. Grace was what is technically known as "earning good money." It had made her uppish. Yes, that was it, thoroughly uppish. A confused fragment out of a poetry book came back to James's mind, something about "thanking heaven fasting, for a good man's love." But there was nothing of that kind of thing observable about

Grace. Well fed on an Esplanade Hotel breakfast, she was ignoring a good man's love utterly. She was indeed accepting the attentions of a poisonous idiot called Claud Sopworth, a man, James felt convinced, of no moral worth whatsoever.

James ground a heel into the earth, and scowled darkly at the horizon. Kimpton-on-Sea. What had possessed him to come to such a place? It was preeminently a resort of the rich and fashionable, it possessed two large hotels, and several miles of picturesque bungalows belonging to fashionable actresses, rich Jews and those members of the English aristocracy who had married wealthy wives. The rent, furnished, of the smallest bungalow was twenty-five guineas a week. Imagination boggled at what the rent of the large ones might amount to. There was one of these palaces immediately behind James's seat. It belonged to that famous sportsman Lord Edward Campion, and there were staying there at the moment a houseful of distinguished guests including the Rajah of Maraputna, whose wealth was fabulous. James had read all about him in the local weekly newspaper that morning; the extent of his Indian possessions, his palaces, his wonderful collection of jewels, with a special mention of one famous emerald which the papers declared enthusiastically was the size of a pigeon's egg. James, being town bred, was somewhat hazy about the size of a pigeon's egg, but the impression left on his mind was good.

"If I had an emerald like that," said James, scowling at the horizon again, "I'd show Grace."

The sentiment was vague, but the enunciation of it made James feel better. Laughing voices hailed him from behind, and he turned abruptly to confront Grace. With her was Clara Sopworth, Alice Sopworth, Dorothy Sopworth and—alas! Claud Sopworth. The girls were arm-in-arm and giggling.

"Why, you are quite a stranger," cried Grace archly.

"Yes," said James.

He could, he felt, have found a more telling retort. You cannot convey the impression of a dynamic personality by the use of the one word "yes." He looked with intense loathing at Claud Sopworth. Claud Sopworth was almost as beautifully dressed as the hero of a musical comedy. James longed passionately for the moment when an enthusiastic beach dog should plant wet, sandy forefeet on the unsullied whiteness of Claud's flannel trousers. He himself wore a serviceable pair of dark-grey flannel trousers which had seen better days.

"Isn't the air beautiful?" said Clara, sniffing it appreciatively. "Quite sets you up, doesn't it?"

She giggled.

"It's ozone," said Alice Sopworth. "It's as good as a tonic, you know." And she giggled also.

James thought:

"I should like to knock their silly heads together. What is the sense of laughing all the time? They are not saying anything funny."

The immaculate Claud murmured languidly:

"Shall we have a bathe, or is it too much of a fag?"

The idea of bathing was accepted shrilly. James fell into line with them. He even managed, with a certain amount of cunning, to draw Grace a little behind the others.

"Look here!" he complained, "I am hardly seeing anything of you."

"Well, I am sure we are all together now," said Grace, "and you can come and lunch with us at the hotel, at least—"

She looked dubiously at James's legs.

"What is the matter?" demanded James ferociously. "Not smart enough for you, I suppose?"

"I do think, dear, you might take a little more pains," said Grace. "Everyone is so fearfully smart here. Look at Claud Sopworth!"

"I have looked at him," said James grimly. "I have never seen a man who looked a more complete ass than he does."

Grace drew herself up.

"There is no need to criticize my friends, James, it's not manners. He's dressed just like any other gentleman at the hotel is dressed."

"Bah!" said James. "Do you know what I read

156

the other day in 'Society Snippets'? Why, that the Duke of—the Duke of, I can't remember, but one duke, anyway, was the worst-dressed man in England, there!"

"I dare say," said Grace, "but then, you see, he is a duke."

"Well?" demanded James. "What is wrong with my being a duke some day? At least, well, not perhaps a duke, but a peer."

He slapped the yellow book in his pocket, and recited to her a long list of peers of the realm who had started life much more obscurely than James Bond. Grace merely giggled.

"Don't be so soft, James," she said. "Fancy you Earl of Kimpton-on-Sea!"

James gazed at her in mingled rage and despair. The air of Kimpton-on-Sea had certainly gone to Grace's head.

The beach at Kimpton is a long, straight stretch of sand. A row of bathing huts and boxes stretched evenly along it for about a mile and a half. The party had just stopped before a row of six huts all labelled imposingly, "For visitors to the Esplanade Hotel only."

"Here we are," said Grace brightly; "but I'm afraid you can't come in with us, James, you'll have to go along to the public tents over there. We'll meet you in the sea. So long!"

"So long!" said James, and he strode off in the direction indicated.

Twelve dilapidated tents stood solemnly confronting the ocean. An aged mariner guarded them, a roll of blue paper in his hand. He accepted a coin of the realm from James, tore him off a blue ticket from his roll, threw him over a towel, and jerked one thumb over his shoulder.

"Take your turn," he said huskily.

It was then that James awoke to the fact of competition. Others besides himself had conceived the idea of entering the sea. Not only was each tent occupied, but outside each tent was a determined-looking crowd of people glaring at each other. James attached himself to the smallest group and waited. The strings of the tent parted, and a beautiful young woman, sparsely clad, emerged on the scene settling her bathing cap with the air of one who had the whole morning to waste. She strolled down to the water's edge, and sat down dreamily on the sands.

"That's no good," said James to himself, and attached himself forthwith to another group.

After waiting five minutes, sounds of activity were apparent in the second tent. With heavings and strainings, the flaps parted asunder and four children and a father and mother emerged. The tent being so small, it had something of the appearance of a conjuring trick. On the instant two women sprang forward each grasping one flap of the tent.

"Excuse me," said the first young woman, panting a little.

158

"Excuse *me*," said the other young woman, glaring.

"I would have you know I was here quite ten minutes before you were," said the first young woman rapidly.

"I have been here a good quarter of an hour, as anyone will tell you," said the second young woman defiantly.

"Now then, now then," said the aged mariner, drawing near.

Both young women spoke to him shrilly. When they had finished, he jerked his thumb at the second young woman, and said briefly:

"It's yours."

Then he departed, deaf to remonstrances. He neither knew nor cared which had been there first, but his decision, as they say in newspaper competitions, was final. The despairing James caught at his arm.

"Look here! I say!"

"Well, mister?"

"How long is it going to be before I get a tent?"

The aged mariner threw a dispassionate glance over the waiting throng.

"Might be an hour, might be an hour and a half, I can't say."

At that moment James espied Grace and the Sopworth girls running lightly down the sands towards the sea.

"Damn!" said James to himself. "Oh, damn!"

He plucked once more at the aged mariner.

"Can't I get a tent anywhere else? What about one of these huts along here? They all seem empty."

"The huts," said the ancient mariner with dignity, "are private."

Having uttered this rebuke, he passed on. With a bitter feeling of having been tricked, James detached himself from the waiting groups, and strode savagely down the beach. It was the limit! It was the absolute, complete limit! He glared savagely at the trim bathing boxes he passed. In that moment from being an Independent Liberal, he became a red-hot Socialist. Why should the rich have bathing boxes and be able to bathe any minute they chose without waiting in a crowd? "This system of ours," said James vaguely, "is all *wrong.*"

From the sea came the coquettish screams of the splashed. Grace's voice! And above her squeaks, the inane "Ha, ha, ha," of Claud Sopworth.

"Damn!" said James, grinding his teeth, a thing which he had never before attempted, only read about in works of fiction.

He came to a stop, twirling his stick savagely, and turning his back firmly on the sea. Instead, he gazed with concentrated hatred upon Eagle's Nest, Buena Vista, and Mon Desir. It was the custom of the inhabitants of Kimpton-on-Sea to label their bathing huts with fancy names. Eagle's

Nest merely struck James as being silly, and Buena Vista was beyond his linguistic accomplishments. But his knowledge of French was sufficient to make him realize the appositeness of the third name.

"Mong Desire," said James. "I should jolly well think it was."

And on that moment he saw that while the doors of the other bathing huts were tightly closed, that of Mon Desir was ajar. James looked thoughtfully up and down the beach, this particular spot was mainly occupied by mothers of large families, busily engaged in superintending their offspring. It was only ten o'clock, too early as yet for the aristocracy of Kimpton-on-Sea to have come down to bathe.

"Eating quails and mushrooms in their beds as likely as not, brought to them on trays by powdered footmen, pah! Not one of them will be down here before twelve o'clock," thought James.

He looked again towards the sea. With the obedience of a well-trained leitmotif, the shrill scream of Grace rose upon the air. It was followed by the "Ha, ha, ha," of Claud Sopworth.

"I will," said James between his teeth.

He pushed open the door of Mon Desir and entered. For the moment he had a fright, as he caught sight of sundry garments hanging from pegs, but he was quickly reassured. The hut was partitioned into two, on the right-hand side, a girl's yellow sweater, a battered panama hat and a pair of beach shoes were depending from a peg. On the left-hand side an old pair of grey flannel trousers, a pullover, and a sou'wester proclaimed the fact that the sexes were segregated. James hastily transferred himself to the gentlemen's part of the hut, and undressed rapidly. Three minutes later, he was in the sea puffing and snorting importantly, doing extremely short bursts of professional-looking swimming—head under the water, arms lashing the sea—that style.

"Oh, there you are!" cried Grace. "I was afraid you wouldn't be in for ages with all that crowd of people waiting there."

"Really?" said James.

He thought with affectionate loyalty of the yellow book, "The strong man can on occasions be discreet." For the moment his temper was quite restored. He was able to say pleasantly but firmly to Claud Sopworth, who was teaching Grace the overarm stroke:

"No, no, old man, you have got it all wrong. *I'll* show her."

And such was the assurance of his tone, that Claud withdrew discomfited. The only pity of it was, that his triumph was short-lived. The temperature of our English waters is not such as to induce bathers to remain in them for any length of time. Grace and the Sopworth girls were already displaying blue chins and chattering teeth. They raced up the beach, and James pursued his solitary way back to Mon Desir. As he towelled himself vigorously and slipped his shirt over his head, he was pleased with himself. He had, he felt, displayed a dynamic personality.

And then suddenly he stood still, frozen with terror. Girlish voices sounded from outside, and voices quite different from those of Grace and her friends. A moment later he had realized the truth, the rightful owners of Mon Desir were arriving. It is possible that if James had been fully dressed, he would have waited their advent in a dignified manner, and attempted an explanation. As it was he acted on panic. The windows of Mon Desir were modestly screened by dark green curtains. James flung himself on the door and held the knob in a desperate clutch. Hands tried ineffectually to turn it from outside.

"It's locked after all," said a girl's voice. "I thought Peg said it was open."

"No, Woggle said so."

"Woggle is the limit," said the other girl. "How perfectly foul, we shall have to go back for the key."

James heard their footsteps retreating. He drew a long, deep breath. In desperate haste he huddled on the rest of his garments. Two minutes later saw him strolling negligently down the beach with an almost aggressive air of innocence. Grace and the Sopworth girls joined him on the beach a quarter of an hour later. The rest of the morning passed agreeably in stone throwing, writing in the sand and light badinage. Then Claud glanced at his watch.

"Lunchtime," he observed. "We'd better be strolling back."

"I'm terribly hungry," said Alice Sopworth.

All the other girls said that they were terribly hungry too.

"Are you coming, James?" asked Grace.

Doubtless James was unduly touchy. He chose to take offence at her tone.

"Not if my clothes are not good enough for you," he said bitterly. "Perhaps, as you are so particular, I'd better not come."

That was Grace's cue for murmured protestations, but the seaside air had affected Grace unfavourably. She merely replied:

"Very well. Just as you like, see you this afternoon then."

James was left dumbfounded.

"Well!" he said, staring after the retreating group. "Well, of all the—"

He strolled moodily into the town. There were two cafés in Kimpton-on-Sea, they are both hot, noisy and overcrowded. It was the affair of the bathing huts once more, James had to wait his turn. He had to wait longer than his turn, an unscrupulous matron who had just arrived forestalling him when a vacant seat did present itself. At last he was seated at a small table. Close to his left ear three raggedly bobbed maidens were making a determined hash of Italian opera. Fortunately James was not musical. He studied the bill of fare dispassionately, his hands thrust deep into his pockets. He thought to himself:

"Whatever I ask for it's sure to be 'off.' That's the kind of fellow I am."

His right hand, groping in the recesses of his pocket, touched an unfamiliar object. It felt like a pebble, a large round pebble.

"What on earth did I want to put a stone in my pockct for?" thought James.

His fingers closed round it. A waitress drifted up to him.

"Fried plaice and chipped potatoes, please," said James.

"Fried plaice is 'off,' " murmured the waitress, her eyes fixed dreamily on the ceiling.

"Then I'll have curried beef," said James.

"Curried beef is 'off.' "

"Is there anything on this beastly menu that isn't 'off'?" demanded James.

The waitress looked pained, and placed a pale-grey forefinger against haricot mutton. James resigned himself to the inevitable and ordered haricot mutton. His mind still seething with resentment against the ways of cafés, he drew his hand out of his pocket, the stone still in it. Unclosing his fingers, he looked absent-mindedly at the object in his palm. Then with a shock all lesser matters passed from his mind, and he stared with all his eyes. The thing he held was not a pebble, it was—he could hardly doubt it—an emerald, an enormous green emerald. James stared at it horror-stricken. No, it couldn't be an emerald, it must be coloured glass. There couldn't be an emerald of that size, unless—printed words danced before James's eyes, "The Rajah of Maraputna—famous emerald the size of a pigeon's egg." Was it—could it be—*that* emerald at which he was now looking? The waitress returned with the haricot mutton, and James closed his fingers spasmodically. Hot and cold shivers chased themselves up and down his spine. He had the sense of being caught in a terrible dilemma. If this was the emerald—but was it? Could it be? He unclosed his fingers and peeped anxiously. James was no expert on precious stones, but the depth and the glow of the jewel convinced him this was the real thing. He put both elbows on the table and leaned forward staring with unseeing eyes at the haricot mutton slowly congealing on the dish in front of him. He had got to think this out. If this was the Rajah's emerald, what was he going to do about it? The word "police" flashed into his mind. If you found anything of value you took it to the police station. Upon this axiom had James been brought up.

Yes, but—how on earth had the emerald got into

his trouser pocket? That was doubtless the question the police would ask. It was an awkward question, and it was moreover a question to which he had at the moment no answer. How had the emerald got into his trouser pocket? He looked despairingly down at his legs, and as he did so a misgiving shot through him. He looked more closely. One pair of old grey flannel trousers is very much like another pair of old grey flannel trousers, but all the same, James had an instinctive feeling that these were not his trousers after all. He sat back in his chair stunned with the force of the discovery. He saw now what had happened, in the hurry of getting out of the bathing hut, he had taken the wrong trousers. He had hung his own, he remembered, on an adjacent peg to the old pair hanging there. Yes, that explained matters so far, he had taken the wrong trousers. But all the same, what on earth was an emerald worth hundreds and thousands of pounds doing there? The more he thought about it, the more curious it seemed. He could, of course, explain to the police—

It was awkward, no doubt about it, it was decidedly awkward. One would have to mention the fact that one had deliberately entered someone else's bathing hut. It was not, of course, a serious offence, but it started him off wrong.

"Can I bring you anything else, sir?"

It was the waitress again. She was looking pointedly at the untouched haricot mutton. James hastily dumped some of it on his plate and asked for his bill. Having obtained it, he paid and went out. As he stood undecidedly in the street, a poster opposite caught his eye. The adjacent town of Harchester possessed an evening paper, and it was the contents bill of this paper that James was looking at. It announced a simple, sensational fact: "The Rajah's Emerald Stolen." "My God," said James faintly, and leaned against a pillar. Pulling himself together he fished out a penny and purchased a copy of the paper. He was not long in finding what he sought. Sensational items of local news were few and far between. Large headlines adorned the front page. "Sensational Burglary at Lord Edward Campion's. Theft of Famous Historical Emerald. Rajah of Maraputna's Terrible Loss." The facts were few and simple. Lord Edward Campion had entertained several friends the evening before. Wishing to show the stone to one of the ladies present, the Rajah had gone to fetch it and had found it missing. The police had been called in. So far no clue had been obtained. James let the paper fall to the ground. It was still not clear to him how the emerald had come to be reposing in the pocket of an old pair of flannel trousers in a bathing hut, but it was borne in upon him every minute that the police would certainly regard his own story as suspicious. What on earth was he to do? Here he was, standing in the principal street of Kimpton-on-Sea with stolen booty worth a king's ransom reposing idly in his pocket, whilst the entire police force of the district were busily searching for just that same booty. There were two courses open to him. Course number one, to go straight to the police station and tell his story—but it must be admitted that James funked that course badly. Course number two, somehow or other to get rid of the emerald. It occurred to him to do it up in a neat little parcel and post it back to the Rajah. Then he shook his head, he had read too many detective stories for that sort of thing. He knew how your supersleuth could get busy with a magnifying glass and every kind of patent device. Any detective worth his salt would get busy on James's parcel and would in half an hour or so have discovered the sender's profession, age, habits and personal appearance. After that it would be a mere matter of hours before he was tracked down.

It was then that a scheme of dazzling simplicity suggested itself to James. It was the luncheon hour, the beach would be comparatively deserted, he would return to Mon Desir, hang up the trousers where he had found them, and regain his own garments. He started briskly towards the beach.

Nevertheless, his conscience pricked him slightly. The emerald *ought* to be returned to the Rajah. He conceived the idea that he might perhaps do a little detective work—once, that is, that he had regained his own trousers and replaced the others. In pursuance of this idea, he directed his steps towards the aged mariner, whom he rightly regarded as being an exhaustible source of Kimpton information.

"Excuse me!" said James politely; "but I believe a friend of mine has a hut on this beach, Mr. Charles Lampton. It is called Mon Desir, I fancy."

The aged mariner was sitting very squarely in a chair, a pipe in his mouth, gazing out to sea. He shifted his pipe a little, and replied without removing his gaze from the horizon:

"Mon Desir belongs to his lordship, Lord Edward Campion, everyone knows that. I never heard of Mr. Charles Lampton, he must be a newcomer."

"Thank you," said James, and withdrew.

The information staggered him. Surely the Rajah could not himself have slipped the stone into the pocket and forgotten it. James shook his head, the theory did not satisfy him, but evidently some member of the house party must be the thief. The situation reminded James of some of his favourite works of fiction.

Nevertheless, his own purpose remained unaltered. All fell out easily enough. The beach was, as he hoped it would be, practically deserted. More fortunate still, the door of Mon Desir remained ajar. To slip in was the work of a moment, Edward was just lifting his own trousers from the hook, when a voice behind him made him spin round suddenly.

"So I have caught you, my man!" said the voice.

James stared openmouthed. In the doorway of Mon Desir stood a stranger; a well-dressed man of about forty years of age, his face keen and hawklike.

"So I have caught you!" the stranger repeated.

"Who—who are you?" stammered James.

"Detective-Inspector Merrilees from the Yard," said the other crisply. "And I will trouble you to hand over that emerald."

"The—the emerald?"

James was seeking to gain time.

"That's what I said, didn't I?" said Inspector Merrilees.

He had a crisp, businesslike enunciation. James tried to pull himself together.

"I don't know what you are talking about," he said with an assumption of dignity.

"Oh, yes, my lad, I think you do."

"The whole thing," said James, "is a mistake. I can explain it quite easily—" He paused.

A look of weariness had settled on the face of the other.

"They always say that," murmured the Scotland Yard man drily. "I suppose you picked it up as you were strolling along the beach, eh? That is the sort of explanation."

It did indeed bear a resemblance to it, James

recognized the fact, but still he tried to gain time.

"How do I know you are what you say you are?" he demanded weakly.

Merrilees flapped back his coat for a moment, showing a badge. Edward stared at him with eyes that popped out of his head.

"And now," said the other almost genially, "you see what you are up against! You are a novice—I can tell that. Your first job, isn't it?"

James nodded.

"I thought as much. Now, my boy, are you going to hand over that emerald, or have I got to search you?"

James found his voice.

"I—I haven't got it on me," he declared.

He was thinking desperately.

"Left it at your lodgings?" queried Merrilees.

James nodded.

"Very well, then," said the detective, "we will go there together."

He slipped his arm through James's.

"I am taking no chances of your getting away from me," he said gently. "We will go to your lodgings, and you will hand that stone over to me."

James spoke unsteadily.

"If I do, will you let me go?" he asked tremulously.

Merrilees appeared embarrassed.

"We know just how that stone was taken," he explained, "and about the lady involved, and, of

172

course, as far as that goes—well, the Rajah wants it hushed up. You know what these native rulers are?"

James, who knew nothing whatsoever about native rulers, except for one cause célèbre, nodded his head with an appearance of eager comprehension.

"It will be most irregular, of course," said the detective; "but you *may* get off scot-free."

Again James nodded. They had walked the length of the Esplanade, and were now turning into the town. James intimated the direction, but the other man never relinquished his sharp grip on James's arm.

Suddenly James hesitated and half spoke. Merrilees looked up sharply, and then laughed. They were just passing the police station, and he noticed James's agonized glances at it.

"I am giving you a chance first," he said good-humouredly.

It was at that moment that things began to happen. A loud bellow broke from James, he clutched the other's arm, and yelled at the top of his voice:

"Help! thief. Help! thief."

A crowd surrounded them in less than a minute. Merrilees was trying to wrench his arm from James's grasp.

"I charge this man," cried James. "I charge this man, he picked my pocket."

"What are you talking about, you fool?" cried the other.

A constable took charge of matters. Mr. Merrilees and James were escorted into the police station. James reiterated his complaint.

"This man has just picked my pocket," he declared excitedly. "He has got my notecase in his right-hand pocket, there!"

"The man is mad," grumbled the other. "You can look for yourself, Inspector, and see if he is telling the truth."

At a sign from the inspector, the constable slipped his hand deferentially into Merrilees's pocket. He drew something out and held it up with a gasp of astonishment.

"My God!" said the inspector, startled out of professional decorum. "It must be the Rajah's emerald."

Merrilees looked more incredulous than anyone else.

"This is monstrous," he spluttered; "monstrous. The man must have put it into my pocket himself as we were walking along together. It's a plant."

The forceful personality of Merrilees caused the inspector to waver. His suspicions swung round to James. He whispered something to the constable, and the latter went out.

"Now then, gentlemen," said the inspector, "let me have your statements please, one at a time."

"Certainly," said James. "I was walking along

the beach, when I met this gentleman, and he pretended he was acquainted with me. I could not remember having met him before, but I was too polite to say so. We walked along together. I had my suspicions of him, and just when we got opposite the police station, I found his hand in my pocket. I held on to him and shouted for help."

The inspector transferred his glance to Merrilees.

"And now you, sir."

Merrilees seemed a little embarrassed.

"The story is very nearly right," he said slowly; "but not quite. It was not I who scraped acquaintance with him, but he who scraped acquaintance with me. Doubtless he was trying to get rid of the emerald, and slipped it into my pocket while we were talking."

The inspector stopped writing.

"Ah!" he said impartially. "Well, there will be a gentleman here in a minute who will help us to get to the bottom of the case."

Merrilees frowned.

"It is really impossible for me to wait," he murmured, pulling out his watch. "I have an appointment. Surely, inspector, you can't be so ridiculous as to suppose I'd steal the emerald and walk along with it in my pocket?"

"It is not likely, sir, I agree," the inspector replied. "But you will have to wait just a matter of five or ten minutes till we get this thing cleared up. Ah! here is his lordship."

A tall man of forty strode into the room. He was wearing a pair of dilapidated trousers and an old sweater.

"Now then, inspector, what is all this?" he said. "You have got hold of the emerald, you say? That's splendid, very smart work. Who are these people you have got here?"

His eyes ranged over James and came to rest on Merrilees. The forceful personality of the latter seemed to dwindle and shrink.

"Why—Jones!" exclaimed Lord Edward Campion.

"You recognize this man, Lord Edward?" asked the inspector sharply.

"Certainly I do," said Lord Edward drily. "He is my valet, came to me a month ago. The fellow they sent down from London was on to him at once, but there was not a trace of the emerald anywhere among his belongings."

"He was carrying it in his coat pocket," the inspector declared. "This gentleman put us on to him." He indicated James.

In another minute James was being warmly congratulated and shaken by the hand.

"My dear fellow," said Lord Edward Campion. "So you suspected him all along, you say?"

"Yes," said James. "I had to trump up the story about my pocket being picked to get him into the police station."

"Well, it is splendid," said Lord Edward,

"absolutely splendid. You must come back and lunch with us, that is if you haven't lunched. It is late, I know, getting on for two o'clock."

"No," said James; "I haven't lunched—but—"

"Not a word, not a word," said Lord Edward. "The Rajah, you know, will want to thank you for getting back his emerald for him. Not that I have quite got the hang of the story yet."

They were out of the police station by now, standing on the steps.

"As a matter of fact," said James, "I think I should like to tell you the true story."

He did so. His lordship was very much entertained.

"Best thing I ever heard in my life," he declared. "I see it all now. Jones must have hurried down to the bathing hut as soon as he had pinched the thing, knowing that the police would make a thorough search of the house. That old pair of trousers I sometimes put on for going out fishing, nobody was likely to touch them, and he could recover the jewel at his leisure. Must have been a shock to him when he came today to find it gone. As soon as you appeared, he realized that you were the person who had removed the stone. I still don't quite see how you managed to see through that detective pose of his, though!"

"A strong man," thought James to himself, "knows when to be frank and when to be discreet."

He smiled deprecatingly whilst his fingers passed gently over the inside of his coat lapel feeling the small silver badge of that little-known club, the Merton Park Super Cycling Club. An astonishing coincidence that the man Jones should also be a member, but there it was!

"Hallo, James!"

He turned. Grace and the Sopworth girls were calling to him from the other side of the road. He turned to Lord Edward.

"Excuse me a moment?"

He crossed the road to them.

"We are going to the pictures," said Grace. "Thought you might like to come."

"I am sorry," said James. "I am just going back to lunch with Lord Edward Campion. Yes, that man over there in the comfortable old clothes. He wants me to meet the Rajah of Maraputna."

He raised his hat politely and rejoined Lord Edward.

Eight

SWAN SONG

"Swan Song" was first published in
Grand Magazine, September 1926.

• • •

It was eleven o'clock on a May morning in London. Mr. Cowan was looking out of the window, behind him was the somewhat ornate splendour of a sitting room in a suite at the Ritz Hotel. The suite in question had been reserved for Mme. Paula Nazorkoff, the famous operatic star, who had just arrived in London. Mr. Cowan, who was Madame's principal man of business, was awaiting an interview with the lady. He turned his head suddenly as the door opened, but it was only Miss Read, Mme. Nazorkoff's secretary, a pale girl with an efficient manner.

"Oh, so it's you, my dear," said Mr. Cowan. "Madame not up yet, eh?"

Miss Read shook her head.

"She told me to come round at ten o'clock," Mr. Cowan said. "I have been waiting an hour."

He displayed neither resentment nor surprise. Mr. Cowan was indeed accustomed to the vagaries of the artistic temperament. He was a tall man, clean-shaven, with a frame rather too well covered, and clothes that were rather too faultless. His hair was very black and shining, and his teeth were aggressively white. When he spoke, he had a way of slurring his "s's" which was not quite a lisp, but came perilously near to it. It required no stretch of imagination to realize that his father's name had probably been Cohen. At that minute a door at the other side of the room opened, and a trim, French girl hurried through.

"Madame getting up?" inquired Cowan hopefully. "Tell us the news, Elise."

Elise immediately elevated both hands to heaven.

"Madame she is like seventeen devils this morning, nothing pleases her! The beautiful yellow roses which monsieur sent to her last night, she says they are all very well for New York, but that it is *imbecile* to send them to her in London. In London, she says, red roses are the only things possible, and straight away she opens the door, and precipitates the yellow roses into the passage, where they descend upon a monsieur, *très comme il faut*, a military gentleman, I think, and he is justly indignant, that one!"

Cowan raised his eyebrows, but displayed no other signs of emotion. Then he took from his pocket a small memorandum book and pencilled in it the words "red roses."

Elise hurried out through the other door, and

Cowan turned once more to the window. Vera Read sat down at the desk, and began opening letters and sorting them. Ten minutes passed in silence, and then the door of the bedroom burst open, and Paula Nazorkoff flamed into the room. Her immediate effect upon it was to make it seem smaller, Vera Read appeared more colourless, and Cowan retreated into a mere figure in the background.

"Ah, ha! My children," said the prima donna, "am I not punctual?"

She was a tall woman, and for a singer not unduly fat. Her arms and legs were still slender, and her neck was a beautiful column. Her hair, which was coiled in a great roll halfway down her neck, was of a dark, glowing red. If it owed some at least of its colour to henna, the result was none the less effective. She was not a young woman, forty at least, but the lines of her face were still lovely, though the skin was loosened and wrinkled round the flashing, dark eyes. She had the laugh of a child, the digestion of an ostrich, and the temper of a fiend, and she was acknowledged to be the greatest dramatic soprano of her day. She turned directly upon Cowan.

"Have you done as I asked you? Have you taken that abominable English piano away, and thrown it into the Thames?"

"I have got another for you," said Cowan, and gestured towards where it stood in the corner.

Nazorkoff rushed across to it, and lifted the lid.

"An Erard," she said, "that is better. Now let us see."

The beautiful soprano voice rang out in an arpeggio, then it ran lightly up and down the scale twice, then took a soft little run up to a high note, held it, its volume swelling louder and louder, then softened again till it died away in nothingness.

"Ah!" said Paula Nazorkoff in naïve satisfaction. "What a beautiful voice I have! Even in London I have a beautiful voice."

"That is so," agreed Cowan in hearty congratulation. "And you bet London is going to fall for you all right, just as New York did."

"You think so?" queried the singer.

There was a slight smile on her lips, and it was evident that for her the question was a mere commonplace.

"Sure thing," said Cowan.

Paula Nazorkoff closed the piano lid down and walked across to the table, with that slow undulating walk that proved so effective on the stage.

"Well, well," she said, "let us get to business. You have all the arrangements there, my friend?"

Cowan took some papers out of the portfolio he had laid on a chair.

"Nothing has been altered much," he remarked. "You will sing five times at Covent Garden, three times in *Tosca*, twice in *Aida*."

"*Aida*! Pah," said the prima donna; "it will be unutterable boredom. *Tosca*, that is different."

"Ah, yes," said Cowan. "*Tosca* is *your* part."

Paula Nazorkoff drew herself up.

"I am the greatest Tosca in the world," she said simply.

"That is so," agreed Cowan. "No one can touch you."

"Roscari will sing 'Scarpia,' I suppose?"

Cowan nodded.

"And Emile Lippi."

"What?" shrieked Nazorkoff. "Lippi, that hideous little barking frog, croak—croak—croak. I will not sing with him, I will bite him, I will scratch his face."

"Now, now," said Cowan soothingly.

"He does not sing, I tell you, he is a mongrel dog who barks."

"Well, we'll see, we'll see," said Cowan.

He was too wise ever to argue with temperamental singers.

"The Cavardossi?" demanded Nazorkoff.

"The American tenor, Hensdale."

The other nodded.

"He is a nice little boy, he sings prettily."

"And Barrère is to sing it once, I believe."

"He is an artist," said Madame generously. "But to let that croaking frog Lippi be Scarpia! Bah—I'll not sing with him."

"You leave it to me," said Cowan soothingly.

He cleared his throat, and took up a fresh set of papers.

"I am arranging for a special concert at the Albert Hall."

Nazorkoff made a grimace.

"I know, I know," said Cowan; "but everybody does it."

"I will be good," said Nazorkoff, "and it will be filled to the ceiling, and I shall have much money. *Ecco!*"

Again Cowan shuffled papers.

"Now here is quite a different proposition," he said, "from Lady Rustonbury. She wants you to go down and sing."

"Rustonbury?"

The prima donna's brow contracted as if in the effort to recollect something.

"I have read that name lately, very lately. It is a town—or a village, isn't it?"

"That's right, pretty little place in Hertfordshire. As for Lord Rustonbury's place, Rustonbury Castle, it's a real dandy old feudal seat, ghosts and family pictures, and secret staircases, and a slap-up private theatre. Rolling in money they are, and always giving some private show. She suggests that we give a complete opera, preferably *Butterfly.*"

"*Butterfly?*"

Cowan nodded.

"And they are prepared to pay. We'll have to

square Covent Garden, of course, but even after that it will be well worth your while financially. In all probability, royalty will be present. It will be a slap-up advertisement."

Madame raised her still beautiful chin.

"Do I need advertisement?" she demanded proudly.

"You can't have too much of a good thing," said Cowan, unabashed.

"Rustonbury," murmured the singer, "where did I see—?"

She sprang up suddenly, and running to the centre table, began turning over the pages of an illustrated paper which lay there. There was a sudden pause as her hand stopped, hovering over one of the pages, then she let the periodical slip to the floor and returned slowly to her seat. With one of her swift changes of mood, she seemed now an entirely different personality. Her manner was very quiet, almost austere.

"Make all arrangements for Rustonbury, I would like to sing there, but there is one condition—the opera must be *Tosca*."

Cowan looked doubtful.

"That will be rather difficult—for a private show, you know, scenery and all that."

"*Tosca* or nothing."

Cowan looked at her very closely. What he saw seemed to convince him, he gave a brief nod and rose to his feet.

"I will see what I can arrange," he said quietly.

Nazorkoff rose too. She seemed more anxious than was usual, with her, to explain her decision.

"It is my greatest rôle, Cowan. I can sing that part as no other woman has ever sung it."

"It is a fine part," said Cowan. "Jeritza made a great hit in it last year."

"Jeritza!" cried the other, a flush mounting in her cheeks. She proceeded to give him at great length her opinion of Jeritza.

Cowan, who was used to listening to singers' opinions of other singers, abstracted his attention till the tirade was over; he then said obstinately:

"Anyway, she sings 'Vissi d'Arte' lying on her stomach."

"And why not?" demanded Nazorkoff. "What is there to prevent her? I will sing it on my back with my legs waving in the air."

Cowan shook his head with perfect seriousness.

"I don't believe that would go down any," he informed her. "All the same, that sort of thing takes on, you know."

"No one can sing 'Vissi d'Arte' as I can," said Nazorkoff confidently. "I sing it in the voice of the convent—as the good nuns taught me to sing years and years ago. In the voice of a choir boy or an angel, without feeling, without passion."

"I know," said Cowan heartily. "I have heard you, you are wonderful."

"That is art," said the prima donna, "to pay the

186

price, to suffer, to endure, and in the end not only to have all knowledge, but also the power to go back, right back to the beginning and recapture the lost beauty of the heart of a child."

Cowan looked at her curiously. She was staring past him with a strange, blank look in her eyes, and something about that look of hers gave him a creepy feeling. Her lips just parted, and she whispered a few words softly to herself. He only just caught them.

"At last," she murmured. "At last—*after all these years.*"

Lady Rustonbury was both an ambitious and an artistic woman, she ran the two qualities in harness with complete success. She had the good fortune to have a husband who cared for neither ambition nor art and who therefore did not hamper her in any way. The Earl of Rustonbury was a large, square man, with an interest in horseflesh and in nothing else. He admired his wife, and was proud of her, and was glad that his great wealth enabled her to indulge all her schemes. The private theatre had been built less than a hundred years ago by his grandfather. It was Lady Rustonbury's chief toy—she had already given an Ibsen drama in it, and a play of the ultra new school, all divorce and drugs, also a poetical fantasy with Cubist scenery. The forthcoming performance of *Tosca* had created widespread interest. Lady Rustonbury was entertaining a very distinguished houseparty for it, and all London that counted was motoring down to attend.

Mme Nazorkoff and her company had arrived just before luncheon. The new young American tenor, Hensdale, was to sing "Cavaradossi," and Roscari, the famous Italian baritone, was to be Scarpia. The expense of the production had been enormous, but nobody cared about that. Paula Nazorkoff was in the best of humours, she was charming, gracious, her most delightful and cosmopolitan self. Cowan was agreeably surprised, and prayed that this state of things might continue.

After luncheon the company went out to the theatre, and inspected the scenery and various appointments. The orchestra was under the direction of Mr. Samuel Ridge, one of England's most famous conductors. Everything seemed to be going without a hitch, and strangely enough, that fact worried Mr. Cowan. He was more at home in an atmosphere of trouble, this unusual peace disturbed him.

"Everything is going a darned sight too smoothly," murmured Mr. Cowan to himself. "Madame is like a cat that has been fed on cream, it's too good to last, something is bound to happen."

Perhaps as the result of his long contact with the operatic world, Mr. Cowan had developed the sixth sense, certainly his prognostications were justified. It was just before seven o'clock that evening when the French maid, Elise, came running to him in great distress.

"Ah, Mr. Cowan, come quickly, I beg of you come quickly."

"What's the matter?" demanded Cowan anxiously. "Madame got her back up about anything—ructions, eh, is that it?"

"No, no, it is not Madame, it is Signor Roscari, he is ill, he is dying!"

"Dying? Oh, come now."

Cowan hurried after her as she led the way to the stricken Italian's bedroom. The little man was lying on his bed, or rather jerking himself all over it in a series of contortions that would have been humorous had they been less grave. Paula Nazorkoff was bending over him; she greeted Cowan imperiously.

"Ah! there you are. Our poor Roscari, he suffers horribly. Doubtless he has eaten something."

"I am dying," groaned the little man. "The pain—it is terrible. Ow!"

He contorted himself again, clasping both hands to his stomach, and rolling about on the bed.

"We must send for a doctor," said Cowan.

Paula arrested him as he was about to move to the door.

"The doctor is already on his way, he will do all that can be done for the poor suffering one, that is

189

arranged for, but never never will Roscari be able to sing tonight."

"I shall never sing again, I am dying," groaned the Italian.

"No, no, you are not dying," said Paula. "It is but an indigestion, but all the same, impossible that you should sing."

"I have been poisoned."

"Yes, it is the ptomaine without doubt," said Paula. "Stay with him, Elise, till the doctor comes."

The singer swept Cowan with her from the room.

"What are we to do?" she demanded.

Cowan shook his head hopelessly. The hour was so far advanced that it would not be possible to get anyone from London to take Roscari's place. Lady Rustonbury, who had just been informed of her guest's illness, came hurrying along the corridor to join them. Her principal concern, like Paula Nazorkoff's, was the success of *Tosca*.

"If there were only someone near at hand," groaned the prima donna.

"Ah!" Lady Rustonbury gave a sudden cry. "Of course! Bréon."

"Bréon?"

"Yes, Edouard Bréon, you know, the famous French baritone. He lives near here, there was a picture of his house in this week's *Country Homes*. He is the very man."

"It is an answer from heaven," cried Nazorkoff. "Bréon as Scarpia, I remember him well, it was one of his greatest rôles. But he has retired, has he not?"

"I will get him," said Lady Rustonbury. "Leave it to me."

And being a woman of decision, she straightway ordered out the *Hispano Suiza*. Ten minutes later, M. Edouard Bréon's country retreat was invaded by an agitated countess. Lady Rustonbury, once she had made her mind up, was a very determined woman, and doubtless M. Bréon realized that there was nothing for it but to submit. Himself a man of very humble origin, he had climbed to the top of his profession, and had consorted on equal terms with dukes and princes, and the fact never failed to gratify him. Yet, since his retirement to this old-world English spot, he had known discontent. He missed the life of adulation and applause, and the English country had not been as prompt to recognize him as he thought they should have been. So he was greatly flattered and charmed by Lady Rustonbury's request.

"I will do my poor best," he said, smiling. "As you know, I have not sung in public for a long time now. I do not even take pupils, only one or two as a great favour. But there—since Signor Roscari is unfortunately indisposed—"

"It was a terrible blow," said Lady Rustonbury.

"Not that he is really a singer," said Bréon.

He told her at some length why this was so. There had been, it seemed, no baritone of distinction since Edouard Bréon retired.

"Mme. Nazorkoff is singing "Tosca," " said Lady Rustonbury. "You know her, I dare say?"

"I have never met her," said Bréon. "I heard her sing once in New York. A great artist—she has a sense of drama."

Lady Rustonbury felt relieved—one never knew with these singers—they had such queer jealousies and antipathies.

She reentered the hall at the castle some twenty minutes later waving a triumphant hand.

"I have got him," she cried, laughing. "Dear M. Bréon has really been too kind, I shall never forget it."

Everyone crowded round the Frenchman, and their gratitude and appreciation were as incense to him. Edouard Bréon, though now close on sixty, was still a fine-looking man, big and dark, with a magnetic personality.

"Let me see," said Lady Rustonbury. "Where is Madame—? Oh! there she is."

Paula Nazorkoff had taken no part in the general welcoming of the Frenchman. She had remained quietly sitting in a high oak chair in the shadow of the fireplace. There was, of course, no fire, for the evening was a warm one and the singer was slowly fanning herself with an immense palm-leaf fan. So aloof and detached was she, that Lady Rustonbury feared she had taken offence.

"M. Bréon." She led him up to the singer. "You have never yet met Madame Nazorkoff, you say."

With a last wave, almost a flourish, of the palm leaf, Paula Nazorkoff laid it down, and stretched out her hand to the Frenchman. He took it and bowed low over it, and a faint sigh escaped from the prima donna's lips.

"Madame," said Bréon, "we have never sung together. That is the penalty of my age! But fate has been kind to me, and come to my rescue."

Paula laughed softly.

"You are too kind, M. Bréon. When I was still but a poor little unknown singer, I have sat at your feet. Your 'Rigoletto'—what art, what perfection! No one could touch you."

"Alas!" said Bréon, pretending to sigh. "My day is over. Scarpia, Rigoletto, Radames, Sharpless, how many times have I not sung them, and now— no more!"

"Yes—tonight."

"True, Madame—I forgot. Tonight."

"You have sung with many 'Toscas,'" said Nazorkoff arrogantly; "but never with *me!*"

The Frenchman bowed.

"It will be an honour," he said softly. "It is a great part, Madame."

"It needs not only a singer, but an actress," put in Lady Rustonbury.

"That is true," Bréon agreed. "I remember when I was a young man in Italy, going to a little out of the way theatre in Milan. My seat cost me only a couple of lira, but I heard as good singing that night as I have heard in the Metropolitan Opera House in New York. Quite a young girl sang 'Tosca,' she sang it like an angel. Never shall I forget her voice in 'Vissi d'Arte,' the clearness of it, the purity. But the dramatic force, that was lacking."

Nazorkoff nodded.

"That comes later," she said quietly.

"True. This young girl—Bianca Capelli, her name was—I interested myself in her career. Through me she had the chance of big engagements, but she was foolish—regrettably foolish."

He shrugged his shoulders.

"How was she foolish?"

It was Lady Rustonbury's twenty-four-year-old daughter, Blanche Amery, who spoke. A slender girl with wide blue eyes.

The Frenchman turned to her at once politely.

"Alas! Mademoiselle, she had embroiled herself with some low fellow, a ruffian, a member of the Camorra. He got into trouble with the police, was condemned to death; she came to me begging me to do something to save her lover."

Blanche Amery was staring at him.

"And did you?" she asked breathlessly.

"Me, Mademoiselle, what could I do? A stranger in the country."

"You might have had influence?" suggested Nazorkoff, in her low vibrant voice.

"If I had, I doubt whether I should have exerted it. The man was not worth it. I did what I could for the girl."

He smiled a little, and his smile suddenly struck the English girl as having something peculiarly disagreeable about it. She felt that, at that moment, his words fell far short of representing his thoughts.

"You did what you could," said Nazorkoff. "That was kind of you, and she was grateful, eh?"

The Frenchman shrugged his shoulders.

"The man was executed," he said, "and the girl entered a convent. Eh, *voilà*! The world has lost a singer."

Nazorkoff gave a low laugh.

"We Russians are more fickle," she said lightly.

Blanche Amery happened to be watching Cowan just as the singer spoke, and she saw his quick look of astonishment, and his lips that half-opened and then shut tight in obedience to some warning glance from Paula.

The butler appeared in the doorway.

"Dinner," said Lady Rustonbury, rising. "You poor things, I am so sorry for you, it must be dreadful always to have to starve yourself before singing. But there will be a very good supper afterwards."

"We shall look forward to it," said Paula Nazorkoff. She laughed softly. *"Afterwards!"*

Inside the theatre, the first act of *Tosca* had just drawn to a close. The audience stirred, spoke to each other. The royalties, charming and gracious, sat in the three velvet chairs in the front row. Everyone was whispering and murmuring to each other, there was a general feeling that in the first act Nazorkoff had hardly lived up to her great reputation. Most of the audience did not realize that in this the singer showed her art, in the first act she was saving her voice and herself. She made of La Tosca a light, frivolous figure, toying with love, coquettishly jealous and exciting. Bréon, though the glory of his voice was past its prime, still struck a magnificent figure as the cynical Scarpia. There was no hint of the decrepit roué in his conception of the part. He made of Scarpia a handsome, almost benign figure, with just a hint of the subtle malevolence that underlay the outward seeming. In the last passage, with the organ and the procession, when Scarpia stands lost in thought, gloating over his plan to secure Tosca, Bréon had displayed a wonderful art. Now the curtain rose up on the second act, the scene in Scarpia's apartments.

This time, when Tosca entered, the art of Nazorkoff at once became apparent. Here was a woman in deadly terror playing her part with the assurance of a fine actress. Her easy greeting of Scarpia, her nonchalance, her smiling replies to him! In this scene, Paula Nazorkoff acted with her eyes, she carried herself with deadly quietness, with an impassive, smiling face. Only her eyes that kept darting glances at Scarpia betrayed her true feelings. And so the story went on, the torture scene, the breaking down of Tosca's composure, and her utter abandonment when she fell at Scarpia's feet imploring him vainly for mercy. Old Lord Leconmere, a connoisseur of music, moved appreciatively, and a foreign ambassador sitting next to him murmured:

"She surpasses herself, Nazorkoff, tonight. There is no other woman on the stage who can let herself go as she does."

Leconmere nodded.

And now Scarpia has named his price, and Tosca, horrified, flies from him to the window. Then comes the beat of drums from afar, and Tosca flings herself wearily down on the sofa. Scarpia standing over her, recites how his people are raising up the gallows—and then silence, and again the far-off beat of drums. Nazorkoff lay prone on the sofa, her head hanging downwards almost touching the floor, masked by her hair. Then, in exquisite contrast to the passion and stress of the last twenty minutes, her voice rang out, high and clear, the voice, as she had told Cowan, of a choir boy or an angel.

• • •

"Vissi d'arte, vissi d'arte, no feci mai male ad anima viva. Con man furtiva quante miserie conobbi, aiutai."

It was the voice of a wondering, puzzled child. Then she is once more kneeling and imploring, till the instant when Spoletta enters. Tosca, exhausted, gives in, and Scarpia utters his fateful words of double-edged meaning. Spoletta departs once more. Then comes the dramatic moment, when Tosca, raising a glass of wine in her trembling hand, catches sight of the knife on the table, and slips it behind her.

Bréon rose up, handsome, saturnine, inflamed with passion. *"Tosca, finalmente mia!"* The lightning stabs with the knife, and Tosca's hiss of vengeance:

"Questo e il bacio di Tosca!" ("It is thus that Tosca kisses.")

Never had Nazorkoff shown such an appreciation of Tosca's act of vengeance. That last fierce whispered *"Muori dannato,"* and then in a strange, quiet voice that filled the theatre:

"Or gli perdono!" ("Now I forgive him!")

The soft death tune began as Tosca set about her ceremonial, placing the candles each side of his head, the crucifix on his breast, her last pause in the doorway looking back, the roll of distant drums, and the curtain fell.

This time real enthusiasm broke out in the

audience, but it was shortlived. Someone hurried out from behind the wings, and spoke to Lord Rustonbury. He rose, and after a minute or two's consultation, turned and beckoned to Sir Donald Calthorp, who was an eminent physician. Almost immediately the truth spread through the audience. Something had happened, an accident, someone was badly hurt. One of the singers appeared before the curtain and explained that M. Bréon had unfortunately met with an accident—the opera could not proceed. Again the rumour went round, Bréon had been stabbed, Nazorkoff had lost her head, she had lived in her part so completely that she had actually stabbed the man who was acting with her. Lord Leconmere, talking to his ambassador friend, felt a touch on his arm, and turned to look into Blanche Amery's eyes.

"It was not an accident," the girl was saying. "I am sure it was not an accident. Didn't you hear, just before dinner, that story he was telling about the girl in Italy? That girl was Paula Nazorkoff. Just after, she said something about being Russian, and I saw Mr. Cowan look amazed. She may have taken a Russian name, but he knows well enough that she is Italian."

"My dear Blanche," said Lord Leconmere.

"I tell you I am sure of it. She had a picture paper in her bedroom opened at the page showing M. Bréon in his English country home. She knew before she came down here. I believe she gave something to that poor little Italian man to make him ill."

"But why?" cried Lord Leconmere. "Why?"

"Don't you see? It's the story of Tosca all over again. He wanted her in Italy, but she was faithful to her lover, and she went to him to try to get him to save her lover, and he pretended he would. Instead he let him die. And now at last her revenge has come. Didn't you hear the way she hissed '*I am Tosca?*' And I saw Bréon's face when she said it, *he knew then*—he recognized her!"

In her dressing room, Paula Nazorkoff sat motionless, a white ermine cloak held round her. There was a knock at the door.

"Come in," said the prima donna.

Elise entered. She was sobbing.

"Madame, Madame, he is dead! And—"

"Yes?"

"Madame, how can I tell you? There are two gentlemen of the police there, they want to speak to you."

Paula Nazorkoff rose to her full height.

"I will go to them," she said quietly.

She untwisted a collar of pearls from her neck, and put them into the French girl's hands.

"Those are for you, Elise, you have been a good girl. I shall not need them now where I am going. You understand, Elise? *I shall not sing 'Tosca' again.*"

She stood a moment by the door, her eyes

sweeping over the dressing room, as though she looked back over the past thirty years of her career.

Then softly between her teeth, she murmured the last line of another opera:

"*La commedia e finita!*"

Nine

THE HOUND OF DEATH

"The Hound of Death"
was first published in the hardback
The Hound of Death and Other Stories
(Odhams Press, 1933). No previous
appearances have been found.

• • •

It was from William P. Ryan, American news-paper correspondent, that I first heard of the affair. I was dining with him in London on the eve of his return to New York and happened to mention that on the morrow I was going down to Folbridge.

He looked up and said sharply: "Folbridge, Cornwall?"

Now only about one person in a thousand knows that there is a Folbridge in Cornwall. They always take it for granted that the Folbridge, Hampshire, is meant. So Ryan's knowledge aroused my curiosity.

"Yes," I said. "Do you know it?"

He merely replied that he was darned. He then asked if I happened to know a house called Trearne down there.

My interest increased.

"Very well indeed. In fact, it's to Trearne I'm going. It's my sister's house."

"Well," said William P. Ryan. "If that doesn't beat the band!"

I suggested that he should cease making cryptic remarks and explain himself.

"Well," he said. "To do that I shall have to go back to an experience of mine at the beginning of the war."

I sighed. The events which I am relating to took place in 1921. To be reminded of the war was the last thing any man wanted. We were, thank God, beginning to forget . . . Besides, William P. Ryan on his war experiences was apt, as I knew, to be unbelievably long-winded.

But there was no stopping him now.

"At the start of the war, as I dare say you know, I was in Belgium for my paper—moving about some. Well, there's a little village—I'll call it X. A one-horse place if there ever was one, but there's quite a big convent there. Nuns in white what do you call 'em—I don't know the name of the order. Anyway, it doesn't matter. Well, this little burgh was right in the way of the German advance. The Uhlans arrived—"

I shifted uneasily. William P. Ryan lifted a hand reassuringly.

"It's all right," he said. "This isn't a German atrocity story. It might have been, perhaps, but it isn't. As a matter of fact, the boot's on the other leg. The Huns made for that convent—they got there and the whole thing blew up."

"Oh!" I said, rather startled.

"Odd business, wasn't it? Of course, off hand, I should say the Huns had been celebrating and had monkeyed round with their own explosives. But it seems they hadn't anything of that kind with them. They weren't the high-explosive johnnies. Well, then, I ask you, what should a pack of nuns know about high explosive? Some nuns, I should say!"

"It is odd," I agreed.

"I was interested in hearing the peasants' account of the matter. They'd got it all cut and dried. According to them it was a slap-up one hundred per cent efficient first-class modern miracle. It seems one of the nuns had got something of a reputation—a budding saint—went into trances and saw visions. And according to them she worked the stunt. She called down the lightning to blast the impious Hun—and it blasted him all right—and everything else within range. A pretty efficient miracle, that!

"I never really got at the truth of the matter—hadn't time. But miracles were all the rage just then—angels at Mons and all that. I wrote up the thing, put in a bit of sob stuff, and pulled the religious stop out well, and sent it to my paper. It went down very well in the States. They were liking that kind of thing just then.

"But (I don't know if you'll understand this) in writing, I got kinder interested. I felt I'd like to know what really had happened. There was nothing to see at the spot itself. Two walls still left standing, and on one of them was a black powder mark that was the exact shape of a great hound.

"The peasants round about were scared to death of that mark. They called it the Hound of Death and they wouldn't pass that way after dark.

"Superstition's always interesting. I felt I'd like to see the lady who worked the stunt. She hadn't perished, it seemed. She'd gone to England with a batch of other refugees. I took the trouble to trace her. I found she'd been sent to Trearne, Folbridge, Cornwall."

I nodded.

"My sister took in a lot of Belgian refugees the beginning of the war. About twenty."

"Well, I always meant, if I had time, to look up the lady. I wanted to hear her own account of the disaster. Then, what with being busy and one thing and another, it slipped my memory. Cornwall's a bit out of the way anyhow. In fact, I'd forgotten the whole thing till your mentioning Folbridge just now brought it back."

"I must ask my sister," I said. "She may have heard something about it. Of course, the Belgians have all been repatriated long ago."

"Naturally. All the same, in case your sister does know anything I'll be glad if you pass it on to me."

"Of course I will," I said heartily.

And that was that.

It was the second day after my arrival at Trearne that the story recurred to me. My sister and I were having tea on the terrace.

"Kitty," I said, "didn't you have a nun among your Belgians?"

"You don't mean Sister Marie Angelique, do you?"

"Possibly I do," I said cautiously. "Tell me about her."

"Oh! my dear, she was the most uncanny creature. She's still here, you know."

"What? In the house?"

"No, no, in the village. Dr. Rose—you remember Dr. Rose?"

I shook my head.

"I remember an old man of about eighty-three."

"Dr. Laird. Oh! he died. Dr. Rose has only been here a few years. He's quite young and very keen on new ideas. He took the most enormous interest in Sister Marie Angelique. She has hallucinations and things, you know, and apparently is most frightfully interesting from a medical point of view. Poor thing, she'd nowhere to go—and really was in my opinion quite potty—only impressive, if you know what I mean—well, as I say, she'd nowhere to go, and Dr. Rose very kindly fixed her up in the village. I believe he's writing a monograph or whatever it is that doctors write, about her."

She paused and then said:

"But what do you know about her?"

"I heard a rather curious story."

I passed on the story as I had received it from Ryan. Kitty was very much interested.

"She looks the sort of person who could blast you—if you know what I mean," she said.

"I really think," I said, my curiosity heightened, "that I must see this young woman."

"Do. I'd like to know what you think of her. Go and see Dr. Rose first. Why not walk down to the village after tea?"

I accepted the suggestion.

I found Dr. Rose at home and introduced myself. He seemed a pleasant young man, yet there was something about his personality that rather repelled me. It was too forceful to be altogether agreeable.

The moment I mentioned Sister Marie Angelique he stiffened to attention. He was evidently keenly interested. I gave him Ryan's account of the matter.

"Ah!" he said thoughtfully. "That explains a great deal."

He looked up quickly at me and went on.

"The case is really an extraordinarily interesting one. The woman arrived here having evidently suffered some severe mental shock. She was in a state of great mental excitement also. She was given to hallucinations of a most startling character. Her personality is most unusual. Perhaps you would like to come with me and call upon her. She is really well worth seeing."

I agreed readily.

We set out together. Our objective was a small cottage on the outskirts of the village. Folbridge is a most picturesque place. It lies at the mouth of the river Fol mostly on the east bank, the west bank is too precipitous for building, though a few cottages do cling to the cliffside there. The doctor's own cottage was perched on the extreme edge of the cliff on the west side. From it you looked down on the big waves lashing against the black rocks.

The little cottage to which we were now proceeding lay inland out of the sight of the sea.

"The district nurse lives here," explained Dr. Rose. "I have arranged for Sister Marie Angelique to board with her. It is just as well that she should be under skilled supervision."

"Is she quite normal in her manner?" I asked curiously.

"You can judge for yourself in a minute," he replied, smiling.

The district nurse, a dumpy pleasant little body, was just setting out on her bicycle when we arrived.

"Good evening, nurse, how's your patient?" called out the doctor.

"She's much as usual, doctor. Just sitting there with her hands folded and her mind far away. Often enough she'll not answer when I speak to her, though for the matter of that it's little enough English she understands even now."

Rose nodded, and as the nurse bicycled away, he went up to the cottage door, rapped sharply and entered.

Sister Marie Angelique was lying in a long chair near the window. She turned her head as we entered.

It was a strange face—pale, transparent looking, with enormous eyes. There seemed to be an infinitude of tragedy in those eyes.

"Good evening, my sister," said the doctor in French.

"Good evening, M. le docteur."

"Permit me to introduce a friend, Mr. Anstruther."

I bowed and she inclined her head with a faint smile.

"And how are you today?" inquired the doctor, sitting down beside her.

"I am much the same as usual." She paused and then went on. "Nothing seems real to me. Are they days that pass—or months—or years? I hardly know. Only my dreams seem real to me."

"You still dream a lot, then?"

"Always—always—and, you understand?—the dreams seem more real than life."

"You dream of your own country—of Belgium?" She shook her head.

"No. I dream of a country that never existed—never. But you know this, M. le docteur. I have told you many times." She stopped and then said abruptly: "But perhaps this gentleman is also a doctor—a doctor perhaps for the diseases of the brain?"

"No, no." Rose said reassuring, but as he smiled I noticed how extraordinarily pointed his canine teeth were, and it occurred to me that there was something wolflike about the man. He went on:

"I thought you might be interested to meet Mr. Anstruther. He knows something of Belgium. He has lately been hearing news of your convent."

Her eyes turned to me. A faint flush crept into her cheeks.

"It's nothing, really," I hastened to explain. "But I was dining the other evening with a friend who was describing the ruined walls of the convent to me."

"So it is ruined!"

It was a soft exclamation, uttered more to herself than to us. Then looking at me once more she asked hesitatingly: "Tell me, Monsieur, did your friend say how—in what way—it was ruined?"

"It was blown up," I said, and added: "The peasants are afraid to pass that way at night."

"Why are they afraid?"

"Because of a black mark on a ruined wall. They have a superstitious fear of it."

She leaned forward.

"Tell me, Monsieur—quick—quick—tell me! What is that mark like?"

"It has the shape of a huge hound," I answered. "The peasants call it the Hound of Death."

"Ah!"

A shrill cry burst from her lips.

"It is true then—it is true. All that I remember is true. It is not some black nightmare. It happened! It happened!"

"What happened, my sister?" asked the doctor in a low voice.

She turned to him eagerly.

"*I remembered.* There on the steps, I remembered. I remembered the way of it. I used the power as we used to use it. I stood on the altar steps and I bade them to come no farther. I told them to depart in peace. They would not listen, they came on although I warned them. And so—" She leaned forward and made a curious gesture. "And so I loosed the Hound of Death on them. . . ."

She lay back on her chair shivering all over, her eyes closed.

The doctor rose, fetched a glass from a cupboard, half-filled it with water, added a drop or two from a little bottle which he produced from his pocket, then took the glass to her.

"Drink this," he said authoritatively.

She obeyed—mechanically as it seemed. Her eyes looked far away as though they contemplated some inner vision of her own.

"But then it is all true," she said. "Everything. The City of the Circles, the People of the Crystal— everything. It is all true."

"It would seem so," said Rose.

His voice was low and soothing, clearly designed to encourage and not to disturb her train of thought.

"Tell me about the City," he said. "The City of Circles, I think you said?"

She answered absently and mechanically.

"Yes—there were three circles. The first circle for the chosen, the second for the priestesses and the outer circle for the priests."

"And in the centre?"

She drew her breath sharply and her voice sank to a tone of indescribable awe.

"The House of the Crystal. . . ."

As she breathed the words, her right hand went to her forehead and her finger traced some figure there.

Her figure seemed to grow more rigid, her eyes closed, she swayed a little—then suddenly she sat upright with a jerk, as though she had suddenly awakened.

"What is it?" she said confusedly. "What have I been saying?"

"It is nothing," said Rose. "You are tired. You want to rest. We will leave you."

She seemed a little dazed as we took our departure.

"Well," said Rose when we were outside. "What do you think of it?"

He shot a sharp glance sideways at me.

"I suppose her mind must be totally unhinged," I said slowly.

"It struck you like that?"

"No—as a matter of fact, she was— well, curiously convincing. When listening to her I had the impression that she actually had done what she claimed to do—worked a kind of gigantic miracle. Her belief that she did so seems genuine enough. That is why—"

"That is why you say her mind must be unhinged. Quite so. But now approach the matter from another angle. Supposing that she did actually work that miracle—supposing that she did, personally, destroy a building and several hundred human beings."

"By the mere exercise of will?" I said with a smile.

"I should not put it quite like that. You will agree that one person could destroy a multitude by touching a switch which controlled a system of mines."

"Yes, but that is mechanical."

"True, that is mechanical, but it is, in essence, the harnessing and controlling of natural forces. The thunderstorm and the power house are, fundamentally, the same thing."

"Yes, but to control the thunderstorm we have to use mechanical means."

Rose smiled.

"I am going off at a tangent now. There is a substance called wintergreen. It occurs in nature in vegetable form. It can also be built up by man synthetically and chemically in the laboratory."

"Well?"

"My point is that there are often two ways of arriving at the same result. Ours is, admittedly, the synthetic way. There might be another. The extraordinary results arrived at by Indian fakirs for instance, cannot be explained away in any easy fashion. The things we call supernatural is only the natural of which the laws are not yet understood."

"You mean?" I asked, fascinated.

"That I cannot entirely dismiss the possibility that a human being *might* be able to tap some vast destructive force and use it to further his or her ends. The means by which this was accomplished might seem to us supernatural—but would not be so in reality."

I stared at him.

He laughed.

"It's a speculation, that's all," he said lightly. "Tell me, did you notice a gesture she made when she mentioned the House of the Crystal?"

"She put her hand to her forehead."

"Exactly. And traced a circle there. Very much as a Catholic makes the sign of the cross. Now, I will tell you something rather interesting, Mr. Anstruther. The word crystal having occurred so often in my patient's rambling, I tried an experiment. I borrowed a crystal from someone and produced it unexpectedly one day to test my patient's reaction to it."

"Well?"

"Well, the result was very curious and suggestive. Her whole body stiffened. She stared at it as though unable to believe her eyes. Then she slid to her knees in front of it, murmured a few words—and fainted."

"What were the few words?"

"Very curious ones. She said: *'The Crystal! Then the Faith still lives!'*"

"Extraordinary!"

"Suggestive, is it not? Now the next curious thing. When she came round from her faint she had forgotten the whole thing. I showed her the crystal and asked her if she knew what it was. She replied that she supposed it was a crystal such as fortune tellers used. I asked her if she had ever seen one before? She replied: 'Never, M. le docteur.' But I saw a puzzled look in her eyes.

'What troubles you, my sister?' I asked. She replied: 'Because it is so strange. I have never seen a crystal before and yet—it seems to me that I know it well. There is something—if only I could remember . . .' The effort at memory was obviously so distressing to her that I forbade her to think any more. That was two weeks ago. I have purposely been biding my time. Tomorrow, I shall proceed to a further experiment."

"With the crystal?"

"With the crystal. I shall get her to gaze into it. I think the result ought to be interesting."

"What do you expect to get hold of?" I asked curiously.

The words were idle ones but they had an unlooked-for result. Rose stiffened, flushed, and his manner when he spoke changed insensibly. It was more formal, more professional.

"Light on certain mental disorders imperfectly understood. Sister Marie Angelique is a most interesting study."

So Rose's interest was purely professional? I wondered.

"Do you mind if I come along too?" I asked.

It may have been my fancy, but I thought he hesitated before he replied. I had a sudden intuition that he did not want me.

"Certainly. I can see no objection."

He added: "I suppose you're not going to be down here very long?"

"Only till the day after tomorrow."

I fancied that the answer pleased him. His brow cleared and he began talking of some recent experiments carried out on guinea pigs.

I met the doctor by appointment the following afternoon, and we went together to Sister Marie Angelique. Today, the doctor was all geniality. He was anxious, I thought, to efface the impression he had made the day before.

"You must not take what I said too seriously," he observed, laughing. "I shouldn't like you to believe me a dabbler in occult sciences. The worst of me is I have an infernal weakness for making out a case."

"Really?"

"Yes, and the more fantastic it is, the better I like it."

He laughed as a man laughs at an amusing weakness.

When we arrived at the cottage, the district nurse had something she wanted to consult Rose about, so I was left with Sister Marie Angelique.

I saw her scrutinizing me closely. Presently she spoke.

"The good nurse here, she tells me that you are the brother of the kind lady at the big house where I was brought when I came from Belgium?"

"Yes," I said.

"She was very kind to me. She is good."

She was silent, as though following out some train of thought. Then she said:

"M. le docteur, he too is a good man?"

I was a little embarrassed.

"Why, yes. I mean—I think so."

"Ah!" She paused and then said: "Certainly he has been very kind to me."

"I'm sure he has."

She looked up at me sharply.

"Monsieur—you—you who speak to me now—do you believe that I am mad?"

"Why, my sister, such an idea never—"

She shook her head slowly—interrupting my protest.

"Am I mad? I do not know—the things I remember—the things I forget. . . ."

She sighed, and at that moment Rose entered the room.

He greeted her cheerily and explained what he wanted her to do.

"Certain people, you see, have a gift for seeing things in a crystal. I fancy you might have such a gift, my sister."

She looked distressed.

"No, no, I cannot do that. To try to read the future—that is sinful."

Rose was taken aback. It was the nun's point of view for which he had not allowed. He changed his ground cleverly.

"One should not look into the future. You are

quite right. But to look into the past—that is different."

"The past?"

"Yes—there are many strange things in the past. Flashes come back to one—they are seen for a moment—then gone again. Do not seek to see anything in the crystal since that is not allowed you. Just take it in your hands—so. Look into it—look deep. Yes—deeper—deeper still. You remember, do you not? You remember. You hear me speaking to you. You can answer my questions. Can you not hear me?"

Sister Marie Angelique had taken the crystal as bidden, handling it with a curious reverence. Then, as she gazed into it, her eyes became blank and unseeing, her head drooped. She seemed to sleep.

Gently the doctor took the crystal from her and put it on the table. He raised the corner of her eyelid. Then he came and sat by me.

"We must wait till she wakes. It won't be long, I fancy."

He was right. At the end of five minutes, Sister Marie Angelique stirred. Her eyes opened dreamily.

"Where am I?"

"You are here—at home. You have had a little sleep. You have dreamt, have you not?"

She nodded.

"Yes, I have dreamt."

"You have dreamt of the Crystal?"

"Yes."

"Tell us about it."

"You will think me mad, M. le docteur. For see you, in my dream, the Crystal was a holy emblem. I even figured to myself a second Christ, a Teacher of the Crystal who died for his faith, his followers hunted down—persecuted . . . But the faith endured.

"Yes—for fifteen thousand full moons—I mean, for fifteen thousand years."

"How long was a full moon?"

"Thirteen ordinary moons. Yes, it was in the fifteen thousandth full moon—of course, I was a Priestess of the Fifth Sign in the House of the Crystal. It was in the first days of the coming of the Sixth Sign. . . ."

Her brows drew together, a look of fear passed over her face.

"Too soon," she murmured. "Too soon. A mistake . . . Ah! yes, I remember! The Sixth Sign. . . ."

She half sprang to her feet, then dropped back, passing her hand over her face and murmuring:

"But what am I saying? I am raving. These things never happened."

"Now don't distress yourself."

But she was looking at him in anguished perplexity.

"M. le docteur, I do not understand. Why should

I have these dreams—these fancies? I was only sixteen when I entered the religious life. I have never travelled. Yet I dream of cities, of strange people, of strange customs. Why?" She pressed both hands to her head.

"Have you ever been hypnotized, my sister? Or been in a state of trance?"

"I have never been hypnotized, M. le docteur. For the other, when at prayer in the chapel, my spirit has often been caught up from my body, and I have been as one dead for many hours. It was undoubtedly a blessed state, the Reverend Mother said—a state of grace. Ah! yes," she caught her breath. *"I remember, we too called it a state of grace."*

"I would like to try an experiment, my sister." Rose spoke in a matter-of-fact voice. "It may dispel those painful half-recollections. I will ask you to gaze once more in the crystal. I will then say a certain word to you. You will answer another. We will continue in this way until you become tired. Concentrate your thoughts on the crystal, not upon the words."

As I once more unwrapped the crystal and gave it into Sister Marie Angelique's hands, I noticed the reverent way her hands touched it. Reposing on the black velvet, it lay between her slim palms. Her wonderful deep eyes gazed into it. There was a short silence, and then the doctor said:

"Hound."

Immediately Sister Marie Angelique answered: *"Death."*

I do not propose to give a full account of the experiment. Many unimportant and meaningless words were purposely introduced by the doctor. Other words he repeated several times, sometimes getting the same answer to them, sometimes a different one.

That evening in the doctor's little cottage on the cliffs we discussed the result of the experiment.

He cleared his throat, and drew his notebook closer to him.

"These results are very interesting—very curious. In answer to the words 'Sixth Sign,' we get variously *Destruction, Purple, Hound, Power,* then again *Destruction,* and finally *Power.* Later, as you may have noticed, I reversed the method, with the following results. In answer to *Destruction,* I get *Hound;* to *Purple, Power;* to *Hound, Death;* again, and to *Power, Hound.* That all holds together, but on a second repetition of *Destruction,* I get *Sea,* which appears utterly irrelevant. To the words 'Fifth Sign,' I get *Blue, Thoughts, Bird, Blue* again, and finally the rather suggestive phrase *Opening of mind to mind.* From the fact that 'Fourth Sign' elicits the word *Yellow,* and later *Light,* and that 'First Sign' is answered by *Blood,* I deduce that each Sign had a particular colour, and possibly a particular symbol, that of the Fifth Sign being a *bird,* and that of the Sixth a *hound.* However, I surmise that the Fifth Sign represented what is familiarly known as telepathy—the opening of mind to mind. The Sixth Sign undoubtedly stands for the Power of Destruction."

"What is the meaning of *Sea?*"

"That I confess I cannot explain. I introduced the word later and got the ordinary answer of *Boat.* To 'Seventh Sign' I got first *Life,* the second time *Love.* To 'Eighth Sign,' I got the answer *None.* I take it therefore that Seven was the sum and number of the signs."

"But the Seventh was not achieved," I said on a sudden inspiration. "Since through the Sixth came *Destruction!*"

"Ah! You think so? But we are taking these— mad ramblings very seriously. They are really only interesting from a medical point of view."

"Surely they will attract the attention of psychic investigators."

The doctor's eyes narrowed. "My dear sir, I have no intention of making them public."

"Then your interest?"

"Is purely personal. I shall make notes on the case, of course."

"I see." But for the first time I felt, like the blind man, that I didn't see at all. I rose to my feet.

"Well, I'll wish you good night, doctor. I'm off to town again tomorrow."

"Ah!" I fancied there was satisfaction, relief perhaps, behind the exclamation.

"I wish you good luck with your investigations," I continued lightly. "Don't loose the Hound of Death on me next time we meet!"

His hand was in mine as I spoke, and I felt the start it gave. He recovered himself quickly. His lips drew back from his long pointed teeth in a smile.

"For a man who loved power, what a power that would be!" he said. "To hold every human being's life in the hollow of your hand!"

And his smile broadened.

That was the end of my direct connection with the affair.

Later, the doctor's notebook and diary came into my hands. I will reproduce the few scant entries in it here, though you will understand that it did not really come into my possession until some time afterwards.

> *Aug. 5th.* Have discovered that by "the Chosen," Sister M.A. means those who reproduced the race. Apparently they were held in the highest honour, and exalted above the Priesthood. Contrast this with early Christians.
>
> *Aug. 7th.* Persuaded Sister M.A. to let me hypnotize her. Succeeded in inducing

hypnoptic sleep and trance, but no *rapport* established.

Aug. 9th. Have there been civilizations in the past to which ours is as nothing? Strange if it should be so, and I the only man with the clue to it. . . .

Aug. 12th. Sister M.A. not at all amenable to suggestion when hypnotized. Yet state of trance easily induced. Cannot understand it.

Aug. 13th. Sister M.A. mentioned today that in "state of grace" the "gate must be closed, lest another should command the body." Interesting—but baffling.

Aug. 18th. So the First Sign is none other than . . . (*words erased here*) . . . then how many centuries will it take to reach the Sixth? But if there should be a shortcut to Power. . . .

Aug. 20th. Have arranged for M.A. to come here with Nurse. Have told her it is necessary to keep patient under morphia. Am I mad? Or shall I be the Superman, with the Power of Death in my hands?

(*Here the entries cease*)

It was, I think, on August 29th that I received the letter. It was directed to me, care of my sister-in-law, in a sloping foreign handwriting. I opened it with some curiosity. It ran as follows:

Cher Monsieur,

I have seen you but twice, but I have felt I could trust you. Whether my dreams are real or not, they have grown clearer of late . . . And, Monsieur, one thing at all events, the Hound of Death is no dream . . . In the days I told you of (Whether they are real or not, I do not know) He who was Guardian of the Crystal revealed the Sixth Sign to the people too soon . . . Evil entered into their hearts. They had the power to slay at will—and they slew without justice—in anger. They were drunk with the lust of Power. When we saw this, We who were yet pure, we knew that once again we should not complete the Circle and come to the Sign of Everlasting Life. He who would have been the next Guardian of the Crystal was bidden to act. That the old might die, and the new, after endless ages, might come again, *he loosed the Hound of Death upon the sea* (being careful not to close the circle), and the sea rose up in the shape of a Hound and swallowed the land utterly. . . .

Once before I remembered this—*on the altar steps in Belgium* . . .

The Dr. Rose, he is of the Brotherhood. He knows the First Sign, and the form of the Second, though its meaning is hidden to all save a chosen few. *He would learn of me the Sixth.* I have withstood him so far—but I grow weak, Monsieur, it is not well that a man should come to power before his time. Many centuries must go by ere the world is ready to have the power of death delivered into its hand . . . I beseech you, Monsieur, you who love goodness and truth, to help me . . . before it is too late.

Your sister in Christ,
Marie Angelique

I let the paper fall. The solid earth beneath me seemed a little less solid than usual. Then I began to rally. The poor woman's belief, genuine enough, had almost affected me! One thing was clear. Dr. Rose, in his zeal for a case, was grossly abusing his professional standing. I would run down and—

Suddenly I noticed a letter from Kitty amongst my other correspondence. I tore it open.

"Such an awful thing has happened," I read. "You remember Dr. Rose's little cottage on the cliff? It was swept away by a landslide last night, the doctor and that poor nun, Sister Marie Angelique, were killed. The debris on the beach is too awful—all piled up in a fantastic mass—from a distance it looks like a great *hound* . . ."

The letter dropped from my hand.

The other facts may be coincidence. A Mr. Rose, whom I discovered to be a wealthy relative of the doctor's, died suddenly that same night— it was said struck by lightning. As far as was known no thunderstorm had occurred in the neighbourhood, but one or two people declared they had heard one peal of thunder. He had an electric burn on him "of a curious shape." His will left everything to his nephew, Dr. Rose.

Now, supposing that Dr. Rose succeeded in obtaining the secret of the Sixth Sign from Sister Marie Angelique. I had always felt him to be an unscrupulous man—he would not shrink at taking his uncle's life if he were sure it could not be brought home to him. But one sentence of Sister Marie Angelique's letter rings in my brain . . . "being careful not to close the Circle . . ." Dr. Rose did not exercise that care—was perhaps unaware of the steps to take, or even of the need for them. So the force he employed returned, completing its circuit. . . .

But of course it is all nonsense! Everything can be accounted for quite naturally. That the doctor believed in Sister Marie Angelique's hallucinations merely proves that *his* mind, too, was slightly unbalanced.

Yet sometimes I dream of a continent under the

seas where men once lived and attained to a degree of civilization far ahead of ours. . . .

Or did Sister Marie Angelique remember *backwards*—as some say is possible—and is this City of the Circles in the future and not in the past?

Nonsense—of course the whole thing was merely hallucination!

Ten

"The Gipsy" was first published in the
hardback *The Hound of Death and Other
Stories* (Odhams Press, 1933). No
previous appearances have been found.

• • •

Macfarlane had often noticed that his friend,
Dickie Carpenter, had a strange aversion to
gipsies. He had never known the reason for it. But
when Dickie's engagement to Esther Lawes was
broken off, there was a momentary tearing down
of reserves between the two men.

Macfarlane had been engaged to the younger
sister, Rachel, for about a year. He had known
both the Lawes girls since they were children.
Slow and cautious in all things, he had been
unwilling to admit to himself the growing
attraction that Rachel's childlike face and honest
brown eyes had for him. Not a beauty like Esther,
no! But unutterably truer and sweeter. With
Dickie's engagement to the elder sister, the bond
between the two men seemed to be drawn closer.

And now, after a few brief weeks, that engagement was off again, and Dickie, simple Dickie,

hard hit. So far in his young life all had gone so smoothly. His career in the Navy had been well chosen. His craving for the sea was inborn. There was something of the Viking about him, primitive and direct, a nature on which subtleties of thought were wasted. He belonged to that inarticulate order of young Englishmen who dislike any form of emotion, and who find it peculiarly hard to explain their mental processes in words.

Macfarlane, that dour Scot, with a Celtic imagination hidden away somewhere, listened and smoked while his friend floundered along in a sea of words. He had known an unburdening was coming. But he had expected the subject matter to be different. To begin with, anyway, there was no mention of Esther Lawes. Only, it seemed, the story of a childish terror.

"It all started with a dream I had when I was a kid. Not a nightmare exactly. She—the gipsy, you know—would just come into any old dream— even a good dream (or a kid's idea of what's good—a party and crackers and things). I'd be enjoying myself no end, and then I'd feel, I'd *know*, that if I looked up, *she'd* be there, standing as she always stood, watching me . . . With sad eyes, you know, as though she understood something that I didn't . . . Can't explain why it rattled me so—but it did! Every time! I used to wake up howling with terror, and my old nurse used to say:

231

'There! Master Dickie's had one of his gipsy dreams again!'"

"Ever been frightened by real gipsies?"

"Never saw one till later. That was queer, too. I was chasing a pup of mine. He'd run away. I got through the garden door, and along one of the forest paths. We lived in the New Forest then, you know. I came to a sort of clearing at the end, with a wooden bridge over a stream. And just beside it a gipsy was standing—with a red handkerchief over her head—just the same as in my dream. And at once I was frightened! She looked at me, you know . . . Just the same look—as though she knew something I didn't, and was sorry about it . . . And then she said quite quietly, nodding her head at me: *'I shouldn't go that way, if I were you.'* I can't tell you why, but it frightened me to death. I dashed past her on to the bridge. I suppose it was rotten. Anyway, it gave way, and I was chucked into the stream. It was running pretty fast, and I was nearly drowned. Beastly to be nearly drowned. I've never forgotten it. And I felt it had all to do with the gipsy. . . ."

"Actually, though, she warned you against it?"

"I suppose you could put it like that," Dickie paused, then went on: "I've told you about this dream of mine, not because it has anything to do with what happened after (at least, I suppose it hasn't), but because it's the jumping off point, as it were. You'll understand now what I mean by the 'gipsy feeling.' So I'll go on to that first night at the Lawes'. I'd just come back from the west coast then. It was awfully rum to be in England again. The Lawes were old friends of my people's. I hadn't seen the girls since I was about seven, but young Arthur was a great pal of mine, and after he died, Esther used to write to me, and send me out papers. Awfully jolly letters, she wrote! Cheered me up no end. I always wished I was a better hand at writing back. I was awfully keen to see her. It seemed odd to know a girl quite well from her letters, and not otherwise. Well, I went down to the Lawes' place first thing. Esther was away when I arrived, but was expected back that evening. I sat next to Rachel at dinner, and as I looked up and down the long table a queer feeling came over me. I felt someone was watching me, and it made me uncomfortable. Then I saw her—"

"Saw who—"

"Mrs. Haworth—what I'm telling you about."

It was on the tip of Macfarlane's tongue to say: "I thought you were telling me about Esther Lawes." But he remained silent, and Dickie went on.

"There was something about her quite different from all the rest. She was sitting next to old Lawes—listening to him very gravely with her head bent down. She had some of that red tulle stuff round her neck. It had got torn, I think, anyway it stood up behind her head like little

233

tongues of flame . . . I said to Rachel: 'Who's that woman over there. Dark—with a red scarf?'

" 'Do you mean Alistair Haworth? She's got a red scarf. But she's fair. *Very* fair.'

"So she was, you know. Her hair was a lovely pale shining yellow. Yet I could have sworn positively she was dark. Queer what tricks one's eyes play on one . . . After dinner, Rachel introduced us, and we walked up and down in the garden. We talked about reincarnation. . . ."

"Rather out of your line, Dickie!"

"I suppose it is. I remember saying that it seemed to be a jolly sensible way of accounting for how one seems to know some people right off—as if you'd met them before. She said: 'You mean lovers . . .' There was something queer about the way she said it—something soft and eager. It reminded me of something—but I couldn't remember what. We went on jawing a bit, and then old Lawes called us from the terrace— said Esther had come, and wanted to see me. Mrs. Haworth put her hand on my arm and said: 'You're going in?' 'Yes,' I said. 'I suppose we'd better,' and then—then—"

"Well?"

"It sounds such rot. Mrs. Haworth said: *'I shouldn't go in if I were you . . .'* " He paused. "It frightened me, you know. It frightened me badly. That's why I told you about the dream . . . Because, you see, she said it just the same way—

quietly, as though she knew something I didn't. It wasn't just a pretty woman who wanted to keep me out in the garden with her. Her voice was just kind—and very sorry. Almost as though she knew what was to come . . . I suppose it was rude, but I turned and left her—almost ran to the house. It seemed like safety. I knew then that I'd been afraid of her from the first. It was a relief to see old Lawes. Esther was there beside him . . ." He hesitated a minute and then muttered rather obscurely: "There was no question—the moment I saw her. I knew I'd got it in the neck."

Macfarlane's mind flew swiftly to Esther Lawes. He had once heard her summed up as "Six foot one of Jewish perfection." A shrewd portrait, he thought, as he remembered her unusual height and the long slenderness of her, the marble whiteness of her face with its delicate down-drooping nose, and the black splendour of hair and eyes. Yes, he did not wonder that the boyish simplicity of Dickie had capitulated. Esther could never have made his own pulses beat one jot faster, but he admitted her magnificence.

"And then," continued Dickie, "we got engaged."

"At once?"

"Well, after about a week. It took her about a fortnight after that to find out that she didn't care after all . . ." He gave a short bitter laugh.

"It was the last evening before I went back to the old ship. I was coming back from the village through the woods—and then I saw *her*—Mrs. Haworth, I mean. She had on a red tam-o'-shanter, and—just for a minute, you know—it made me jump! I've told you about my dream, so you'll understand . . . Then we walked along a bit. Not that there was a word Esther couldn't have heard, you know. . . ."

"No?" Macfarlane looked at his friend curiously. Strange how people told you things of which they themselves were unconscious!

"And then, when I was turning to go back to the house, she stopped me. She said: 'You'll be home soon enough. *I shouldn't go back too soon if I were you* . . .' And then *I knew*—that there was something beastly waiting for me . . . and . . . as soon as I got back Esther met me, and told me—that she'd found out she didn't really care. . . ."

Macfarlane grunted sympathetically. "And Mrs. Haworth?" he asked.

"I never saw her again—until tonight."

"Tonight?"

"Yes. At the doctor johnny's nursing home. They had a look at my leg, the one that got messed up in that torpedo business. It's worried me a bit lately. The old chap advised an operation—it'll be quite a simple thing. Then as I left the place, I ran into a girl in a red jumper over her nurse's things, and she said: '*I wouldn't have that operation, if I were you* . . .' Then I saw it was Mrs. Haworth. She passed on so quickly I couldn't stop her. I met another nurse, and asked about her. But she said there wasn't anyone of that name in the home . . . Queer. . . ."

"Sure it was her?"

"Oh! yes, you see—she's very beautiful . . ." He paused, and then added: "I shall have the old op, of course—but—but in case my number *should* be up—"

"Rot!"

"Of course it's rot. But all the same I'm glad I told you about this gipsy business . . . You know, there's more of it if only I could remember. . . ."

Macfarlane walked up the steep moorland road. He turned in at the gate of the house near the crest of the hill. Setting his jaw squarely, he pulled the bell.

"Is Mrs. Haworth in?"

"Yes, sir. I'll tell her." The maid left him in a low long room, with windows that gave on the wildness of the moorland. He frowned a little. Was he making a colossal ass of himself?

Then he started. A low voice was singing overhead:

"The gipsy woman
Lives on the moor—"

The voice broke off. Macfarlane's heart beat a shade faster. The door opened.

The bewildering, almost Scandinavian fairness

of her came as a shock. In spite of Dickie's description, he had imagined her gipsy dark . . . And he suddenly remembered Dickie's words, and the peculiar tone of them. *"You see, she's very beautiful . . ."* Perfect unquestionable beauty is rare, and perfect unquestionable beauty was what Alistair Haworth possessed.

He caught himself up, and advanced towards her. "I'm afraid you don't know me from Adam. I got your address from the Lawes. But—I'm a friend of Dickie Carpenter's."

She looked at him closely for a minute or two. Then she said: "I was going out. Up on the moor. Will you come too?"

She pushed open the window, and stepped out on the hillside. He followed her. A heavy, rather foolish-looking man was sitting in a basket chair smoking.

"My husband! We're going out on the moor, Maurice. And then Mr. Macfarlane will come back to lunch with us. You will, won't you?"

"Thanks very much." He followed her easy stride up the hill, and thought to himself: "Why? Why, on God's earth, marry *that?*"

Alistair made her way to some rocks. "We'll sit here. And you shall tell me—what you came to tell me."

"You knew?"

"I always know when bad things are coming. It is bad, isn't it? About Dickie?"

238

"He underwent a slight operation—quite success-fully. But his heart must have been weak. He died under the anaesthetic."

What he expected to see on her face, he scarcely knew—hardly that look of utter eternal weariness . . . He heard her murmur: "Again—to wait—so long—so long . . ." She looked up: "Yes, what were you going to say?"

"Only this. Someone warned him against this operation. A nurse. He thought it was you. Was it?"

She shook her head. "No, it wasn't me. But I've got a cousin who is a nurse. She's rather like me in a dim light. I dare say that was it." She looked up at him again. "It doesn't matter, does it?" And then suddenly her eyes widened. She drew in her breath. "Oh!" she said. "Oh! How funny! You don't understand. . . ."

Macfarlane was puzzled. She was still staring at him.

"I thought you did . . . You *should* do. You look as though you'd got it, too. . . ."

"Got what?"

"The gift—curse—call it what you like. I believe you have. Look hard at that hollow in the rocks. Don't think of anything, just look . . . Ah!" she marked his slight start. "Well—you saw something?"

"It must have been imagination. Just for a second I saw it full of blood!"

She nodded. "I knew you had it. That's the place where the old sun worshippers sacrificed victims. I knew that before anyone told me. And there are times when I know just how they felt about it—almost as though I'd been there myself . . . And there's something about the moor that makes me feel as though I were coming back home . . . Of course it's natural that I should have the gift. I'm a Ferguesson. There's second sight in the family. And my mother was a medium until my father married her. Cristing was her name. She was rather celebrated."

"Do you mean by 'the gift' the power of being able to see things before they happen?"

"Yes, forwards or backwards—it's all the same. For instance, I saw you wondering why I married Maurice—oh! yes, you did!—It's simply because I've always known that there's something dreadful hanging over him . . . I wanted to save him from it . . . Women are like that. With my gift, I ought to be able to prevent it happening . . . if one ever can . . . I couldn't help Dickie. And Dickie wouldn't understand . . . He was afraid. He was very young."

"Twenty-two."

"And I'm thirty. But I didn't mean that. There are so many ways of being divided, length and height and breadth . . . but to be divided by time is the worst way of all . . . ." She fell into a long brooding silence.

The low peal of a gong from the house below roused them.

At lunch, Macfarlane watched Maurice Haworth. He was undoubtedly madly in love with his wife. There was the unquestioning happy fondness of a dog in his eyes. Macfarlane marked also the tenderness of her response, with its hint of maternity. After lunch he took his leave.

"I'm staying down at the inn for a day or so. May I come and see you again? Tomorrow, perhaps?"

"Of course. But—"

"But what—"

She brushed her hand quickly across her eyes. "I don't know. I—I fancied that we shouldn't meet again—that's all . . . Goodbye."

He went down the road slowly. In spite of himself, a cold hand seemed tightening round his heart. Nothing in her words, of course, but—

A motor swept round the corner. He flattened himself against the hedge . . . only just in time. A curious greyish pallor crept across his face. . . .

"Good Lord, my nerves are in a rotten state," muttered Macfarlane, as he awoke the following morning. He reviewed the events of the afternoon before dispassionately. The motor, the shortcut to the inn and the sudden mist that had made him lose his way with the knowledge that a dangerous bog was no distance off. Then the chimney pot that had fallen off the inn, and the smell of burning in the night which he had traced to a cinder on his hearthrug. Nothing in it at all! Nothing at all—but for her words, and that deep unacknowledged certainty in his heart that she *knew*. . . .

He flung off his bedclothes with sudden energy. He must go up and see her first thing. That would break the spell. That is, *if he got there safely* . . . Lord, what a fool he was!

He could eat little breakfast. Ten o'clock saw him starting up the road. At ten-thirty his hand was on the bell. Then, and not till then, he permitted himself to draw a long breath of relief.

"Is Mr. Haworth in?"

It was the same elderly woman who had opened the door before. But her face was different—ravaged with grief.

"Oh! sir, oh! sir, you haven't heard then?"

"Heard what?"

"Miss Alistair, the pretty lamb. It was her tonic. She took it every night. The poor captain is beside himself, he's nearly mad. He took the wrong bottle off the shelf in the dark . . . They sent for the doctor, but he was too late—"

And swiftly there recurred to Macfarlane the words: *"I've always known there was something dreadful hanging over him. I ought to be able to prevent it happening*—if one ever can—" Ah! but one couldn't cheat Fate . . . Strange fatality of vision that had destroyed where it sought to save. . . .

The old servant went on: "My pretty lamb! So sweet and gentle she was, and so sorry for anything in trouble. Couldn't bear anyone to be hurt." She hesitated, then added: "Would you like to go up and see her, sir? I think, from what she said, that you must have known her long ago. A *very* long time ago, she said. . . ."

Macfarlane followed the old woman up the stairs, into the room over the drawing room where he had heard the voice singing the day before. There was stained glass at the top of the windows. It threw a red light on the head of the bed . . . *A gipsy with a red handkerchief over her head . . .* Nonsense, his nerves were playing tricks again. He took a long last look at Alistair Haworth.

"There's a lady to see you, sir."

"Eh?" Macfarlane looked at the landlady abstractedly. "Oh! I beg your pardon, Mrs. Rowse, I've been seeing ghosts."

"Not really, sir? There's queer things to be seen on the moor after nightfall, I know. There's the white lady, and the Devil's blacksmith, and the sailor and the gipsy—"

"What's that? A sailor and a gipsy?"

"So they say, sir. It was quite a tale in my young days. Crossed in love they were, a while back . . . But they've not walked for many a long day now."

"No? I wonder if perhaps—they will again now. . . ."

"Lor! sir, what things you do say! About that young lady—"

"What young lady?"

"The one that's waiting to see you. She's in the parlour. Miss Lawes, she said her name was."

"Oh!"

Rachel! He felt a curious feeling of contraction, a shifting of perspective. He had been peeping through at another world. He had forgotten Rachel, for Rachel belonged to this life only . . . Again that curious shifting of perspective, that slipping back to a world of three dimensions only.

He opened the parlour door. Rachel—with her honest brown eyes. And suddenly, like a man awakening from a dream, a warm rush of glad reality swept over him. He was alive—alive! He thought: "There's only one life one can be sure about! This one!"

"Rachel!" he said, and, lifting her chin, he kissed her lips.

Eleven

"The Lamp" was first published in the
hardback *The Hound of Death and Other
Stories* (Odhams Press, 1933). No
previous appearances have been found.

• • •

It was undoubtedly an old house. The whole
square was old, with that disapproving dignified
old age often met with in a cathedral town. But
No. 19 gave the impression of an elder among
elders; it had a veritable patriarchal solemnity;
it towered greyest of the grey, haughtiest of
the haughty, chillest of the chill. Austere,
forbidding, and stamped with that particular
desolation attaching to all houses that have been
long untenanted, it reigned above the other
dwellings.

In any other town it would have been freely
labelled "haunted," but Weyminster was averse
from ghosts and considered them hardly respectable except at the appanage of a "county family."
So No. 19 was never alluded to as a haunted
house; but nevertheless it remained, year after
year, TO BE LET OR SOLD.

· · ·

Mrs. Lancaster looked at the house with approval as she drove up with the talkative house agent, who was in an unusually hilarious mood at the idea of getting No. 19 off his books. He inserted the key in the door without ceasing his appreciative comments.

"How long has the house been empty?" inquired Mrs. Lancaster, cutting short his flow of language rather brusquely.

Mr. Raddish (of Raddish and Foplow) became slightly confused.

"E—er—some time," he remarked blandly.

"So I should think," said Mrs. Lancaster drily.

The dimly lighted hall was chill with a sinister chill. A more imaginative woman might have shivered, but this woman happened to be eminently practical. She was tall with much dark brown hair just tinged with grey and rather cold blue eyes.

She went over the house from attic to cellar, asking a pertinent question from time to time. The inspection over, she came back into one of the front rooms looking out on the square and faced the agent with a resolute mien.

"What is the matter with the house?"

Mr. Raddish was taken by surprise.

"Of course, an unfurnished house is always a little gloomy," he parried feebly.

"Nonsense," said Mrs. Lancaster. "The rent is

ridiculously low for such a house—purely nominal. There must be some reason for it. I suppose the house is haunted?"

Mr. Raddish gave a nervous little start but said nothing.

Mrs. Lancaster eyed him keenly. After a few moments she spoke again.

"Of course that is all nonsense, I don't believe in ghosts or anything of that sort, and personally it is no deterrent to my taking the house; but servants, unfortunately, are very credulous and easily frightened. It would be kind of you to tell me exactly what—what thing *is* supposed to haunt this place."

"I—er—really don't know," stammered the house agent.

"I am sure you must," said the lady quietly. "I cannot take the house without knowing. What was it? A murder?"

"Oh! no," cried Mr. Raddish, shocked by the idea of anything so alien to the respectability of the square. "It's—it's only a child."

"A child?"

"Yes."

"I don't know the story exactly," he continued reluctantly. "Of course, there are all kinds of different versions, but I believe that about thirty years ago a man going by the name of Williams took No. 19. Nothing was known of him; he kept no servants; he had no friends; he seldom went out in the day time. He had one child, a little boy. After he had been there about two months, he went up to London, and had barely set foot in the metropolis before he was recognized as being a man 'wanted' by the police on some charge—exactly what, I do not know. But it must have been a grave one, because, sooner than give himself up he shot himself. Meanwhile, the child lived on here, alone in the house. He had food for a little time, and he waited day after day for his father's return. Unfortunately, it had been impressed upon him that he was never under any circumstances to go out of the house or speak to anyone. He was a weak, ailing, little creature, and did not dream of disobeying this command. In the night, the neighbours, not knowing that his father had gone away, often heard him sobbing in the awful loneliness and desolation of the empty house."

Mr. Raddish paused.

"And—er—the child starved to death," he concluded, in the same tones as he might have announced that it had just begun to rain.

"And it is the child's ghost that is supposed to haunt the place?" asked Mrs. Lancaster.

"It is nothing of consequence really," Mr. Raddish hastened to assure her. "There's nothing *seen,* not *seen,* only people say, ridiculous, of course, but they do say they hear—the child—crying, you know."

Mrs. Lancaster moved towards the front door.

"I like the house very much," she said. "I shall get nothing as good for the price. I will think it over and let you know."

"It really looks very cheerful, doesn't it, Papa?"

Mrs. Lancaster surveyed her new domain with approval. Gay rugs, well-polished furniture, and many knickknacks, had quite transformed the gloomy aspect of No. 19.

She spoke to a thin, bent old man with stooping shoulders and a delicate mystical face. Mr. Winburn did not resemble his daughter; indeed no greater contrast could be imagined than that presented by her resolute practicalness and his dreamy abstraction.

"Yes," he answered with a smile, "no one would dream the house was haunted."

"Papa, don't talk nonsense! On our first day too."

Mr. Winburn smiled.

"Very well, my dear, we will agree that there are no such things as ghosts."

"And please," continued Mrs. Lancaster, "don't say a word before Geoff. He's so imaginative."

Geoff was Mrs. Lancaster's little boy. The family consisted of Mr. Winburn, his widowed daughter, and Geoffrey.

Rain had begun to beat against the window— pitter-patter, pitter-patter.

"Listen," said Mr. Winburn. "Is it not like little footsteps?"

"It is more like rain," said Mrs. Lancaster, with a smile.

"But *that, that* is a footstep," cried her father, bending forward to listen.

Mrs. Lancaster laughed outright.

Mr. Winburn was obliged to laugh too. They were having tea in the hall, and he had been sitting with his back to the staircase. He now turned his chair round to face it.

Little Geoffrey was coming down, rather slowly and sedately, with a child's awe of a strange place. The stairs were of polished oak, uncarpeted. He came across and stood by his mother. Mr. Winburn gave a slight start. As the child was crossing the floor, he distincty heard another pair of footsteps on the stairs, as of someone following Geoffrey. Dragging footsteps, curiously painful they were. Then he shrugged his shoulders incredulously. "The rain, no doubt," he thought.

"I'm looking at the spongecakes," remarked Geoff with the admirably detached air of one who points out an interesting fact.

His mother hastened to comply with the hint.

"Well, Sonny, how do you like your new home?" she asked.

"Lots," replied Geoffrey with his mouth generously filled. "Pounds and pounds and pounds." After this last assertion, which was evidently expressive of the deepest contentment, he relapsed into silence, only anxious to remove the spongecake from the sight of man in the least time possible.

Having bolted the last mouthful, he burst forth into speech.

"Oh! Mummy, there's attics here, Jane says; and can I go at once and *eggz*plore them? And there might be a secret door, Jane says there isn't, but I think there must be, and, anyhow, I know there'll be *pipes, water pipes* (with a face full of ecstasy) and can I play with them, and, oh! can I go and see the Boi-i-ler?" He spun out the last word with such evident rapture that his grandfather felt ashamed to reflect that this peerless delight of childhood only conjured up to his imagination the picture of hot water that wasn't hot, and heavy and numerous plumber's bills.

"We'll see about the attics tomorrow, darling," said Mrs. Lancaster. "Suppose you fetch your bricks and build a nice house, or an engine."

"Don't want to build an 'ouse."

"House."

"House, or h'engine h'either."

"Build a boiler," suggested his grandfather.

Geoffrey brightened.

"With pipes?"

"Yes, lots of pipes."

Geoffrey ran away happily to fetch his bricks.

The rain was still falling. Mr. Winburn listened. Yes, it must have been the rain he had heard; but it did sound like footsteps.

251

He had a queer dream that night.

He dreamt that he was walking through a town, a great city it seemed to him. But it was a children's city; there werc no grown-up people there, nothing but children, crowds of them. In his dream they all rushed to the stranger crying: "Have you brought him?" It seemed that he understood what they meant and shook his head sadly. When they saw this, the children turned away and began to cry, sobbing bitterly.

The city and the children faded away and he awoke to find himself in bed, but the sobbing was still in his ears. Though wide awake, he heard it distinctly; and he remembered that Geoffrey slept on the floor below, while this sound of a child's sorrow descended from above. He sat up and struck a match. Instantly the sobbing ceased.

Mr. Winburn did not tell his daughter of the dream or its sequel. That it was no trick of his imagination, he was convinced; indeed soon afterwards he heard it again in the day time. The wind was howling in the chimney but *this* was a separate sound—distinct, unmistakable; pitiful little heartbroken sobs.

He found out too, that he was not the only one to hear them. He overheard the housemaid saying to the parlour maid that she "didn't think as that there nurse was kind to Master Geoffrey, she'd 'eard 'im crying 'is little 'eart out only that morning." Geoffrey had come down to breakfast and lunch beaming with health and happiness; and Mr. Winburn knew that it was not Geoff who had been crying, but that other child whose dragging footsteps had startled him more than once.

Mrs. Lancaster alone never heard anything. Her ears were not perhaps attuned to catch sounds from another world.

Yet one day she also received a shock.

"Mummy," said Geoff plaintively. "I wish you'd let me play with that little boy."

Mrs. Lancaster looked up from her writing table with a smile.

"What little boy, dear?"

"I don't know his name. He was in a attic, sitting on the floor crying, but he ran away when he saw me. I suppose he was *shy* (with slight contempt), not like a *big* boy, and then, when I was in the nursery building, I saw him standing in the door watching me build, and he looked so awful lonely and as though he wanted to play wiv me. I said: 'Come and build a h'engine,' but he didn't say nothing, just looked as—as though he saw a lot of chocolates, and his Mummy had told him not to touch them." Geoff sighed, sad personal reminiscences evidently recurring to him. "But when I asked Jane who he was and told her I wanted to play wiv him, she said there wasn't no little boy in the 'ouse and not to tell naughty stories. I don't love Jane at all."

Mrs. Lancaster got up.

"Jane was right. There was no little boy."

"But I saw him. Oh! Mummy, do let me play wiv him, he did look so awful lonely and unhappy. I *do* want to do something to 'make him better.'"

Mrs. Lancaster was about to speak again, but her father shook his head.

"Geoff," he said very gently, "that poor little boy *is* lonely, and perhaps you may do something to comfort him; but you must find out how by yourself—like a puzzle—do you see?"

"Is it because I am getting *big* I must do it all my lone?"

"Yes, because you are getting big."

As the boy left the room, Mrs. Lancaster turned to her father impatiently.

"Papa, this is absurd. To encourage the boy to believe the servants' idle tales!"

"No servant has told the child anything," said the old man gently. "He's seen—what I *hear*, what I could see perhaps if I were his age."

"But it's such nonsense! Why don't I see it or hear it?"

Mr. Winburn smiled, a curiously tired smile, but did not reply.

"Why?" repeated his daughter. "And why did you tell him he could help the—the—thing. It's—it's all so impossible."

The old man looked at her with his thoughtful glance.

"Why not?" he said. "Do you remember these words:

'What Lamp has Destiny to guide
Her little Children stumbling in the Dark?
"A Blind Understanding," Heaven replied.'

"Geoffrey has that—a blind understanding. All children possess it. It is only as we grow older that we lose it, that we cast it away from us. Sometimes, when we are quite old, a faint gleam comes back to us, but the Lamp burns brightest in childhood. That is why I think Geoffrey may help."

"I don't understand," murmured Mrs. Lancaster feebly.

"No more do I. That—that child is in trouble and wants—to be set free. But how? I do not know, but— it's awful to think of it—sobbing its heart out—a *child*."

A month after this conversation Geoffrey fell very ill. The east wind had been severe, and he was not a strong child. The doctor shook his head and said that it was a grave case. To Mr. Winburn he divulged more and confessed that the case was quite hopeless. "The child would never have lived to grow up, under any circumstances," he added.

"There has been serious lung trouble for a long time."

It was when nursing Geoff that Mrs. Lancaster became aware of that—other child. At first the sobs were an indistinguishable part of the wind, but gradually they became more distinct, more unmistakable. Finally she heard them in moments of dead calm: a child's sobs—dull, hopeless, heartbroken.

Geoff grew steadily worse and in his delirium he spoke of the "little boy" again and again. "I do want to help him get away, I do!" he cried.

Succeeding the delirium there came a state of lethargy. Geoffrey lay very still, hardly breathing, sunk in oblivion. There was nothing to do but wait and watch. Then there came a still night, clear and calm, without one breath of wind.

Suddenly the child stirred. His eyes opened. He looked past his mother toward the open door. He tried to speak and she bent down to catch the half breathed words.

"All right, I'm comin'," he whispered; then he sank back.

The mother felt suddenly terrified, she crossed the room to her father. Somewhere near them the other child was laughing. Joyful, contented, triumphant and silvery laughter echoed through the room.

"I'm frightened; I'm frightened," she moaned.

He put his arm round her protectingly. A sudden gust of wind made them both start, but it passed swiftly and left the air quiet as before.

The laughter had ceased and there crept to them a faint sound, so faint as hardly to be heard, but growing louder till they could distinguish it. Footsteps—light footsteps, swiftly departing.

Pitter-patter, pitter-patter, they ran—those well-known halting little feet. Yet—surely—now *other* footsteps suddenly mingled with them, moving with a quicker and a lighter tread.

With one accord they hastened to the door.

Down, down, down, past the door, close to them, pitter-patter, pitter-patter, went the unseen feet of the little children *together.*

Mrs. Lancaster looked up wildly.

"There are *two* of them—*two!*"

Grey with sudden fear, she turned towards the cot in the corner, but her father restrained her gently, and pointed away.

"There," he said simply.

Pitter-patter, pitter-patter—fainter and fainter.

And then—silence.

Twelve

THE STRANGE CASE
OF SIR ARTHUR CARMICHAEL

"The Strange Case of Sir Arthur
Carmichael" was first published in the
hardback *The Hound of Death and Other
Stories* (Odhams Press, 1933). No
previous appearances have been found.

• • •

(Taken from the notes of the late Dr. Edward
Carstairs, M.D., the eminent psychologist.)

I am perfectly aware that there are two distinct
ways of looking at the strange and tragic events
which I have set down here. My own opinion has
never wavered. I have been persuaded to write the
story out in full, and indeed I believe it to be due
to science that such strange and inexplicable facts
should not be buried in oblivion.

It was a wire from my friend, Dr. Settle, that first
introduced me to the matter. Beyond mentioning
the name Carmichael, the wire was not explicit,
but in obedience to it I took the 12:20 train from
Paddington to Wolden, in Hertfordshire.

The name of Carmichael was not unfamiliar to

me. I had been slightly acquainted with the late Sir William Carmichael of Wolden, though I had seen nothing of him for the last eleven years. He had, I knew, one son, the present baronet, who must now be a young man of about twenty-three. I remembered vaguely having heard some rumours about Sir William's second marriage, but could recall nothing definite unless it were a vague impression detrimental to the second Lady Carmichael.

Settle met me at the station.

"Good of you to come," he said as he wrung my hand.

"Not at all. I understand this is something in my line?"

"Very much so."

"A mental case, then?" I hazarded. "Possessing some unusual features?"

We had collected my luggage by this time and were seated in a dogcart driving away from the station in the direction of Wolden, which lay about three miles away. Settle did not answer for a minute or two. Then he burst out suddenly.

"The whole thing's incomprehensible! Here is a young man, twenty-three years of age, thoroughly normal in every respect. A pleasant amiable boy, with no more than his fair share of conceit, not brilliant intellectually perhaps, but an excellent type of the ordinary upper-class young English-man. Goes to bed in his usual health one evening, and is found the next morning wandering about the village in a semi-idiotic condition, incapable of recognizing his nearest and dearest."

"Ah!" I said, stimulated. This case promised to be interesting. "Complete loss of memory? And this occurred—?"

"Yesterday morning. The ninth of August."

"And there has been nothing—no shock that you know of—to account for this state?"

"Nothing."

I had a sudden suspicion.

"Are you keeping anything back?"

"N—no."

His hesitation confirmed my suspicion.

"I must know everything."

"It's nothing to do with Arthur. It's to do with— with the house."

"With the house," I repeated, astonished.

"You've had a great deal to do with that sort of thing, haven't you, Carstairs? You've 'tested' so-called haunted houses. What's your opinion of the whole thing?"

"In nine cases out of ten, fraud," I replied. "But the tenth—well, I have come across phenomena that are absolutely unexplainable from the ordinary materialistic standpoint. I am a believer in the occult."

Settle nodded. We were just turning in at the park gates. He pointed with his whip at a low-lying white mansion on the side of a hill.

"That's the house," he said. "And—there's *something* in that house, something uncanny—horrible. We all feel it . . . And I'm not a superstitious man. . . ."

"What form does it take?" I asked.

He looked straight in front of him. "I'd rather you knew nothing. You see, if you—coming here unbiased—knowing nothing about it—see it too—well—"

"Yes," I said, "it's better so. But I should be glad if you will tell me a little more about the family."

"Sir William," said Settle, "was twice married. Arthur is the child of his first wife. Nine years ago he married again, and the present Lady Carmichael is something of a mystery. She is only half English, and, I suspect, has Asiatic blood in her veins."

He paused.

"Settle," I said, "you don't like Lady Carmichael."

He admitted it frankly. "No, I don't. There has always seemed to be something sinister about her. Well, to continue, by his second wife Sir William had another child, also a boy, who is now eight years old. Sir William died three years ago, and Arthur came into the title and place. His step-mother and half brother continued to live with him at Wolden. The estate, I must tell you, is very much impoverished. Nearly the whole of Sir Arthur's income goes to keeping it up. A few hundreds a year was all Sir William could leave his wife, but fortunately Arthur has always got on splendidly with his stepmother, and has been only too delighted to have her live with him. Now—"

"Yes?"

"Two months ago Arthur became engaged to a charming girl, a Miss Phyllis Patterson." He added, lowering his voice with a touch of emotion: "They were to have been married next month. She is staying here now. You can imagine her distress—"

I bowed my head silently.

We were driving up close to the house now. On our right the green lawn sloped gently away. And suddenly I saw a most charming picture. A young girl was coming slowly across the lawn to the house. She wore no hat, and the sunlight enhanced the gleam of her glorious golden hair. She carried a great basket of roses, and a beautiful grey Persian cat twined itself lovingly round her feet as she walked.

I looked at Settle interrogatively.

"That is Miss Patterson," he said.

"Poor girl," I said, "poor girl. What a picture she makes with the roses and her grey cat."

I heard a faint sound and looked quickly round at my friend. The reins had slipped out of his fingers, and his face was quite white.

"What's the matter?" I exclaimed.

He recovered himself with an effort.

In a few moments more we had arrived, and I

was following him into the green drawing room, where tea was laid out.

A middle-aged but still beautiful woman rose as we entered and came forward with an outstretched hand.

"This is my friend, Dr. Carstairs, Lady Carmichael."

I cannot explain the instinctive wave of repulsion that swept over me as I took the proffered hand of this charming and stately woman who moved with the dark and languorous grace that recalled Settle's surmise of Oriental blood.

"It is very good of you to come, Dr. Carstairs," she said in a low musical voice, "and to try and help us in our great trouble."

I made some trivial reply and she handed me my tea.

In a few minutes the girl I had seen on the lawn outside entered the room. The cat was no longer with her, but she still carried the basket of roses in her hand. Settle introduced me and she came forward impulsively.

"Oh! Dr. Carstairs, Dr. Settle has told us so much about you. I have a feeling that you will be able to do something for poor Arthur."

Miss Patterson was certainly a very lovely girl, though her cheeks were pale, and her frank eyes were outlined with dark circles.

"My dear young lady," I said reassuringly, "indeed you must not despair. These cases of lost memory, or secondary personality, are often of very short duration. At any minute the patient may return to his full powers."

She shook her head. "I can't believe in this being a second personality," she said. "*This* isn't Arthur at all. It is *no* personality of his. It isn't *him*. I—"

"Phyllis, dear," said Lady Carmichael's soft voice, "here is your tea."

And something in the expression of her eyes as they rested on the girl told me that Lady Carmichael had little love for her prospective daughter-in-law.

Miss Patterson declined the tea, and I said, to ease the conversation: "Isn't the pussycat going to have a saucer of milk?"

She looked at me rather strangely.

"The—pussycat?"

"Yes, your companion of a few moments ago in the garden—"

I was interrupted by a crash. Lady Carmichael had upset the tea kettle, and the hot water was pouring all over the floor. I remedied the matter, and Phyllis Patterson looked questioningly at Settle. He rose.

"Would you like to see your patient now, Carstairs?"

I followed him at once. Miss Patterson came with us. We went upstairs and Settle took a key from his pocket.

"He sometimes has a fit of wandering," he explained. "So I usually lock the door when I'm away from the house."

He turned the key in the lock and went in.

The young man was sitting on the window seat where the last rays of the westerly sun struck broad and yellow. He sat curiously still, rather hunched together, with every muscle relaxed. I thought at first that he was quite unaware of our presence until I suddenly saw that, under immovable lids, he was watching us closely. His eyes dropped as they met mine, and he blinked. But he did not move.

"Come, Arthur," said Settle cheerfully. "Miss Patterson and a friend of mine have come to see you."

But the young fellow in the window seat only blinked. Yet a moment or two later I saw him watching us again—furtively and secretly.

"Want your tea?" asked Settle, still loudly and cheerfully, as though talking to a child.

He set on the table a cup full of milk. I lifted my eyebrows in surprise, and Settle smiled.

"Funny thing," he said, "the only drink he'll touch is milk."

In a moment or two, without undue haste, Sir Arthur uncoiled himself, limb by limb, from his huddled position, and walked slowly over to the table. I recognized suddenly that his movements were absolutely silent, his feet made no sound as they trod. Just as he reached the table he gave a tremendous stretch, poised on one leg forward, the other stretching out behind him. He prolonged this exercise to its utmost extent, and then yawned. Never have I seen such a yawn! It seemed to swallow up his entire face.

He now turned his attention to the milk, bending down to the table until his lips touched the fluid.

Settle answered my inquiring look.

"Won't make use of his hands at all. Seems to have returned to a primitive state. Odd, isn't it?"

I felt Phyllis Patterson shrink against me a little, and I laid my hand soothingly on her arm.

The milk was finished at last, and Arthur Carmichael stretched himself once more, and then with the same quiet noiseless footsteps he regained the window seat, where he sat, huddled up as before, blinking at us.

Miss Patterson drew us out into the corridor. She was trembling all over.

"Oh! Dr. Carstairs," she cried. "It *isn't* him— that thing in there isn't Arthur! I should feel—I should know—"

I shook my head sadly.

"The brain can play strange tricks, Miss Patterson."

I confess that I was puzzled by the case. It presented unusual features. Though I had never seen young Carmichael before there was something about his peculiar manner of walking, and the way he blinked, that reminded me of someone or something that I could not quite place.

Our dinner that night was a quiet affair, the burden of conversation being sustained by Lady Carmichael and myself. When the ladies had withdrawn Settle asked me my impression of my hostess.

"I must confess," I said, "that for no cause or reason I dislike her intensely. You are quite right, she has Eastern blood, and, I should say, possesses marked occult powers. She is a woman of extraordinary magnetic force."

Settle seemed on the point of saying something, but checked himself and merely remarked after a minute or two: "She is absolutely devoted to her little son."

We sat in the green drawing room again after dinner. We had just finished coffee and were conversing rather stiffly on the topics of the day when the cat began to miaow piteously for admission outside the door. No one took any notice, and, as I am fond of animals, after a moment or two I rose.

"May I let the poor thing in?" I asked Lady Carmichael.

Her face seemed very white, I thought, but she made a faint gesture of the head which I took as assent and, going to the door, I opened it. But the corridor outside was quite empty.

"Strange," I said, "I could have sworn I heard a cat."

As I came back to my chair I noticed they were all watching me intently. It somehow made me feel a little uncomfortable.

We retired to bed early. Settle accompanied me to my room.

"Got everything you want?" he asked, looking around.

"Yes, thanks."

He still lingered rather awkwardly as though there was something he wanted to say but could not quite get out.

"By the way," I remarked, "you said there was something uncanny about this house? As yet it seems most normal."

"You call it a cheerful house?"

"Hardly that, under the circumstances. It is obviously under the shadow of a great sorrow. But as regards any abnormal influence, I should give it a clean bill of health."

"Good night," said Settle abruptly. "And pleasant dreams."

Dream I certainly did. Miss Patterson's grey cat seemed to have impressed itself upon my brain. All night long, it seemed to me, I dreamt of the wretched animal.

Awaking with a start, I suddenly realized what had brought the cat so forcibly into my thoughts. The creature was miaowing persistently outside my door. Impossible to sleep with that racket going on. I lit my candle and went to the door. But the passage outside my room was empty, though the miaowing still continued. A new idea struck me. The unfortunate animal was shut up somewhere, unable to get out. To the left was the end of the passage, where Lady Carmichael's room was situated. I turned therefore to the right and had taken but a few paces when the noise broke out again from behind me. I turned sharply and the sound came again, this time distinctly on the *right* of me.

Something, probably a draught in the corridor, made me shiver, and I went sharply back to my room. Everything was silent now, and I was soon asleep once more—to wake to another glorious summer's day.

As I was dressing I saw from my window the disturber of my night's rest. The grey cat was creeping slowly and stealthily across the lawn. I judged its object of attack to be a small flock of birds who were busy chirruping and preening themselves not far away.

And then a very curious thing happened. The cat came straight on and passed through the midst of the birds, its fur almost brushing against them— and the birds did not fly away. I could not understand it—the thing seemed incomprehensible.

So vividly did it impress me that I could not refrain from mentioning it at breakfast.

"Do you know?" I said to Lady Carmichael, "that you have a very unusual cat?"

I heard the quick rattle of a cup on a saucer, and I saw Phyllis Patterson, her lips parted and her breath coming quickly, gazing earnestly at me.

There was a moment's silence, and then Lady Carmichael said in a distinctly disagreeable manner: "I think you must have made a mistake. There is no cat here. I have never had a cat."

It was evident that I had managed to put my foot in it badly, so I hastily changed the subject.

But the matter puzzled me. Why had Lady Carmichael declared there was no cat in the house? Was it perhaps Miss Patterson's, and its presence concealed from the mistress of the house? Lady Carmichael might have one of those strange antipathies to cats which are so often met with nowadays. It hardly seemed a plausible explanation, but I was forced to rest content with it for the moment.

Our patient was still in the same condition. This time I made a thorough examination and was able to study him more closely than the night before. At my suggestion it was arranged that he should spend as much time with the family as possible. I hoped not only to have a better opportunity of observing him when he was off his guard, but the ordinary everyday routine might awaken some gleam of intelligence. His demeanour, however, remained unchanged. He was quiet and docile, seemed vacant, but was in point of fact, intensely and rather slyly watchful. One thing certainly came as a surprise to me, the intense affection he displayed towards his stepmother. Miss Patterson he ignored completely, but he always managed to sit as near Lady Carmichael as possible, and once I saw him rub his head against her shoulder in a dumb expression of love.

I was worried about the case. I could not but feel that there was some clue to the whole matter which had so far escaped me.

"This is a very strange case," I said to Settle.

"Yes," said he, "it's very—suggestive."

He looked at me rather furtively, I thought.

"Tell me," he said. "He doesn't—remind you of anything?"

The words struck me disagreeably, reminding me of my impression of the day before.

"Remind me of what?" I asked.

He shook his head.

"Perhaps it's my fancy," he muttered. "Just my fancy."

And he would say no more on the matter.

Altogether there was mystery shrouding the affair. I was still obsessed with that baffling feeling of having missed the clue that should elucidate it to me. And concerning a lesser matter there was also mystery. I mean that trifling affair of the grey cat. For some reason or other the thing was getting on my nerves. I dreamed of cats—I continually fancied I heard him. Now and then in the distance I caught a glimpse of the beautiful animal. And the fact that there was some mystery connected with it fretted me unbearably. On a sudden impulse I applied one afternoon to the footman for information.

"Can you tell me anything," I said, "about the cat I see?"

"The cat, sir?" He appeared politely surprised.

"Wasn't there—isn't there—a cat?"

"Her ladyship *had* a cat, sir. A great pet. Had to be put away though. A great pity, as it was a beautiful animal."

"A grey cat?" I asked slowly.

"Yes, sir. A Persian."

"And you say it was destroyed?"

"Yes, sir."

"You're quite sure it was destroyed?"

"Oh! quite sure, sir. Her ladyship wouldn't have him sent to the vet—but did it herself. A little less than a week ago now. He's buried out there under the copper beech, sir." And he went out of the room, leaving me to my meditations.

Why had Lady Carmichael affirmed so positively that she had never had a cat?

I felt an intuition that this trifling affair of the cat was in some way significant. I found Settle and took him aside.

"Settle," I said. "I want to ask you a question.

Have you, or have you not, both seen and heard a cat in this house?"

He did not seem surprised at the question. Rather did he seem to have been expecting it.

"I've heard it," he said. "I've not seen it."

"But the first day," I cried. "On the lawn with Miss Patterson!"

He looked at me very steadily.

"I saw Miss Patterson walking across the lawn. Nothing else."

I began to understand. "Then," I said, "the cat—?"

He nodded.

"I wanted to see if you—unprejudiced—would hear what we all hear . . . ?"

"You all hear it then?"

He nodded again.

"It's strange," I murmured thoughtfully. "I never heard of a cat haunting a place before."

I told him what I had learnt from the footman, and he expressed surprise.

"That's news to me. I didn't know that."

"But what does it mean?" I asked helplessly.

He shook his head. "Heaven only knows! But I'll tell you, Carstairs—I'm afraid. The—thing's voice sounds—menacing."

"Menacing?" I said sharply. "To whom?"

He spread out his hands. "I can't say."

It was not till that evening after dinner that I realized the meaning of his words. We were sitting in the green drawing room, as on the night of my arrival, when it came—the loud insistent miaowing of a cat outside the door. But this time it was unmistakably angry in its tone—a fierce cat yowl, long-drawn and menacing. And then as it ceased the brass hook outside the door was rattled violently as by a cat's paw.

Settle started up.

"I swear that's real," he cried.

He rushed to the door and flung it open.

There was nothing there.

He came back mopping his brow. Phyllis was pale and trembling, Lady Carmichael deathly white. Only Arthur, squatting contentedly like a child, his head against his stepmother's knee, was calm and undisturbed.

Miss Patterson laid her hand on my arm and we went upstairs.

"Oh! Dr. Carstairs," she cried. "What is it? What does it all mean?"

"We don't know yet, my dear young lady," I said. "But I mean to find out. But you mustn't be afraid. I am convinced there is no danger to you personally."

She looked at me doubtfully. "You think that?"

"I am sure of it," I answered firmly. I remembered the loving way the grey cat had twined itself round her feet, and I had no misgivings. The menace was not for her.

I was some time dropping off to sleep, but at length I fell into an uneasy slumber from which I awoke with a sense of shock. I heard a scratching sputtering noise as of something being violently ripped or torn. I sprang out of bed and rushed out into the passage. At the same moment Settle burst out of his room opposite. The sound came from our left.

"You hear it, Carstairs?" he cried. "You hear it?"

We came swiftly up to Lady Carmichael's door. Nothing had passed us, but the noise had ceased. Our candles glittered blankly on the shiny panels of Lady Carmichael's door. We stared at one another.

"You know what it was?" he half whispered.

I nodded. "A cat's claws ripping and tearing something." I shivered a little. Suddenly I gave an exclamation and lowered the candle I held.

"Look here, Settle."

"Here" was a chair that rested against the wall—and the seat of it was ripped and torn in long strips. . . .

We examined it closely. He looked at me and I nodded.

"Cat's claws," he said, drawing in his breath sharply. "Unmistakable." His eyes went from the chair to the closed door. "That's the person who is menaced. Lady Carmichael!"

I slept no more that night. Things had come to a pass where something must be done. As far as I knew there was only one person who had the key to the situation. I suspected Lady Carmichael of knowing more than she chose to tell.

She was deathly pale when she came down the next morning, and only toyed with the food on her plate. I was sure that only an iron determination kept her from breaking down. After breakfast I requested a few words with her. I went straight to the point.

"Lady Carmichael," I said. "I have reason to believe that you are in very grave danger."

"Indeed?" She braved it out with wonderful unconcern.

"There is in this house," I continued, "A Thing—a Presence—that is obviously hostile to you."

"What nonsense," she murmured scornfully. "As if I believed in any rubbish of that kind."

"The chair outside your door," I remarked drily, "was ripped to ribbons last night."

"Indeed?" With raised eyebrows she pretended surprise, but I saw that I had told her nothing she did not know. "Some stupid practical joke, I suppose."

"It was not that," I replied with some feeling. "And I want you to tell me—for your own sake—" I paused.

"Tell you what?" she queried.

"Anything that can throw light on the matter," I said gravely.

She laughed.

"I know nothing," she said. "Absolutely nothing."

And no warnings of danger could induce her to relax the statement. Yet I was convinced that she *did* know a great deal more than any of us, and held some clue to the affair of which we were absolutely ignorant. But I saw that it was quite impossible to make her speak.

I determined, however, to take every precaution that I could, convinced as I was that she was menaced by a very real and immediate danger. Before she went to her room the following night Settle and I made a thorough examination of it. We had agreed that we would take it in turns to watch the passage.

I took the first watch, which passed without incident, and at three o'clock Settle relieved me. I was tired after my sleepless night the day before, and dropped off at once. And I had a very curious dream.

I dreamed that the grey cat was sitting at the foot of my bed and that its eyes were fixed on mine with a curious pleading. Then, with the ease of dreams, I knew that the creature wanted me to follow it. I did so, and it led me down the great staircase and right to the opposite wing of the house to a room which was obviously the library. It paused there at one side of the room and raised its front paws till they rested on one of the lower shelves of books, while it gazed at me once more with that same moving look of appeal.

Then—cat and library faded, and I awoke to find that morning had come.

Settle's watch had passed without incident, but he was keenly interested to hear of my dream. At my request he took me to the library, which coincided in every particular with my vision of it. I could even point out the exact spot where the animal had given me that last sad look.

We both stood there in silent perplexity. Suddenly an idea occurred to me, and I stooped to read the title of the book in that exact place. I noticed that there was a gap in the line.

"Some book has been taken out of here," I said to Settle.

He stooped also to the shelf.

"Hallo," he said. "There's a nail at the back here that has torn off a fragment of the missing volume."

He detached the little scrap of paper with care. It was not more than an inch square—but on it were printed two significant words: "The cat. . . ."

"This thing gives me the creeps," said Settle. "It's simply horribly uncanny."

"I'd give anything to know," I said, "what book it is that is missing from here. Do you think there is any way of finding out?"

"May be a catalogue somewhere. Perhaps Lady Carmichael—"

I shook my head.

"Lady Carmichael will tell you nothing."

"You think so?"

"I am sure of it. While we are guessing and feeling about in the dark Lady Carmichael *knows*. And for reasons of her own she will say nothing. She prefers to run a most horrible risk sooner than break silence."

The day passed with an uneventfulness that reminded me of the calm before a storm. And I had a strange feeling that the problem was near solution. I was groping about in the dark, but soon I should see. The facts were all there, ready, waiting for the little flash of illumination that should weld them together and show out their significance.

And come it did! In the strangest way!

It was when we were all sitting together in the green drawing room as usual after dinner. We had been very silent. So noiseless indeed was the room that a little mouse ran across the floor—and in an instant the thing happened.

With one long spring Arthur Carmichael leapt from his chair. His quivering body was swift as an arrow on the mouse's track. It had disappeared behind the wainscoting, and there he crouched—watchful—his body still trembling with eagerness.

It was horrible! I have never known such a paralysing moment. I was no longer puzzled as to that something that Arthur Carmichael reminded me of with his stealthy feet and watching eyes. And in a flash an explanation, wild, incredible, unbelievable, swept into my mind. I rejected it as impossible—unthinkable! But I could not dismiss it from my thoughts.

I hardly remember what happened next. The whole thing seemed blurred and unreal. I know that somehow we got upstairs and said our good nights briefly, almost with a dread of meeting each other's eyes, lest we should see there some confirmation of our own fears.

Settle established himself outside Lady Carmichael's door to take the first watch, arranging to call me at 3 a.m. I had no special fears for Lady Carmichael; I was too taken up with my fantastic impossible theory. I told myself it was impossible—but my mind returned to it, fascinated.

And then suddenly the stillness of the night was disturbed. Settle's voice rose in a shout, calling me. I rushed out to the corridor.

He was hammering and pounding with all his might on Lady Carmichael's door.

"Devil take the woman!" he cried. "She's locked it!"

"But—"

"It's in there, man! In with her! Can't you hear it?"

From behind the locked door a long-drawn cat yowl sounded fiercely. And then following it a horrible scream—and another . . . I recognized Lady Carmichael's voice.

"The door!" I yelled. "We must break it in. In another minute we shall be too late."

We set our shoulders against it, and heaved with all our might. It gave with a crash—and we almost fell into the room.

Lady Carmichael lay on the bed bathed in blood. I have seldom seen a more horrible sight. Her heart was still beating, but her injuries were terrible, for the skin of the throat was all ripped and torn . . . Shuddering, I whispered: "The Claws . . ." A thrill of superstitious horror ran over me.

I dressed and bandaged the wounds carefully and suggested to Settle that the exact nature of the injuries had better be kept secret, especially from Miss Patterson. I wrote out a telegram for a hospital nurse, to be despatched as soon as the telegraph office was open.

The dawn was now stealing in at the window. I looked out on the lawn below.

"Get dressed and come out," I said abruptly to Settle. "Lady Carmichael will be all right now."

He was soon ready, and we went out into the garden together.

"What are you going to do?"

"Dig up the cat's body," I said briefly. "I must be sure—"

I found a spade in a toolshed and we set to work beneath the large copper beech tree. At last our digging was rewarded. It was not a pleasant job.

The animal had been dead a week. But I saw what I wanted to see.

"That's the cat," I said. "The identical cat I saw the first day I came here."

Settle sniffed. An odour of bitter almonds was still perceptible.

"Prussic acid," he said.

I nodded.

"What are you thinking?" he asked curiously.

"What you think too!"

My surmise was no new one to him—it had passed through his brain also, I could see.

"It's impossible," he murmured. "Impossible! It's against all science—all nature . . ." His voice tailed off in a shudder. "That mouse last night," he said. "But—oh! it couldn't be!"

"Lady Carmichael," I said, "is a very strange woman. She has occult powers—hypnotic powers. Her forebears came from the East. Can we know what use she might have made of these powers over a weak lovable nature such as Arthur Carmichael's? And remember, Settle, if Arthur Carmichael remains a hopeless imbecile, devoted to her, the whole property is practically hers and her son's—whom you have told me she adores. And Arthur was going to be married!"

"But what are we going to do, Carstairs?"

"There's nothing to be done," I said. "We'll do our best though to stand between Lady Carmichael and vengeance."

Lady Carmichael improved slowly. Her injuries healed themselves as well as could be expected—the scars of that terrible assault she would probably bear to the end of her life.

I had never felt more helpless. The power that defeated us was still at large, undefeated, and though quiescent for the minute we could hardly regard it as doing otherwise than biding its time. I was determined upon one thing. As soon as Lady Carmichael was well enough to be moved she must be taken away from Wolden. There was just a chance that the terrible manifestation might be unable to follow her. So the days went on.

I had fixed September 18th as the date of Lady Carmichael's removal. It was on the morning of the 14th when the unexpected crisis arose.

I was in the library discussing details of Lady Carmichael's case with Settle when an agitated housemaid rushed into the room.

"Oh! sir," she cried. "Be quick! Mr. Arthur—he's fallen into the pond. He stepped on the punt and it pushed off with him, and he overbalanced and fell in! I saw it from the window."

I waited for no more, but ran straight out of the room followed by Settle. Phyllis was just outside and had heard the maid's story. She ran with us.

"But you needn't be afraid," she cried. "Arthur is a magnificent swimmer."

I felt forebodings, however, and redoubled my pace. The surface of the pond was unruffled. The empty punt floated lazily about—but of Arthur there was no sign.

Settle pulled off his coat and his boots. "I'm going in," he said. "You take the boat hook and fish about from the other punt. It's not very deep."

Very long the time seemed as we searched vainly. Minute followed minute. And then, just as we were despairing, we found him, and bore the apparently lifeless body of Arthur Carmichael to shore.

As long as I live I shall never forget the hopeless agony of Phyllis's face.

"Not—not—" her lips refused to frame the dreadful word.

"No, no, my dear," I cried. "We'll bring him round, never fear."

But inwardly I had little hope. He had been under water for half an hour. I sent off Settle to the house for hot blankets and other necessaries, and began myself to apply artificial respiration.

We worked vigorously with him for over an hour but there was no sign of life. I motioned to Settle to take my place again, and I approached Phyllis.

"I'm afraid," I said gently, "that it is no good. Arthur is beyond our help."

She stayed quite still for a moment and then suddenly flung herself down on the lifeless body.

"Arthur!" she cried desperately. "Arthur! Come

back to me! Arthur—come back—come back!"

Her voice echoed away into silence. Suddenly I touched Settle's arm. "Look!" I said.

A faint tinge of colour crept into the drowned man's face. I felt his heart.

"Go on with the respiration," I cried. "He's coming round!"

The moments seemed to fly now. In a marvellously short time his eyes opened.

Then suddenly I realized a difference. *These were intelligent eyes, human eyes . . .*

They rested on Phyllis.

"Hallo! Phil," he said weakly. "Is it you? I thought you weren't coming until tomorrow."

She could not yet trust herself to speak but she smiled at him. He looked round with increasing bewilderment.

"But, I say, where am I? And—how rotten I feel! What's the matter with me? Hallo, Dr. Settle!"

"You've been nearly drowned—that's what's the matter," returned Settle grimly.

Sir Arthur made a grimace.

"I've always heard it was beastly coming back afterwards! But how did it happen? Was I walking in my sleep?"

Settle shook his head.

"We must get him to the house," I said, stepping forward.

He stared at me, and Phyllis introduced me. "Dr. Carstairs, who is staying here."

We supported him between us and started for the house. He looked up suddenly as though struck by an idea.

"I say, doctor, this won't knock me up for the 12th, will it?"

"The 12th?" I said slowly, "you mean the 12th of August?"

"Yes—next Friday."

"Today is the 14th of September," said Settle abruptly. His bewilderment was evident.

"But—but I thought it was the 8th of August? I must have been ill then?"

Phyllis interposed rather quickly in her gentle voice.

"Yes," she said, "you've been very ill."

He frowned. "I can't understand it. I was perfectly all right when I went to bed last night—at least of course it wasn't really last night. I had dreams though. I remember, dreams . . ." His brow furrowed itself still more as he strove to remember. "Something—what was it? Something dreadful—someone had done it to me—and I was angry—desperate . . . And then I dreamed I was a cat—yes, a cat! Funny, wasn't it? But it wasn't a funny dream. It was more—horrible! But I can't remember. It all goes when I think."

I laid my hand on his shoulder. "Don't try to think, Sir Arthur," I said gravely. "Be content—to forget."

He looked at me in a puzzled way and nodded.

I heard Phyllis draw a breath of relief. We had reached the house.

"By the way," said Sir Arthur suddenly, "where's the mater?"

"She has been—ill," said Phyllis after a momentary pause.

"Oh! poor old mater!" His voice rang with genuine concern. "Where is she? In her room?"

"Yes," I said, "but you had better not disturb—"

The words froze on my lips. The door of the drawing room opened and Lady Carmichael, wrapped in a dressing gown, came out into the hall.

Her eyes were fixed on Arthur, and if ever I have seen a look of absolute guilt-stricken terror I saw it then. Her face was hardly human in its frenzied terror. Her hand went to her throat.

Arthur advanced towards her with boyish affection.

"Hello, mater! So you've been knocked up too? I say, I'm awfully sorry."

She shrank back before him, her eyes dilating. Then suddenly, with a shriek of a doomed soul, she fell backwards through the open door.

I rushed and bent over her, then beckoned to Settle.

"Hush," I said. "Take him upstairs quietly and then come down again. Lady Carmichael is dead."

He returned in a few minutes.

"What was it?" he asked. "What caused it?"

"Shock," I said grimly. "The shock of seeing Arthur Carmichael, restored to life! Or you may call it, as I prefer to, the judgment of God!"

"You mean—" he hesitated.

I looked at him in the eyes so that he understood.

"A life for a life," I said significantly.

"But—"

"Oh! I know that a strange and unforeseen accident permitted the spirit of Arthur Carmichael to return to his body. But, nevertheless, Arthur Carmichael was murdered."

He looked at me half fearfully. "With prussic acid?" he asked in a low tone.

"Yes," I answered. "With prussic acid."

Settle and I have never spoken our belief. It is not one likely to be credited. According to the orthodox point of view Arthur Carmichael merely suffered from loss of memory, Lady Carmichael lacerated her own throat in a temporary fit of mania, and the apparition of the Grey Cat was mere imagination.

But there are two facts that to my mind are unmistakable. One is the ripped chair in the corridor. The other is even more significant. A catalogue of the library was found, and after exhaustive search it was proved that the missing volume was an ancient and curious work on the possibilities of the metamorphosis of human beings into animals!

One thing more. I am thankful to say that Arthur knows nothing. Phyllis has locked the secret of those weeks in her own heart, and she will never, I am sure, reveal them to the husband she loves so dearly, and who came back across the barrier of the grave at the call of her voice.

Thirteen

The Call of Wings

"The Call of Wings" was first published in the hardback *The Hound of Death and Other Stories* (Odhams Press, 1933). No previous appearances have been found.

• • •

Silas Hamer heard it first on a wintry night in February. He and Dick Borrow had walked from a dinner given by Bernard Seldon, the nerve specialist. Borrow had been unusually silent, and Silas Hamer asked him with some curiosity what he was thinking about. Borrow's answer was unexpected.

"I was thinking, that of all these men tonight, only two amongst them could lay claim to happiness. And that these two, strangely enough, were you and I!"

The word "strangely" was apposite, for no two men could be more dissimilar than Richard Borrow, the hardworking East End parson, and Silas Hamer, the sleek complacent man whose millions were a matter of household knowledge.

"It's odd, you know," mused Borrow, "I believe you're the only contented millionaire I've ever met."

Hamer was silent a moment. When he spoke his tone had altered.

"I used to be a wretched shivering little newspaper boy. I wanted then—what I've got now!—the comfort and the luxury of money, not its power. I wanted money, not to wield as a force, but to spend lavishly—on myself! I'm frank about it, you see. Money can't buy everything, they say. Very true. But it can buy everything I want—therefore I'm satisfied. I'm a materialist, Borrow, out and out a materialist!"

The broad glare of the lighted thoroughfare confirmed this confession of faith. The sleek lines of Silas Hamer's body were amplified by the heavy fur-lined coat, and the white light emphasized the thick rolls of flesh beneath his chin. In contrast to him walked Dick Borrow, with the thin ascetic face and the star-gazing fanatical eyes.

"It's *you*," said Hamer with emphasis, "that I can't understand."

Borrow smiled.

"I live in the midst of misery, want, starvation—all the ills of the flesh! And a predominant Vision upholds me. It's not easy to understand unless you believe in Visions, which I gather you don't."

"I don't believe," said Silas Hamer stolidly, "in anything I can't see, hear and touch."

"Quite so. That's the difference between us. Well, good-bye, the earth now swallows me up!"

291

They had reached the doorway of a lighted tube station, which was Borrow's route home.

Hamer proceeded alone. He was glad he had sent away the car tonight and elected to walk home. The air was keen and frosty, his senses were delightfully conscious of the enveloping warmth of the fur-lined coat.

He paused for an instant on the kerbstone before crossing the road. A great motor bus was heavily ploughing its way towards him. Hamer, with the feeling of infinite leisure, waited for it to pass. If he were to cross in front of it he would have to hurry—and hurry was distasteful to him.

By his side a battered derelict of the human race rolled drunkenly off the pavement. Hamer was aware of a shout, an ineffectual swerve of the motor bus, and then—he was looking stupidly, with a gradually awakening horror, at a limp inert heap of rags in the middle of the road.

A crowd gathered magically, with a couple of policemen and the bus driver as its nucleus. But Hamer's eyes were riveted in horrified fascination on that lifeless bundle that had once been a man— a man like himself! He shuddered as at some menace.

"Dahn't yer blime yerself, guv'nor," remarked a rough-looking man at his side. "Yer couldn't 'a done nothin'. 'E was done for anyways."

Hamer stared at him. The idea that it was possible in any way to save the man had quite

292

honestly never occurred to him. He scouted the notion now as an absurdity. Why if he had been so foolish, he might at this moment . . . His thoughts broke off abruptly, and he walked away from the crowd. He felt himself shaking with a nameless unquenchable dread. He was forced to admit to himself that he was *afraid*—horribly afraid—of Death . . . Death that came with dreadful swiftness and remorseless certainty to rich and poor alike. . . .

He walked faster, but the new fear was still with him, enveloping him in its cold and chilling grasp.

He wondered at himself, for he knew that by nature he was no coward. Five years ago, he reflected, this fear would not have attacked him. For then Life had not been so sweet . . . Yes, that was it; love of Life was the key to the mystery. The zest of living was at its height for him; it knew but one menace, Death, the destroyer!

He turned out of the lighted thoroughfare. A narrow passageway, between high walls, offered a shortcut to the Square where his house, famous for its art treasures, was situated.

The noise of the street behind him lessened and faded, the soft thud of his own footsteps was the only sound to be heard.

And then out of the gloom in front of him came another sound. Sitting against the wall was a man playing the flute. One of the enormous tribe of street musicians, of course, but why had he chosen such a peculiar spot? Surely at this time of night the police—Hamer's reflections were interrupted suddenly as he realized with a shock that the man had no legs. A pair of crutches rested against the wall beside him. Hamer saw now that it was not a flute he was playing but a strange instrument whose notes were much higher and clearer than those of a flute.

The man played on. He took no notice of Hamer's approach. His head was flung far back on his shoulders, as though uplifted in the joy of his own music, and the notes poured out clearly and joyously, rising higher and higher. . . .

It was a strange tune—strictly speaking, it was not a tune at all, but a single phrase, not unlike the slow turn given out by the violins of *Rienzi*, repeated again and again, passing from key to key, from harmony to harmony, but always rising and attaining each time to a greater and more boundless freedom.

It was unlike anything Hamer had ever heard. There was something strange about it, something inspiring—and uplifting . . . it . . . He caught frantically with both hands to a projection in the wall beside him. He was conscious of one thing only—*that he must keep down*—at all costs he must *keep down* . . .

He suddenly realized that the music had stopped. The legless man was reaching out for his crutches. And here was he, Silas Hamer, clutching like a lunatic at a stone buttress, for the simple reason that he had had the utterly preposterous notion—absurd on the face of it!—that he was rising from the ground—that the music was carrying him upwards. . . .

He laughed. What a wholly mad idea! Of course his feet had never left the earth for a moment, but what a strange hallucination! The quick tap-tapping of wood on the pavement told him that the cripple was moving away. He looked after him until the man's figure was swallowed up in the gloom. An odd fellow!

He proceeded on his way more slowly; he could not efface from his mind the memory of that strange impossible sensation when the ground had failed beneath his feet. . . .

And then on an impulse he turned and followed hurriedly in the direction the other had taken. The man could not have gone far—he would soon overtake him.

He shouted as soon as he caught sight of the maimed figure swinging itself slowly along.

"Hi! One minute."

The man stopped and stood motionless until Hamer came abreast of him. A lamp burned just over his head and revealed every feature. Silas Hamer caught his breath in involuntary surprise. The man possessed the most singularly beautiful head he had ever seen. He might have been any age; assuredly he was not a boy, yet youth was the most predominant characteristic—youth and vigour in passionate intensity!

Hamer found an odd difficulty in beginning his conversation.

"Look here," he said awkwardly, "I want to know what was that thing you were playing just now?"

The man smiled . . . With his smile the world seemed suddenly to leap into joyousness. . . .

"It was an old tune—a very old tune . . . Years old—centuries old."

He spoke with an odd purity and distinctness of enunciation, giving equal value to each syllable. He was clearly not an Englishman, yet Hamer was puzzled as to his nationality.

"You're not English? Where do you come from?"

Again the broad joyful smile.

"From over the sea, sir. I came—a long time ago—a very long time ago."

"You must have had a bad accident. Was it lately?"

"Some time now, sir."

"Rough luck to lose both legs."

"It was well," said the man very calmly. He turned his eyes with a strange solemnity on his interlocutor. "They were evil."

Hamer dropped a shilling in his hand and turned away. He was puzzled and vaguely disquieted. "They were evil"! What a strange thing to say!

Evidently an operation for some form of disease, but—how odd it had sounded.

Hamer went home thoughtful. He tried in vain to dismiss the incident from his mind. Lying in bed, with the first incipient sensation of drowsiness stealing over him, he heard a neighbouring clock strike one. One clear stroke and then silence— silence that was broken by a faint familiar sound . . . Recognition came leaping. Hamer felt his heart beating quickly. It was the man in the passageway playing, somewhere not far distant. . . .

The notes came gladly, the slow turn with its joyful call, the same haunting little phrase . . . "It's uncanny," murmured Hamer, "it's uncanny. It's got wings to it. . . ."

Clearer and clearer, higher and higher—each wave rising above the last, and catching *him* up with it. This time he did not struggle, he let himself go . . . Up—up . . . The waves of sound were carrying him higher and higher . . . Triumphant and free, they swept on.

Higher and higher . . . They had passed the limits of human sound now, but they still continued—rising, ever rising . . . Would they reach the final goal, the full perfection of height?

Rising. . . .

Something was pulling—pulling him down- wards. Something big and heavy and insistent. It pulled remorselessly—pulled him back, and down . . . down. . . .

He lay in bed gazing at the window opposite. Then, breathing heavily and painfully, he stretched an arm out of bed. The movement seemed curiously cumbrous to him. The softness of the bed was oppressive, oppressive too were the heavy curtains over the window that blocked out the light and air. The ceiling seemed to press down upon him. He felt stifled and choked. He moved slightly under the bed clothes, and the weight of his body seemed to him the most oppressive of all. . . .

"I want your advice, Seldon."

Seldon pushed back his chair an inch or so from the table. He had been wondering what was the object of this tête-à-tête dinner. He had seen little of Hamer since the winter, and he was aware tonight of some indefinable change in his friend.

"It's just this," said the millionaire. "I'm worried about myself."

Seldon smiled as he looked across the table.

"You're looking in the pink of condition."

"It's not that." Hamer paused a minute, then added quietly. "I'm afraid I'm going mad."

The nerve specialist glanced up with a sudden keen interest. He poured himself out a glass of port with a rather slow movement, and then said quietly, but with a sharp glance at the other man: "What makes you think that?"

"Something that's happened to me. Something

inexplicable, unbelievable. It can't be true, so I must be going mad."

"Take your time," said Seldon, "and tell me about it."

"I don't believe in the supernatural," began Hamer. "I never have. But this thing . . . Well, I'd better tell you the whole story from the beginning. It began last winter one evening after I had dined with you."

Then briefly and concisely he narrated the events of his walk home and the strange sequel.

"That was the beginning of it all. I can't explain it to you properly—the feeling, I mean—but it was wonderful! Unlike anything I've ever felt or dreamed. Well, it's gone on ever since. Not every night, just now and then. The music, the feeling of being uplifted, the soaring flight . . . and then the terrible drag, the pull back to earth, and afterwards the pain, the actual physical pain of the awakening. It's like coming down from a high mountain—you know the pains in the ears one gets? Well, this is the same thing, but intensified—and with it goes the awful sense of *weight*—of being hemmed in, stifled. . . ."

He broke off and there was a pause.

"Already the servants think I'm mad. I couldn't bear the roof and the walls—I've had a place arranged up at the top of the house, open to the sky, with no furniture or carpets, or any stifling things . . . But even then the houses all round are nearly as bad. It's open country I want, some-where where one can breathe . . ." He looked across at Seldon. "Well, what do you say? Can you explain it?"

"H'm," said Seldon. "Plenty of explanations. You've been hypnotized, or you've hypnotized yourself. Your nerves have gone wrong. Or it may be merely a dream."

Hamer shook his head. "None of those explanations will do."

"And there are others," said Seldon slowly, "but they're not generally admitted."

"*You* are prepared to admit them?"

"On the whole, yes! There's a great deal we can't understand which can't possibly be explained normally. We've any amount to find out still, and I for one believe in keeping an open mind."

"What do you advise me to do?" asked Hamer after a silence.

Seldon leaned forward briskly. "One of several things. Go away from London, seek out your 'open country.' The dreams may cease."

"I can't do that," said Hamer quickly. "It's come to this, that I can't do without them. I don't want to do without them."

"Ah! I guessed as much. Another alternative, find this fellow, this cripple. You're endowing him now with all sorts of supernatural attributes. Talk to him. Break the spell."

Hamer shook his head again.

"Why not?"

"I'm afraid," said Hamer simply.

Seldon made a gesture of impatience. "Don't believe in it all so blindly! This tune now, the medium that starts it all, what is it like?"

Hamer hummed it, and Seldon listened with a puzzled frown.

"Rather like a bit out of the Overture to *Rienzi*. There *is* something uplifting about it—it has wings. But I'm not carried off the earth! Now, these flights of yours, are they all exactly the same?"

"No, no." Hamer leaned forward eagerly. "They develop. Each time I see a little more. It's difficult to explain. You see, I'm always conscious of reaching a certain point—the music carries me there—not direct, but a succession of *waves,* each reaching higher than the last, until the highest point where one can go no further. I stay there until I'm dragged back. It isn't a place, it's more a *state.* Well, not just at first, but after a little while, I began to understand that there were other things all round me waiting until I was able to perceive them. Think of a kitten. It has eyes, but at first it can't see with them. It's blind and has to learn to see. Well, that was what it was to me. Mortal eyes and ears were no good to me, but there was something corresponding to them that hadn't yet been developed—something that wasn't *bodily* at

301

all. And little by little that grew . . . there were sensations of light . . . then of sound . . . then of colour . . . All very vague and unformulated. It was more the knowledge of things than seeing or hearing them. First it was light, a light that grew stronger and clearer . . . then sand, great stretches of reddish sand . . . and here and there straight long lines of water like canals—"

Seldon drew in his breath sharply. "*Canals!* That's interesting. Go on."

"But these things didn't matter—they didn't count any longer. The real things were the things I couldn't see yet—but I heard them . . . It was a sound like the rushing of wings . . . somehow, I can't explain why, it was glorious! There's nothing like it here. And then came another glory—*I saw them*—the Wings! Oh, Seldon, the Wings!"

"But what were they? Men—angels—birds?"

"I don't know. I couldn't see—not yet. But the colour of them! *Wing colour*—we haven't got it here—it's a wonderful colour."

"Wing colour?" repeated Seldon. "What's it like?" Hamer flung up his hands impatiently. "How can I tell you? Explain the colour blue to a blind person! It's a colour you've never seen— Wing colour!"

"Well?"

"Well? That's all. That's as far as I've got. But each time the coming back has been worse—more painful. I can't understand that. I'm convinced my body never leaves the bed. In this place I get to I'm convinced I've got no *physical* presence. Why should it hurt so confoundly then?"

Seldon shook his head in silence.

"It's something awful—the coming back. The *pull* of it—then the pain, pain in every limb and every nerve, and my ears feel as though they were bursting. Then everything *presses* so, the weight of it all, the dreadful sense of imprisonment. I want light, air, space—above all *space* to breathe in! And I want freedom."

"And what," asked Seldon, "of all the other things that used to mean so much to you?"

"That's the worst of it. I care for them still as much as, if not more than, ever. And these things, comfort, luxury, pleasure, seem to pull opposite ways to the Wings. It's a perpetual struggle between them—and I can't see how it's going to end."

Seldon sat silent. The strange tale he had been listening to was fantastic enough in all truth. Was it all a delusion, a wild hallucination—or could it by any possibility be true? And if so, why *Hamer,* of all men . . . ? Surely the materialist, the man who loved the flesh and denied the spirit, was the last man to see the sights of another world.

Across the table Hamer watched him anxiously.

"I suppose," said Seldon slowly, "that you can only wait. Wait and see what happens."

"I can't! I tell you I can't! Your saying that shows you don't understand. It's tearing me in two, this awful struggle—this killing long-drawn-out fight between—between—" He hesitated.

"The flesh and the spirit?" suggested Seldon.

Hamer stared heavily in front of him. "I suppose one might call it that. Anyway, it's unbearable . . . I can't get free. . . ."

Again Bernard Seldon shook his head. He was caught up in the grip of the inexplicable. He made one more suggestion.

"If I were you," he advised, "I would get hold of that cripple."

But as he went home he muttered to himself: "*Canals*—I wonder."

Silas Hamer went out of the house the following morning with a new determination in his step. He had decided to take Seldon's advice and find the legless man. Yet inwardly he was convinced that his search would be in vain and that the man would have vanished as completely as though the earth had swallowed him up.

The dark buildings on either side of the passageway shut out the sunlight and left it dark and mysterious. Only in one place, halfway up it, there was a break in the wall, and through it there fell a shaft of golden light that illuminated with radiance a figure sitting on the ground. A figure— yes, it was the man!

The instrument of pipes leaned against the wall beside his crutches, and he was covering the paving stones with designs in coloured chalk. Two were completed, sylvan scenes of marvellous beauty and delicacy, swaying trees and a leaping brook that seemed alive.

And again Hamer doubted. Was this man a mere street musician, a pavement artist? Or was he something more. . . .

Suddenly the millionaire's self-control broke down, and he cried fiercely and angrily: "Who are you? For God's sake, who are you?"

The man's eyes met his, smiling.

"Why don't you answer? Speak, man, speak!"

Then he noticed that the man was drawing with incredible rapidity on a bare slab of stone. Hamer followed the movement with his eyes . . . A few bold strokes, and giant trees took form. Then, seated on a boulder . . . a man . . . playing an instrument of pipes. A man with a strangely beautiful face—*and goat's legs* . . .

The cripple's hand made a swift movement. The man still sat on the rock, but the goat's legs were gone. Again his eyes met Hamer's.

"They were evil," he said.

Hamer stared, fascinated. For the face before him was the face of the picture, but strangely and incredibly beautified . . . Purified from all but an intense and exquisite joy of living.

Hamer turned and almost fled down the

passageway into the bright sunlight, repeating to himself incessantly: "It's impossible. Impossible . . . I'm mad—dreaming!" But the face haunted him the face of Pan. . . .

He went into the Park and sat on a chair. It was a deserted hour. A few nursemaids with their charges sat in the shade of the trees, and dotted here and there in the stretches of green, like islands in a sea, lay the recumbent forms of men. . . .

The words "a wretched tramp" were to Hamer an epitome of misery. But suddenly, today, he envied them. . . .

They seemed to him of all created beings the only free ones. The earth beneath them, the sky above them, the world to wander in . . . they were not hemmed in or chained.

Like a flash it came to him that that which bound him so remorselessly was the thing he had worshipped and prized above all others—wealth! He had thought it the strongest thing on earth, and now, wrapped round by its golden strength, he saw the truth of his words. It was his money that held him in bondage. . . .

But was it? Was that really it? Was there a deeper and more pointed truth that he had not seen? Was it the money or was it his own love of the money? He was bound in fetters of his own making; not wealth itself, but love of wealth was the chain.

He knew now clearly the two forces that were tearing at him, the warm composite strength of materialism that enclosed and surrounded him, and, opposed to it, the clear imperative call—he named it to himself the Call of the Wings.

And while the one fought and clung the other scorned war and would not stoop to struggle. It only called—called unceasingly . . . He heard it so clearly that it almost spoke in words.

"You cannot make terms with me," it seemed to say.

. "For I am above all other things. If you follow my call you must give up all else and cut away the forces that hold you. For only the Free shall follow where I lead. . . ."

"I can't," cried Hamer. "I can't. . . ."

A few people turned to look at the big man who sat talking to himself.

So sacrifice was being asked of him, the sacrifice of that which was most dear to him, that which was part of himself.

Part of himself—he remembered the man without legs. . . .

"What in the name of Fortune brings you here?" asked Borrow.

Indeed the East End mission was an unfamiliar background to Hamer.

"I've listened to a good many sermons," said the millionaire, "all saying what could be done if you people had funds. I've come to tell you this: you can have funds."

"Very good of you," answered Borrow, with some surprise. "A big subscription, eh?"

Hamer smiled drily. "I should say so. Just every penny I've got."

"What?"

Hamer rapped out details in a brisk businesslike manner. Borrow's head was whirling.

"You—you mean to say that you're making over your entire fortune to be devoted to the relief of the poor in the East End with myself appointed as trustee?"

"That's it."

"But why—*why?*"

"I can't explain," said Hamer slowly. "Remember our talk about vision last February? Well, a vision has got hold of me."

"It's splendid!" Borrow leaned forward, his eyes gleaming.

"There's nothing particularly splendid about it," said Hamer grimly. "I don't care a button about poverty in the East End. All they want is grit! *I* was poor enough—and I got out of it. But I've got to get rid of the money, and these tomfool societies shan't get hold of it. You're a man I can trust. Feed bodies or souls with it—preferably the former. I've been hungry, but you can do as you like."

"There's never been such a thing known," stammered Borrow.

"The whole thing's done and finished with," continued Hamer. "The lawyers have fixed it up

308

at last, and I've signed everything. I can tell you I've been busy this last fortnight. It's almost as difficult getting rid of a fortune as making one."

"But you—you've kept *something*?"

"Not a penny," said Hamer cheerfully. "At least—that's not quite true. I've just two pence in my pocket." He laughed.

He said goodbye to his bewildered friend, and walked out of the mission into the narrow evil-smelling streets. The words he had said so gaily just now came back to him with an aching sense of loss. "Not a penny!" Of all his vast wealth he had kept nothing. He was afraid now—afraid of poverty and hunger and cold. Sacrifice had no sweetness for him.

Yet behind it all he was conscious that the weight and menace of things had lifted, he was no longer oppressed and bound down. The severing of the chain had seared and torn him, but the vision of freedom was there to strengthen him. His material needs might dim the Call, but they could not deaden it, for he knew it to be a thing of immortality that could not die.

There was a touch of autumn in the air, and the wind blew chill. He felt the cold and shivered, and then, too, he was hungry—he had forgotten to have any lunch. It brought the future very near to him. It was incredible that he should have given it all up; the ease, the comfort, the warmth! His body cried out impotently . . . And then once again there came to him a glad and uplifting sense of freedom.

Hamer hesitated. He was near the Tube station. He had twopence in his pocket. The idea came to him to journey by it to the Park where he had watched the recumbent idlers a fortnight ago. Beyond this whim he did not plan for the future. He believed honestly enough now that he was mad—sane people did not act as he had done. Yet, if so, madness was a wonderful and amazing thing.

Yes, he would go now to the open country of the Park, and there was a special significance to him in reaching it by Tube. For the Tube represented to him all the horrors of buried, shut-in life . . . He would ascend from its imprisonment free to the wide green and the trees that concealed the menace of the pressing houses.

The lift bore him swiftly and relentlessly downward. The air was heavy and lifeless. He stood at the extreme end of the platform, away from the mass of people. On his left was the opening of the tunnel from which the train, snakelike, would presently emerge. He felt the whole place to be subtly evil. There was no one near him but a hunched-up lad sitting on a seat, sunk, it seemed, in a drunken stupor.

In the distance came the faint menacing roar of the train. The lad rose from his seat and shuffled unsteadily to Hamer's side, where he stood on the edge of the platform peering into the tunnel.

Then—it happened so quickly as to be almost incredible—he lost his balance and fell. . . .

A hundred thoughts rushed simultaneously to Hamer's brain. He saw a huddled heap run over by a motor bus, and heard a hoarse voice saying: "Dahn't yer blime yerself, guv'nor. Yer couldn't 'a done nothin'." And with that came the knowledge that *this* life could only be saved, if it were saved, by himself. There was no one else near, and the train was close . . . It all passed through his mind with lightning rapidity. He experienced a curious calm lucidity of thought.

He had one short second in which to decide, and he knew in that moment that his fear of Death was unabated. He was horribly afraid. And then the train, rushing round the curve of the tunnel, powerless to pull up in time.

Swiftly Hamer caught up the lad in his arms. No natural gallant impulse swayed him, his shivering flesh was but obeying the command of the alien spirit that called for sacrifice. With a last effort he flung the lad forward on to the platform, falling himself. . . .

Then suddenly his Fear died. The material world held him down no longer. He was free of his shackles. He fancied for a moment that he heard the joyous piping of Pan. Then—nearer and louder—swallowing up all else—came the glad rushing of innumerable Wings . . . enveloping and encircling him. . . .

Fourteen

MAGNOLIA BLOSSOM

"Magnolia Blossom" was first published
in *Royal Magazine*, March 1926.

• • •

Vincent Easton was waiting under the clock at
Victoria Station. Now and then he glanced up at it
uneasily. He thought to himself: "How many other
men have waited here for a woman who didn't
come?"

A sharp pang shot through him. Supposing that
Theo didn't come, that she had changed her mind?
Women did that sort of thing. Was he sure of
her—had he ever been sure of her? Did he really
know anything at all about her? Hadn't she
puzzled him from the first? There had seemed to
be two women—the lovely, laughing creature who
was Richard Darrell's wife, and the other—silent,
mysterious, who had walked by his side in the
garden of Haymer's Close. Like a magnolia
flower—that was how he thought of her—perhaps
because it was under the magnolia tree that they
had tasted their first rapturous, incredulous kiss.
The air had been sweet with the scent of magnolia
bloom, and one or two petals, velvety-soft and

fragrant, had floated down, resting on that upturned face that was as creamy and as soft and as silent as they. Magnolia blossom—exotic, fragrant, mysterious.

That had been a fortnight ago—the second day he had met her. And now he was waiting for her to come to him forever. Again incredulity shot through him. She wouldn't come. How could he ever have believed it? It would be giving up so much. The beautiful Mrs. Darrell couldn't do this sort of thing quietly. It was bound to be a nine days' wonder, a far-reaching scandal that would never quite be forgotten. There were better, more expedient ways of doing these things—a discreet divorce, for instance.

But they had never thought of that for a moment—at least he had not. Had she? he wondered. He had never known anything of her thoughts. He had asked her to come away with him almost timorously—for after all, what was he? Nobody in particular—one of a thousand orange growers in the Transvaal. What a life to take her to—after the brilliance of London! And yet, since he wanted her so desperately, he must needs ask.

She had consented very quietly, with no hesitations or protests, as though it were the simplest thing in the world that he was asking her.

"Tomorrow?" he had said, amazed, almost unbelieving.

And she had promised in that soft, broken voice that was so different from the laughing brilliance of her social manner. He had compared her to a diamond when he first saw her a thing of flashing fire, reflecting light from a hundred facets. But at that first touch, that first kiss, she had changed miraculously to the clouded softness of a pearl—a pearl like a magnolia blossom, creamy pink.

She had promised. And now he was waiting for her to fulfil that promise.

He looked again at the clock. If she did not come soon, they would miss the train.

Sharply a wave of reaction set in. She wouldn't come! Of course she wouldn't come. Fool that he had been ever to expect it! What were promises? He would find a letter when he got back to his rooms—explaining, protesting, saying all the things that women do when they are excusing themselves for lack of courage.

He felt anger—anger and the bitterness of frustration.

Then he saw her coming towards him down the platform, a faint smile on her face. She walked slowly, without haste or fluster, as one who had all eternity before her. She was in black—soft black that clung, with a little black hat that framed the wonderful creamy pallor of her face.

He found himself grasping her hand, muttering stupidly:

"So you've come—you have come. After all!"

"Of course."

How calm her voice sounded! How calm!

"I thought you wouldn't," he said, releasing her hand and breathing hard.

Her eyes opened—wide, beautiful eyes. There was wonder in them, the simple wonder of a child.

"Why?"

He didn't answer. Instead he turned aside and requisitioned a passing porter. They had not much time. The next few minutes were all bustle and confusion. Then they were sitting in their reserved compartment and the drab houses of southern London were drifting by them.

Theodora Darrell was sitting opposite him. At last she was his. And he knew now how incredulous, up to the very last minute, he had been. He had not dared to let himself believe. That magical, elusive quality about her had frightened him. It had seemed impossible that she should ever belong to him.

Now the suspense was over. The irrevocable step was taken. He looked across at her. She lay back in the corner, quite still. The faint smile lingered on her lips, her eyes were cast down, the long, black lashes swept the creamy curve of her cheek.

He thought: "What's in her mind now? What is she thinking of? Me? Her husband? What does she think about him anyway? Did she care for him once? Or did she never care? Does she hate him, or is she indifferent to him?" And with a pang the thought swept through him: "I don't know. I never shall know. I love her, and I don't know anything about her—what she thinks or what she feels."

His mind circled round the thought of Theodora Darrell's husband. He had known plenty of married women who were only too ready to talk about their husbands—of how they were misunderstood by them, of how their finer feelings were ignored. Vincent Easton reflected cynically that it was one of the best-known opening gambits.

But except casually, Theo had never spoken of Richard Darrell. Easton knew of him what everybody knew. He was a popular man, handsome, with an engaging, carefree manner. Everybody liked Darrell. His wife always seemed on excellent terms with him. But that proved nothing, Vincent reflected. Theo was well-bred—she would not air her grievances in public.

And between them, no word had passed. From that second evening of their meeting, when they had walked together in the garden, silent, their shoulders touching, and he had felt the faint tremor that shook her at his touch, there had been no explainings, no defining of the position. She had returned his kisses, a dumb, trembling creature, shorn of all that hard brilliance which, together with her cream-and-rose beauty, had made her famous. Never once had she spoken of her husband. Vincent had been thankful for that at the time. He had been glad to be spared the arguments of a woman who wished to assure herself and her lover that they were justified in yielding to their love.

Yet now the tacit conspiracy of silence worried him. He had again that panic-stricken sense of knowing nothing about this strange creature who was willingly linking her life to his. He was afraid.

In the impulse to reassure himself, he bent forward and laid a hand on the black-clad knee opposite him. He felt once again the faint tremor that shook her, and he reached up for her hand. Bending forward, he kissed the palm, a long, lingering kiss. He felt the response of her fingers on his and, looking up, met her eyes, and was content.

He leaned back in his seat. For the moment, he wanted no more. They were together. She was his. And presently he said in a light, almost bantering tone:

"You're very silent?"

"Am I?"

"Yes." He waited a minute, then said in a graver tone: "You're sure you don't—regret?"

Her eyes opened wide at that. "Oh, no!"

317

He did not doubt the reply. There was an assurance of sincerity behind it.

"What are you thinking about? I want to know."

In a low voice she answered: "I think I'm afraid."

"Afraid?"

"Of happiness."

He moved over beside her then, held her to him and kissed the softness of her face and neck.

"I love you," he said. "I love you—love you."

Her answer was in the clinging of her body, the abandon of her lips.

Then he moved back to his own corner. He picked up a magazine and so did she. Every now and then, over the top of the magazines, their eyes met. Then they smiled.

They arrived at Dover just after five. They were to spend the night there, and cross to the Continent on the following day. Theo entered their sitting room in the hotel with Vincent close behind her. He had a couple of evening papers in his hand which he threw down on the table. Two of the hotel servants brought in the luggage and withdrew.

Theo turned from the window where she had been standing looking out. In another minute they were in each other's arms.

There was a discreet tap on the door and they drew apart again.

"Damn it all," said Vincent, "it doesn't seem as though we were ever going to be alone."

Theo smiled. "It doesn't look like it," she said softly. Sitting down on the sofa, she picked up one of the papers.

The knock proved to be a waiter bearing tea. He laid it on the table, drawing the latter up to the sofa on which Theo was sitting, cast a deft glance round, inquired if there were anything further, and withdrew.

Vincent, who had gone into the adjoining room, came back into the sitting room.

"Now for tea," he said cheerily, but stopped suddenly in the middle of the room. "Anything wrong?" he asked.

Theo was sitting bolt upright on the sofa. She was staring in front of her with dazed eyes, and her face had gone deathly white.

Vincent took a quick step towards her.

"What is it, sweetheart?"

For answer she held out the paper to him, her finger pointing to the headline.

Vincent took the paper from her. "Failure of Hobson, Jekyll and Lucas," he read. The name of the big city firm conveyed nothing to him at the moment, though he had an irritating conviction in the back of his mind that it ought to do so. He looked inquiringly at Theo.

"Richard is Hobson, Jekyll and Lucas," she explained.

"Your husband?"

"Yes."

Vincent returned to the paper and read the bald information it conveyed carefully. Phrases such as "sudden crash," "serious revelations to follow," "other houses affected" struck him disagreeably.

Roused by a movement, he looked up. Theo was adjusting her little black hat in front of the mirror. She turned at the movement he made. Her eyes looked steadily into his.

"Vincent—I must go to Richard."

He sprang up.

"Theo—don't be absurd."

She repeated mechanically:

"I must go to Richard."

"But, my dear—"

She made a gesture towards the paper on the floor.

"That means ruin—bankruptcy. I can't choose this day of all others to leave him."

"You had left him before you heard of this. Be reasonable!"

She shook her head mournfully.

"You don't understand. I must go to Richard."

And from that he could not move her. Strange that a creature so soft, so pliant, could be so unyielding. After the first, she did not argue. She let him say what he had to say unhindered. He held her in his arms, seeking to break her will by enslaving her senses, but though her soft mouth returned his kisses, he felt in her something aloof and invincible that withstood all his pleadings.

He let her go at last, sick and weary of the vain endeavour. From pleading he had turned to bitterness, reproaching her with never having loved him. That, too, she took in silence, without protest, her face, dumb and pitiful, giving the lie to his words. Rage mastered him in the end; he hurled at her every cruel word he could think of, seeking only to bruise and batter her to her knees.

At last the words gave out; there was nothing more to say. He sat, his head in his hands, staring down at the red pile carpet. By the door, Theodora stood, a black shadow with a white face.

It was all over.

She said quietly: "Goodbye, Vincent."

He did not answer.

The door opened—and shut again.

The Darrells lived in a house in Chelsea—an intriguing, old-world house, standing in a little garden of its own. Up the front of the house grew a magnolia tree, smutty, dirty, begrimed, but still a magnolia.

Theo looked up at it, as she stood on the doorstep some three hours later. A sudden smile twisted her mouth in pain.

She went straight to the study at the back of the house. A man was pacing up and down in the room—a young man, with a handsome face and a haggard expression.

He gave an ejaculation of relief as she came in.

"Thank God you've turned up, Theo. They said you'd taken your luggage with you and gone off out of town somewhere."

"I heard the news and came back."

Richard Darrell put an arm about her and drew her to the couch. They sat down upon it side by side. Theo drew herself free of the encircling arm in what seemed a perfectly natural manner.

"How bad is it, Richard?" she asked quietly.

"Just as bad as it can be—and that's saying a lot."

"Tell me!"

He began to walk up and down again as he talked. Theo sat and watched him. He was not to know that every now and then the room went dim, and his voice faded from her hearing, while another room in a hotel at Dover came clearly before her eyes.

Nevertheless she managed to listen intelligently enough. He came back and sat down on the couch by her.

"Fortunately," he ended, "they can't touch your marriage settlement. The house is yours also."

Theo nodded thoughtfully.

"We shall have that at any rate," she said. "Then things will not be too bad? It means a fresh start, that is all."

"Oh! Quite so. Yes."

But his voice did not ring true, and Theo thought suddenly: "There's something else. He hasn't told me everything."

"There's nothing more, Richard?" she said gently. "Nothing worse?"

He hesitated for just half a second, then: "Worse? What should there be?"

"I don't know," said Theo.

"It'll be all right," said Richard, speaking more as though to reassure himself than Theo. "Of course, it'll be all right."

He flung an arm about her suddenly.

"I'm glad you're here," he said. "It'll be all right now that you're here. Whatever else happens, I've got you, haven't I?"

She said gently: "Yes, you've got me." And this time she left his arm round her.

He kissed her and held her close to him, as though in some strange way he derived comfort from her nearness.

"I've got you, Theo," he said again presently, and she answered as before: "Yes, Richard."

He slipped from the couch to the floor at her feet.

"I'm tired out," he said fretfully. "My God, it's been a day. Awful! I don't know what I should do if you weren't here. After all, one's wife is one's wife, isn't she?"

She did not speak, only bowed her head in assent.

He laid his head on her lap. The sigh he gave was like that of a tired child.

Theo thought again: "There's something he hasn't told me. What is it?"

Mechanically her hand dropped to his smooth, dark head, and she stroked it gently, as a mother might comfort a child.

Richard murmured vaguely:

"It'll be all right now you're here. You won't let me down."

His breathing grew slow and even. He slept. Her hand still smoothed his head.

But her eyes looked steadily into the darkness in front of her, seeing nothing.

"Don't you think, Richard," said Theodora, "that you'd better tell me everything?"

It was three days later. They were in the drawing room before dinner.

Richard started, and flushed.

"I don't know what you mean," he parried.

"Don't you?"

He shot a quick glance at her.

"Of course there are—well—details."

"I ought to know everything, don't you think, if I am to help?"

He looked at her strangely.

"What makes you think I want you to help?"

She was a little astonished.

"My dear Richard, I'm your wife."

He smiled suddenly, the old, attractive, carefree smile.

"So you are, Theo. And a very good-looking wife, too. I never could stand ugly women."

He began walking up and down the room, as was his custom when something was worrying him.

"I won't deny you're right in a way," he said presently. "There is something."

He broke off.

"Yes?"

"It's so damned hard to explain things of this kind to women. They get hold of the wrong end of the stick—fancy a thing is—well, what it isn't."

Theo said nothing.

"You see," went on Richard, "the law's one thing, and right and wrong are quite another. I may do a thing that's perfectly right and honest, but the law wouldn't take the same view of it. Nine times out of ten, everything pans out all right, and the tenth time you—well, hit a snag."

Theo began to understand. She thought to herself: "Why am I not surprised? Did I always know, deep down, that he wasn't straight?"

Richard went on talking. He explained himself at unnecessary lengths. Theo was content for him to cloak the actual details of the affair in this mantle of verbosity. The matter concerned a large tract of South African property. Exactly what Richard had done, she was not concerned to know.

Morally, he assured her, everything was fair and aboveboard; legally—well, there it was; no getting away from the fact, he had rendered himself liable to criminal prosecution.

He kept shooting quick glances at his wife as he talked. He was nervous and uncomfortable. And still he excused himself and tried to explain away that which a child might have seen in its naked truth. Then finally in a burst of justification, he broke down. Perhaps Theo's eyes, momentarily scornful, had something to do with it. He sank down in a chair by the fireplace, his head in his hands.

"There it is, Theo," he said brokenly. "What are you going to do about it?"

She came over to him with scarcely a moment's pause and, kneeling down by the chair, put her face against his.

"What can be done, Richard? What can we do?"

He caught her to him.

"You mean it? You'll stick to me?"

"Of course. My dear, of course."

He said, moved to sincerity in spite of himself: "I'm a thief, Theo. That's what it means, shorn of fine language—just a thief."

"Then I'm a thief's wife, Richard. We'll sink or swim together."

They were silent for a little while. Presently Richard recovered something of his jaunty manner.

"You know, Theo, I've got a plan, but we'll talk of that later. It's just on dinnertime. We must go and change. Put on that creamy thingummybob of yours, you know—the Caillot model."

Theo raised her eyebrows quizzically.

"For an evening at home?"

"Yes, yes, I know. But I like it. Put it on, there's a good girl. It cheers me up to see you looking your best."

Theo came down to dinner in the Caillot. It was a creation in creamy brocade, with a faint pattern of gold running through it and an undernote of pale pink to give warmth to the cream. It was cut daringly low in the back, and nothing could have been better designed to show off the dazzling whiteness of Theo's neck and shoulders. She was truly now a magnolia flower.

Richard's eye rested upon her in warm approval. "Good girl. You know, you look simply stunning in that dress."

They went in to dinner. Throughout the evening Richard was nervous and unlike himself, joking and laughing about nothing at all, as if in a vain attempt to shake off his cares. Several times Theo tried to lead him back to the subject they had been discussing before, but he edged away from it.

Then suddenly, as she rose to go to bed, he came to the point.

"No, don't go yet. I've got something to say. You know, about this miserable business."

She sat down again.

He began talking rapidly. With a bit of luck, the whole thing could be hushed up. He had covered his tracks fairly well. So long as certain papers didn't get into the receiver's hands—

He stopped significantly.

"Papers?" asked Theo perplexedly. "You mean you will destroy them?"

Richard made a grimace.

"I'd destroy them fast enough if I could get hold of them. That's the devil of it all!"

"Who has them, then?"

"A man we both know—Vincent Easton."

A very faint exclamation escaped Theo. She forced it back, but Richard had noticed it.

"I've suspected he knew something of the business all along. That's why I've asked him here a good bit. You may remember that I asked you to be nice to him?"

"I remember," said Theo.

"Somehow I never seem to have got on really friendly terms with him. Don't know why. But he likes you. I should say he likes you a good deal."

Theo said in a very clear voice: "He does."

"Ah!" said Richard appreciatively. "That's good. Now you see what I'm driving at. I'm convinced that if you went to Vincent Easton and asked him to give you those papers, he wouldn't refuse. Pretty woman, you know—all that sort of thing."

"I can't do that," said Theo quickly.

"Nonsense."

"It's out of the question."

The red came slowly out in blotches on Richard's face. She saw that he was angry.

"My dear girl, I don't think you quite realize the position. If this comes out, I'm liable to go to prison. It's ruin—disgrace."

"Vincent Easton will not use those papers against you. I am sure of that."

"That's not quite the point. He mayn't realize that they incriminate me. It's only taken in conjunction with—with my affairs—with the figures they're bound to find. Oh! I can't go into details. He'll ruin me without knowing what he's doing unless somebody puts the position before him."

"You can do that yourself, surely. Write to him."

"A fat lot of good that would be! No, Theo, we've only got one hope. You're the trump card. You're my wife. You must help me. Go to Easton tonight—"

A cry broke from Theo.

"Not tonight. Tomorrow perhaps."

"My God, Theo, can't you realize things? Tomorrow may be too late. If you could go now— at once—to Easton's rooms." He saw her flinch, and tried to reassure her. "I know, my dear girl, I know. It's a beastly thing to do. But it's life or death. Theo, you won't fail me? You said you'd do anything to help me—"

Theo heard herself speaking in a hard, dry voice. "Not this thing. There are reasons."

"It's life or death, Theo. I mean it. See here."

He snapped open a drawer of the desk and took out a revolver. If there was something theatrical about that action, it escaped her notice.

"It's that or shooting myself. I can't face the racket. If you won't do as I ask you, I'll be a dead man before morning. I swear to you solemnly that that's the truth."

Theo gave a low cry. "No, Richard, not that!"

"Then help me."

He flung the revolver down on the table and knelt by her side. "Theo my darling—if you love me—if you've ever loved me—do this for me. You're my wife, Theo, I've no one else to turn to."

On and on his voice went, murmuring, pleading. And at last Theo heard her own voice saying: "Very well—yes."

Richard took her to the door and put her into a taxi.

"Theo!"

Vincent Easton sprang up in incredulous delight. She stood in the doorway. Her wrap of white ermine was hanging from her shoulders. Never, Easton thought, had she looked so beautiful.

"You've come after all."

She put out a hand to stop him as he came towards her.

"No, Vincent, this isn't what you think."

She spoke in a low, hurried voice.

"I'm here from my husband. He thinks there are some papers which may—do him harm. I have come to ask you to give them to me."

Vincent stood very still, looking at her. Then he gave a short laugh.

"So that's it, is it? I thought Hobson, Jekyll and Lucas sounded familiar the other day, but I couldn't place them at the minute. Didn't know your husband was connected with the firm. Things have been going wrong there for some time. I was commissioned to look into the matter. I suspected some underling. Never thought of the man at the top."

Theo said nothing. Vincent looked at her curiously.

"It makes no difference to you, this?" he asked. "That—well, to put it plainly, that your husband's a swindler?"

She shook her head.

"It beats me," said Vincent. Then he added quietly: "Will you wait a minute or two? I will get the papers."

Theo sat down in a chair. He went into the other room. Presently he returned and delivered a small package into her hand.

"Thank you," said Theo. "Have you a match?"

Taking the matchbox he proffered, she knelt down by the fireplace. When the papers were reduced to a pile of ashes, she stood up.

"Thank you," she said again.

"Not at all," he answered formally. "Let me get you a taxi."

He put her into it, saw her drive away. A strange, formal little interview. After the first, they had not even dared look at each other. Well, that was that, the end. He would go away, abroad, try and forget.

Theo leaned her head out of the window and spoke to the taxi driver. She could not go back at once to the house in Chelsea. She must have a breathing space. Seeing Vincent again had shaken her horribly. If only—if only. But she pulled herself up. Love for her husband she had none— but she owed him loyalty. He was down, she must stick by him. Whatever else he might have done, he loved her; his offence had been committed against society, not against her.

The taxi meandered on through the wide streets of Hampstead. They came out on the heath, and a breath of cool, invigorating air fanned Theo's cheeks. She had herself in hand again now. The taxi sped back towards Chelsea.

Richard came out to meet her in the hall.

"Well," he demanded, "you've been a long time."

"Have I?"

"Yes—a very long time. Is it—all right?"

He followed her, a cunning look in his eyes. His hands were shaking.

"It's—it's all right, eh?" he said again.

"I burnt them myself."

"Oh!"

She went on into the study, sinking into a big armchair. Her face was dead white and her whole body drooped with fatigue. She thought to herself: "If only I could go to sleep now and never, never wake up again!"

Richard was watching her. His glance, shy, furtive, kept coming and going. She noticed nothing. She was beyond noticing.

"It went off quite all right, eh?"

"I've told you so."

"You're sure they were the right papers? Did you look?"

"No."

"But then—"

"I'm sure, I tell you. Don't bother me, Richard. I can't bear any more tonight."

Richard shifted nervously.

"No, no. I see."

He fidgeted about the room. Presently he came over to her, laid a hand on her shoulder. She shook it off.

"Don't touch me." She tried to laugh. "I'm sorry, Richard. My nerves are on edge. I feel I can't bear to be touched."

"I know. I understand."

Again he wandered up and down.

"Theo," he burst out suddenly. "I'm damned sorry."

"What?" She looked up, vaguely startled.

"I oughtn't to have let you go there at this time of night. I never dreamed that you'd be subjected to any—unpleasantness."

"Unpleasantness?" She laughed. The word seemed to amuse her. "You don't know! Oh, Richard, you don't know!"

"I don't know what?"

She said very gravely, looking straight in front of her: "What this night has cost me."

"My God! Theo! I never meant—You—you did that, for me? The swine! Theo—Theo—I couldn't have known. I couldn't have guessed. My God!"

He was kneeling by her now stammering, his arms round her, and she turned and looked at him with faint surprise, as though his words had at last really penetrated to her attention.

"I—I never meant—"

"You never meant what, Richard?"

Her voice startled him.

"Tell me. What was it that you never meant?"

"Theo, don't let us speak of it. I don't want to know. I want never to think of it."

She was staring at him, wide awake now, with every faculty alert. Her words came clear and distinct:

"You never meant—What do you think happened?"

"It didn't happen, Theo. Let's say it didn't happen."

And still she stared, till the truth began to come to her.

"You think that—"

"I don't want—"

She interrupted him: "You think that Vincent Easton asked a price for those letters? You think that I—paid him?"

Richard said weakly and unconvincingly: "I—I never dreamed he was that kind of man."

"Didn't you?" She looked at him searchingly. His eyes fell before hers. "Why did you ask me to put on this dress this evening? Why did you send me there alone at this time of night? You guessed he—cared for me. You wanted to save your skin—save it at any cost—even at the cost of my honour." She got up.

"I see now. You meant that from the beginning—or at least you saw it as a possibility, and it didn't deter you."

"Theo—"

"You can't deny it. Richard, I thought I knew all there was to know about you years ago. I've known almost from the first that you weren't straight as regards the world. But I thought you were straight with me."

"Theo—"

"Can you deny what I've just been saying?"

He was silent, in spite of himself.

"Listen, Richard. There is something I must tell you. Three days ago when this blow fell on you, the servants told you I was away—gone to the country. That was only partly true. I had gone away with Vincent Easton—"

Richard made an inarticulate sound. She held out a hand to stop him.

"Wait. We were at Dover. I saw a paper—I realized what had happened. Then, as you know, I came back."

She paused.

Richard caught her by the wrist. His eyes burnt into hers.

"You came back—in time?"

Theo gave a short, bitter laugh.

"Yes, I came back, as you say, 'in time,' Richard."

Her husband relinquished his hold on her arm. He stood by the mantelpiece, his head thrown back. He looked handsome and rather noble.

"In that case," he said, "I can forgive."

"I cannot."

The two words came crisply. They had the semblance and the effect of a bomb in the quiet room. Richard started forward, staring, his jaw dropped with an almost ludicrous effect.

"You—er—what did you say, Theo?"

"I said I cannot forgive! In leaving you for

another man, I sinned—not technically, perhaps, but in intention, which is the same thing. But if I sinned, I sinned through love. You, too, have not been faithful to me since our marriage. Oh, yes, I know. That I forgave, because I really believed in your love for me. But the thing you have done tonight is different. It is an ugly thing, Richard—a thing no woman should forgive. You sold me, your own wife, to purchase safety!"

She picked up her wrap and turned towards the door.

"Theo," he stammered out, "where are you going?"

She looked back over her shoulder at him.

"We all have to pay in this life, Richard. For my sin I must pay in loneliness. For yours—well, you gambled with the thing you love, and you have lost it!"

"You are going?"

She drew a long breath.

"To freedom. There is nothing to bind me here."

He heard the door shut. Ages passed, or was it a few minutes? Something fluttered down outside the window—the last of the magnolia petals, soft, fragrant.

Fifteen

NEXT TO A DOG

"Next to a Dog" was first published in
Grand Magazine, September 1929.

• • •

The ladylike woman behind the Registry Office
table cleared her throat and peered across at the
girl who sat opposite.

"Then you refuse to consider the post? It only
came in this morning. A very nice part of Italy, I
believe, a widower with a little boy of three and an
elderly lady, his mother or aunt."

Joyce Lambert shook her head.

"I can't go out of England," she said in a tired
voice; "there are reasons. If only you could find
me a daily post?"

Her voice shook slightly—ever so slightly, for
she had it well under control. Her dark blue eyes
looked appealingly at the woman opposite her.

"It's very difficult, Mrs. Lambert. The only kind
of daily governess required is one who has full
qualifications. You have none. I have hundreds on
my books—literally hundreds." She paused. "You
have someone at home you can't leave?"

Joyce nodded.

338

"A child?"

"No, not a child." And a faint smile flickered across her face.

"Well, it is very unfortunate. I will do my best, of course, but—"

The interview was clearly at an end. Joyce rose. She was biting her lip to keep the tears from springing to her eyes as she emerged from the frowsy office into the street.

"You mustn't," she admonished herself sternly. "Don't be a snivelling little idiot. You're panicking—that's what you're doing—panicking. No good ever came of giving way to panic. It's quite early in the day still and lots of things may happen. Aunt Mary ought to be good for a fortnight anyway. Come on, girl, step out, and don't keep your well-to-do relations waiting."

She walked down Edgware Road, across the park, and then down to Victoria Street, where she turned into the Army and Navy Stores. She went to the lounge and sat down glancing at her watch. It was just half past one. Five minutes sped by and then an elderly lady with her arms full of parcels bore down upon her.

"Ah! There you are, Joyce. I'm a few minutes late, I'm afraid. The service is not as good as it used to be in the luncheon room. You've had lunch, of course?"

Joyce hesitated a minute or two, then she said quietly: "Yes, thank-you."

"I always have mine at half past twelve," said Aunt Mary, settling herself comfortably with her parcels. "Less rush and a clearer atmosphere. The curried eggs here are excellent."

"Are they?" said Joyce faintly. She felt that she could hardly bear to think of curried eggs—the hot steam rising from them—the delicious smell! She wrenched her thoughts resolutely aside.

"You look peaky, child," said Aunt Mary, who was herself of a comfortable figure. "Don't go in for this modern fad of eating no meat. All fal-de-lal. A good slice off the joint never did anyone any harm."

Joyce stopped herself from saying, "It wouldn't do me any harm now." If only Aunt Mary would stop talking about food. To raise your hopes by asking you to meet her at half past one and then to talk of curried eggs and slices of roast meat—oh! cruel—cruel.

"Well, my dear," said Aunt Mary. "I got your letter—and it was very nice of you to take me at my word. I said I'd be pleased to see you anytime and so I should have been—but as it happens, I've just had an extremely good offer to let the house. Quite too good to be missed, and bringing their own plate and linen. Five months. They come in on Thursday and I go to Harrogate. My rheumatism's been troubling me lately."

"I see," said Joyce. "I'm so sorry."

"So it'll have to be for another time. Always pleased to see you, my dear."

"Thank you, Aunt Mary."

"You know, you do look peaky," said Aunt Mary, considering her attentively. "You're thin, too; no flesh on your bones, and what's happened to your pretty colour? You always had a nice healthy colour. Mind you take plenty of exercise."

"I'm taking plenty of exercise today," said Joyce grimly. She rose. "Well, Aunt Mary, I must be getting along."

Back again—through St. James's Park this time, and so on through Berkeley Square and across Oxford Street and up Edgware Road, past Praed Street to the point where the Edgware Road begins to think of becoming something else. Then aside, through a series of dirty little streets till one particular dingy house was reached.

Joyce inserted her latchkey and entered a small frowsy hall. She ran up the stairs till she reached the top landing. A door faced her and from the bottom of this door a snuffling noise proceeded succeeded in a second by a series of joyful whines and yelps.

"Yes, Terry darling—it's Missus come home."

As the door opened, a white body precipitated itself upon the girl—an aged wire-haired terrier very shaggy as to coat and suspiciously bleary as to eyes. Joyce gathered him up in her arms and sat down on the floor.

"Terry darling! Darling, darling Terry. Love your Missus, Terry; love your Missus a lot!"

And Terry obeyed, his eager tongue worked busily, he licked her face, her ears, her neck and all the time his stump of a tail wagged furiously.

"Terry darling, what are we going to do? What's going to become of us? Oh! Terry darling, I'm so tired."

"Now then, miss," said a tart voice behind her. "If you'll give over hugging and kissing that dog, here's a cup of nice hot tea for you."

"Oh! Mrs. Barnes, how good of you."

Joyce scrambled to her feet. Mrs. Barnes was a big, formidable-looking woman. Beneath the exterior of a dragon she concealed an unexpectedly warm heart.

"A cup of hot tea never did anyone any harm," enunciated Mrs. Barnes, voicing the universal sentiment of her class.

Joyce sipped gratefully. Her landlady eyed her covertly.

"Any luck, miss—ma'am, I should say?"

Joyce shook her head, her face clouded over.

"Ah!" said Mrs. Barnes with a sigh. "Well, it doesn't seem to be what you might call a lucky day."

Joyce looked up sharply.

"Oh, Mrs. Barnes—you don't mean—"

Mrs. Barnes was nodding gloomily.

"Yes—it's Barnes. Out of work again. What we're going to do, I'm sure I don't know."

"Oh, Mrs. Barnes—I must—I mean you'll want—"

"Now don't you fret, my dear. I'm not denying but that I'd be glad if you'd found something— but if you haven't—you haven't. Have you finished that tea? I'll take the cup."

"Not quite."

"Ah!" said Mrs. Barnes accusingly. "You're going to give what's left to that dratted dog—I know you."

"Oh, please, Mrs. Barnes. Just a little drop. You don't mind really, do you?"

"It wouldn't be any use if I did. You're crazy about that cantankerous brute. Yes, that's what I say—and that's what he is. As near as nothing bit me this morning, he did."

"Oh, no, Mrs. Barnes! Terry wouldn't do such a thing."

"Growled at me—showed his teeth. I was just trying to see if there was anything could be done to those shoes of yours."

"He doesn't like anyone touching my things. He thinks he ought to guard them."

"Well, what does he want to think for? It isn't a dog's business to think. He'd be well enough in his proper place, tied up in the yard to keep off burglars. All this cuddling! He ought to be put away, miss—that's what I say."

"No, no, no. Never. Never!"

"Please yourself," said Mrs. Barnes. She took the cup from the table, retrieved the saucer from the floor where Terry had just finished his share, and stalked from the room.

"Terry," said Joyce. "Come here and talk to me. What are we going to do, my sweet?"

She settled herself in the rickety armchair, with Terry on her knees. She threw off her hat and leaned back. She put one of Terry's paws on each side of her neck and kissed him lovingly on his nose and between his eyes. Then she began talking to him in a soft low voice, twisting his ears gently between her fingers.

"What are we going to do about Mrs. Barnes, Terry? We owe her four weeks—and she's such a lamb, Terry—such a lamb. She'd never turn us out. But we can't take advantage of her being a lamb, Terry. We can't do that. Why does Barnes want to be out of work? I hate Barnes. He's always getting drunk. And if you're always getting drunk, you are usually out of work. But I don't get drunk, Terry, and yet I'm out of work.

"I can't leave you, darling. I can't leave you. There's not even anyone I could leave you with—nobody who'd be good to you. You're getting old, Terry—twelve years old—and nobody wants an old dog who's rather blind and a little deaf and a little—yes, just a little—bad-tempered. You're sweet to me, darling, but you're not sweet to

344

everyone, are you? You growl. It's because you know the world's turning against you. We've just got each other, haven't we, darling?"

Terry licked her cheek delicately.

"Talk to me, darling."

Terry gave a long lingering groan—almost a sigh, then he nuzzled his nose in behind Joyce's ear.

"You trust me, don't you, angel? You know I'd never leave you. But what are we going to do? We're right down to it now, Terry."

She settled back further in the chair, her eyes half closed.

"Do you remember, Terry, all the happy times we used to have? You and I and Michael and Daddy. Oh, Michael—Michael! It was his first leave, and he wanted to give me a present before he went back to France. And I told him not to be extravagant. And then we were down in the country—and it was all a surprise. He told me to look out of the window, and there you were, dancing up the path on a long lead. The funny little man who brought you, a little man who smelt of dogs. How he talked. 'The goods, that's what he is. Look at him, ma'am, ain't he a picture? I said to myself, as soon as the lady and gentleman see him they'll say: "That dog's the goods!" '"

"He kept on saying that—and we called you that for quite a long time—the Goods! Oh, Terry, you were such a darling of a puppy, with your little head on one side, wagging your absurd tail! And Michael went away to France and I had you—the darlingest dog in the world. You read all Michael's letters with me, didn't you? You'd sniff them, and I'd say—'From Master,' and you'd understand. We were so happy—so happy. You and Michael and I. And now Michael's dead, and you're old, and I—I'm so tired of being brave."

Terry licked her.

"You were there when the telegram came. If it hadn't been for you, Terry—if I hadn't had you to hold on to. . . ."

She stayed silent for some minutes.

"And we've been together ever since—been through all the ups and downs together—there have been a lot of downs, haven't there? And now we've come right up against it. There are only Michael's aunts, and they think I'm all right. They don't know he gambled that money away. We must never tell anyone that. *I* don't care—why shouldn't he? Everyone has to have some fault. He loved us both, Terry, and that's all that matters. His own relations were always inclined to be down on him and to say nasty things. We're not going to give them the chance. But I wish I had some relations of my own. It's very awkward having no relations at all.

"I'm so tired, Terry—and remarkably hungry. I can't believe I'm only twenty-nine—I feel sixty-nine. I'm not really brave—I only pretend to be.

346

And I'm getting awfully mean ideas. I walked all the way to Ealing yesterday to see Cousin Charlotte Green. I thought if I got there at half past twelve she'd be sure to ask me to stop to lunch. And then when I got to the house, I felt it was too cadging for anything. I just couldn't. So I walked all the way back. And that's foolish. You should be a determined cadger or else not even think of it. I don't think I'm a strong character."

Terry groaned again and put a black nose into Joyce's eye.

"You've got a lovely nose still, Terry—all cold like ice cream. Oh, I do love you so! I can't part from you. I can't have you 'put away,' I can't . . . I can't . . . I can't. . . ."

The warm tongue licked eagerly.

"You understand so, my sweet. You'd do anything to help Missus, wouldn't you?"

Terry clambered down and went unsteadily to a corner. He came back holding a battered bowl between his teeth.

Joyce was midway between tears and laughter.

Was he doing his only trick? The only thing he could think of to help Missus. "Oh, Terry—Terry—nobody shall part us! I'd do anything. Would I, though? One says that—and then when you're shown the thing, you say, 'I didn't mean anything like *that*.' Would I do anything?"

She got down on the floor beside the dog.

"You see, Terry, it's like this. Nursery governesses

can't have dogs, and companions to elderly ladies can't have dogs. Only married women can have dogs, Terry—little fluffy expensive dogs that they take shopping with them   and if one preferred an old blind terrier—well, why not?"

She stopped frowning and at that minute there was a double knock from below.

"The post. I wonder."

She jumped up and hurried down the stairs, returning with a letter.

"It might be. If only. . . ."

She tore it open.

Dear Madam,
    We have inspected the picture and our opinion is that it is not a genuine Cuyp and that its value is practically nil.
    Yours truly,
    Sloane & Ryder

Joyce stood holding it. When she spoke, her voice had changed.

"That's that," she said. "The last hope gone. But we won't be parted. There's a way—and it won't be cadging. Terry darling, I'm going out. I'll be back soon."

Joyce hurried down the stairs to where the telephone stood in a dark corner. There she asked for a certain number. A man's voice answered her, its tone changing as he realized her identity.

"Joyce, my dear girl. Come out and have some dinner and dance tonight."

"I can't," said Joyce lightly. "Nothing fit to wear."

And she smiled grimly as she thought of the empty pegs in the flimsy cupboard.

"How would it be if I came along and saw you now? What's the address? Good Lord, where's that? Rather come off your high horse, haven't you?"

"Completely."

"Well, you're frank about it. So long."

Arthur Halliday's car drew up outside the house about three quarters of an hour later. An awestruck Mrs. Barnes conducted him upstairs.

"My dear girl—what an awful hole. What on earth has got you into this mess?"

"Pride and a few other unprofitable emotions."

She spoke lightly enough; her eyes looked at the man opposite her sardonically.

Many people called Halliday handsome. He was a big man with square shoulders, fair, with small, very pale blue eyes and a heavy chin.

He sat down on the rickety chair she indicated.

"Well," he said thoughtfully. "I should say you'd had your lesson. I say—will that brute bite?"

"No, no, he's all right. I've trained him to be rather a—a watchdog."

Halliday was looking her up and down.

"Going to climb down, Joyce," he said softly. "Is that it?"

Joyce nodded.

"I told you before, my dear girl. I always get what I want in the end. I knew you'd come in time to see which way your bread was buttered."

"It's lucky for me you haven't changed your mind," said Joyce.

He looked at her suspiciously. With Joyce you never knew quite what she was driving at.

"You'll marry me?"

She nodded. "As soon as you please."

"The sooner, the better, in fact." He laughed, looking round the room. Joyce flushed.

"By the way, there's a condition."

"A condition?" He looked suspicious again.

"My dog. He must come with me."

"This old scarecrow? You can have any kind of a dog you choose. Don't spare expense."

"I want Terry."

"Oh! All right, please yourself."

Joyce was staring at him.

"You do know—don't you—that I don't love you? Not in the least."

"I'm not worrying about that. I'm not thin-skinned. But no hanky-panky, my girl. If you marry me, you play fair."

The colour flashed into Joyce's cheeks.

"You will have your money's worth," she said.

"What about a kiss now?"

He advanced upon her. She waited, smiling. He took her in his arms, kissing her face, her lips, her neck. She neither stiffened nor drew back. He released her at last.

"I'll get you a ring," he said. "What would you like, diamonds or pearls?"

"A ruby," said Joyce. "The largest ruby possible—the colour of blood."

"That's an odd idea."

"I should like it to be a contrast to the little half hoop of pearls that was all that Michael could afford to give me."

"Better luck this time, eh?"

"You put things wonderfully, Arthur."

Halliday went out chuckling.

"Terry," said Joyce. "Lick me—lick hard—all over my face and my neck—particularly my neck."

And as Terry obeyed, she murmured reflectively:

"Thinking of something else very hard—that's the only way. You'd never guess what I thought of—jam—jam in a grocer's shop. I said it over to myself. Strawberry, blackcurrant, raspberry, damson. And perhaps, Terry, he'll get tired of me fairly soon. I hope so, don't you? They say men do when they're married to you. But Michael wouldn't have tired of me—never—never—never—Oh! Michael. . . ."

Joyce rose the next morning with a heart like lead. She gave a deep sigh and immediately Terry, who

351

slept on her bed, had moved up and was kissing her affectionately.

"Oh, darling—darling! We've got to go through with it. But if only someting would happen. Terry darling, can't you help Missus? You would if you could, I know."

Mrs. Barnes brought up some tea and bread and butter and was heartily congratulatory.

"There now, ma'am, to think of you going to marry that gentleman. It was a Rolls he came in. It was indeed. It quite sobered Barnes up to think of one of them Rolls standing outside our door. Why, I declare that dog's sitting out on the window sill."

"He likes the sun," said Joyce. "But it's rather dangerous. Terry, come in."

"I'd have the poor dear put out of his misery if I was you," said Mrs. Barnes, "and get your gentleman to buy you one of them plumy dogs as ladies carry in their muffs."

Joyce smiled and called again to Terry. The dog rose awkwardly and just at that moment the noise of a dog fight rose from the street below. Terry craned his neck forward and added some brisk barking. The window sill was old and rotten. It tilted and Terry, too old and stiff to regain his balance, fell.

With a wild cry, Joyce ran down the stairs and out of the front door. In a few seconds she was kneeling by Terry's side. He was whining pitifully and his position showed her that he was badly hurt. She bent over him.

"Terry—Terry darling—darling, darling, darling—"

Very feebly, he tried to wag his tail.

"Terry boy—Missus will make you better—darling boy—"

A crowd, mainly composed of small boys, was pushing round.

"Fell from the window, 'e did."

"My, 'e looks bad."

"Broke 'is back as likely as not."

Joyce paid no heed.

"Mrs. Barnes, where's the nearest vet?"

"There's Jobling—round in Mere Street—if you could get him there."

"A taxi."

"Allow me."

It was the pleasant voice of an elderly man who had just alighted from a taxi. He knelt down by Terry and lifted the upper lip, then passed his hand down the dog's body.

"I'm afraid he may be bleeding internally," he said. "There don't seem to be any bones broken. We'd better get him along to the vet's."

Between them, he and Joyce lifted the dog. Terry gave a yelp of pain. His teeth met in Joyce's arm.

"Terry—it's all right—all right, old man."

They got him into the taxi and drove off. Joyce

wrapped a handkerchief round her arm in an absentminded way. Terry, distressed, tried to lick it.

"I know, darling; I know. You didn't mean to hurt me. It's all right. It's all right, Terry."

She stroked his head. The man opposite watched her but said nothing.

They arrived at the vet's fairly quickly and found him in. He was a red-faced man with an unsympathetic manner.

He handled Terry none too gently while Joyce stood by, agonized. The tears were running down her face. She kept on talking in a low, reassuring voice.

"It's all right, darling. It's all right. . . ."

The vet straightened himself.

"Impossible to say exactly. I must make a proper examination. You must leave him here."

"Oh! I can't."

"I'm afraid you must. I must take him below. I'll telephone you in—say—half an hour."

Sick at heart, Joyce gave in. She kissed Terry on his nose. Blind with tears, she stumbled down the steps. The man who had helped her was still there. She had forgotten him.

"The taxi's still here. I'll take you back." She shook her head.

"I'd rather walk."

"I'll walk with you."

He paid off the taxi. She was hardly conscious

of him as he walked quietly by her side without speaking. When they arrived at Mrs. Barnes', he spoke.

"Your wrist. You must see to it."

She looked down at it.

"Oh! That's all right."

"It wants properly washing and tying up. I'll come in with you."

He went with her up the stairs. She let him wash the place and bind it up with a clean handkerchief. She only said one thing.

"Terry didn't mean to do it. He would never, *never* mean to do it. He just didn't realize it was me. He must have been in dreadful pain."

"I'm afraid so, yes."

"And perhaps they're hurting him dreadfully now?"

"I'm sure that everything that can be done for him is being done. When the vet rings up, you can go and get him and nurse him here."

"Yes, of course."

The man paused, then moved towards the door.

"I hope it will be all right," he said awkwardly. "Good-bye."

"Good-bye."

Two or three minutes later it occurred to her that he had been kind and that she had never thanked him.

Mrs. Barnes appeared, cup in hand.

"Now, my poor lamb, a cup of hot tea. You're all to pieces, I can see that."

"Thank you, Mrs. Barnes, but I don't want any tea."

"It would do you good, dearie. Don't take on so now. The doggie will be all right and even if he isn't that gentleman of yours will give you a pretty new dog—"

"Don't, Mrs. Barnes. Don't. Please, if you don't mind, I'd rather be left alone."

"Well, I never—there's the telephone."

Joyce sped down to it like an arrow. She lifted the receiver. Mrs. Barnes panted down after her. She heard Joyce say, "Yes—speaking. What? Oh! Oh! Yes. Yes, thank you."

She put back the receiver. The face she turned to Mrs. Barnes startled that good woman. It seemed devoid of any life or expression.

"Terry's dead, Mrs. Barnes," she said. "He died alone there without me."

She went upstairs and, going into her room, shut the door very decisively.

"Well, I never," said Mrs. Barnes to the hall wallpaper.

Five minutes later she poked her head into the room. Joyce was sitting bolt upright in a chair. She was not crying.

"It's your gentleman, miss. Shall I send him up?"

A sudden light came into Joyce's eyes.

"Yes, please. I'd like to see him."

Halliday came in boisterously.

"Well, here we are. I haven't lost much time, have I? I'm prepared to carry you off from this dreadful place here and now. You can't stay here. Come on, get your things on."

"There's no need, Arthur."

"No need? What do you mean?"

"Terry's dead. I don't need to marry you now."

"What are you talking about?"

"My dog—Terry. He's dead. I was only marrying you so that we could be together."

Halliday stared at her, his face growing redder and redder. "You're mad."

"I daresay. People who love dogs are."

"You seriously tell me that you were only marrying me because—Oh, it's absurd!"

"Why did you think I was marrying you? You knew I hated you."

"You were marrying me because I could give you a jolly good time—and so I can."

"To my mind," said Joyce, "that is a much more revolting motive than mine. Anyway, it's off. I'm not marrying you!"

"Do you realize that you are treating me damned badly?"

She looked at him coolly but with such a blaze in her eyes that he drew back before it.

"I don't think so. I've heard you talk about getting a kick out of life. That's what you got out of me—and my dislike of you heightened it. You knew I hated you and you enjoyed it. When I let you kiss me yesterday, you were disappointed because I didn't flinch or wince. There's something brutal in you, Arthur, something cruel— something that likes hurting . . . Nobody could treat you as badly as you deserve. And now do you mind getting out of my room? I want it to myself."

He spluttered a little.

"Wh—what are you going to do? You've no money."

"That's my business. Please go."

"You little devil. You absolutely maddening little devil. You haven't done with me yet."

Joyce laughed.

The laugh routed him as nothing else had done. It was so unexpected. He went awkwardly down the stairs and drove away.

Joyce heaved a sigh. She pulled on her shabby black felt hat and in her turn went out. She walked along the streets mechanically, neither thinking nor feeling. Somewhere at the back of her mind there was pain—pain that she would presently feel, but for the moment everything was mercifully dulled.

She passed the Registry Office and hesitated.

"I must do something. There's the river, of course. I've often thought of that. Just finish everything. But it's so cold and wet. I don't think I'm brave enough. I'm not brave really."

She turned into the Registry Office.

"Good morning, Mrs. Lambert. I'm afraid we've no daily post."

"It doesn't matter," said Joyce. "I can take any kind of post now. My friend, whom I lived with, has—gone away."

"Then you'd consider going abroad?"

Joyce nodded.

"Yes, as far away as possible."

"Mr. Allaby is here now, as it happens, interviewing candidates. I'll send you in to him."

In another minute Joyce was sitting in a cubicle answering questions. Something about her interlocutor seemed vaguely familiar to her, but she could not place him. And then suddenly her mind awoke a little, aware that the last question was faintly out of the ordinary.

"Do you get on well with old ladies?" Mr. Allaby was asking.

Joyce smiled in spite of herself.

"I think so."

"You see my aunt, who lives with me, is rather difficult. She is very fond of me and she is a great dear really, but I fancy that a young woman might find her rather difficult sometimes."

"I think I'm patient and good-tempered," said Joyce, "and I have always got on with elderly people very well."

"You would have to do certain things for my aunt and otherwise you would have the charge of my little boy, who is three. His mother died a year ago."

"I see."

There was a pause.

"Then if you think you would like the post, we will consider that settled. We travel out next week. I will let you know the exact date, and I expect you would like a small advance of salary to fit yourself out."

"Thank you very much. That would be very kind of you."

They had both risen. Suddenly Mr. Allaby said awkwardly:

"I—hate to butt in—I mean I wish—I would like to know—I mean, is your dog all right?"

For the first time Joyce looked at him. The colour came into her face, her blue eyes deepened almost to black. She looked straight at him. She had thought him elderly, but he was not so very old. Hair turning grey, a pleasant weatherbeaten face, rather stooping shoulders, eyes that were brown and something of the shy kindliness of a dog's. He looked a little like a dog, Joyce thought.

"Oh, it's *you*," she said. "I thought afterwards—I never thanked you."

"No need. Didn't expect it. Knew what you were feeling like. What about the poor old chap?"

The tears came into Joyce's eyes. They streamed down her cheeks. Nothing on earth could have kept them back.

"He's dead."

"Oh!"

He said nothing else, but to Joyce that Oh! was one of the most comforting things she had ever heard. There was everything in it that couldn't be put into words.

After a minute or two he said jerkily:

"Matter of fact, I had a dog. Died two years ago. Was with a crowd of people at the time who couldn't understand making heavy weather about it. Pretty rotten to have to carry on as though nothing had happened."

Joyce nodded.

"I *know*—" said Mr. Allaby.

He took her hand, squeezed it hard and dropped it. He went out of the little cubicle. Joyce followed in a minute or two and fixed up various details with the ladylike person. When she arrived home, Mrs. Barnes met her on the doorstep with that relish in gloom typical of her class.

"They've sent the poor little doggie's body home," she announced. "It's up in your room. I was saying to Barnes, and he's ready to dig a nice little hole in the back garden—"

About the Author

Agatha Christie is the most widely published author of all time and in any language, outsold only by the Bible and Shakespeare. Her books have sold more than a billion copies in English and another billion in a hundred foreign languages. She is the author of eighty crime novels and short-story collections, nineteen plays, two memoirs, and six novels written under the name Mary Westmacott.

She first tried her hand at detective fiction while working in a hospital dispensary during World War I, creating the now legendary Hercule Poirot with her debut novel *The Mysterious Affair at Styles*. With *The Murder at the Vicarage*, published in 1930, she introduced another beloved sleuth, Miss Jane Marple. Additional series characters include the husband-and-wife crime-fighting team of Tommy and Tuppence Beresford, private investigator Parker Pyne, and Scotland Yard detectives Superintendent Battle and Inspector Japp.

Many of Christie's novels and short stories were adapted into plays, films, and television series. *The Mousetrap*, her most famous play of all, opened in 1952 and is the longest-running play in history. Among her best-known film adaptations are *Murder on the Orient Express* (1974) and *Death on the Nile* (1978), with Albert Finney and Peter Ustinov playing Hercule Poirot, respectively. On the small screen Poirot has been most memorably portrayed by David Suchet, and Miss Marple by Joan Hickson and subsequently Geraldine McEwan and Julia McKenzie.

Christie was first married to Archibald Christie and then to archaeologist Sir Max Mallowan, whom she accompanied on expeditions to countries that would also serve as the settings for many of her novels. In 1971 she achieved one of Britain's highest honors when she was made a Dame of the British Empire. She died in 1976 at the age of eighty-five. Her one hundred and twentieth anniversary was celebrated around the world in 2010.

www.AgathaChristie.com

Also by Agatha Christie and available from Center Point Large Print:

Crooked House
They Came to Baghdad
Endless Night
Ordeal by Innocence
Towards Zero
Death Comes as the End
The Pale Horse
Destination Unknown
Parker Pyne Investigates
The Secret of Chimneys
The Seven Dials Mystery
The Sittaford Mystery
Why Didn't They Ask Evans?
The Mysterious Mr. Quin
Sparkling Cyanide
The Harlequin Tea Set and Other Stories
The Man in the Brown Suit
Double Sin and Other Stories
Three Blind Mice and Other Stories
The Regatta Mystery and Other Stories
The Witness for the Prosecution
  and Other Stories
Murder Is Easy
Passenger to Frankfurt

Miss Marple Mystery Series:
The Murder at the Vicarage
The Body in the Library
The Moving Finger
A Murder Is Announced
They Do It with Mirrors
4:50 from Paddington
A Caribbean Mystery
A Pocket Full of Rye
At Bertram's Hotel
Nemesis
Miss Marple: The Complete Short Stories
The Mirror Crack'd from Side to Side

Hercule Poirot Mystery Series:
The Murder of Roger Ackroyd
Death on the Nile
The A.B.C. Murders
Five Little Pigs
The Big Four
Poirot Investigates
Dead Man's Folly
One, Two, Buckle My Shoe
Murder in Mesopotamia
Lord Edgware Dies
Taken at the Flood
The Murder on the Links
The Hollow
Hallowe'en Party
After the Funeral
Cards on the Table
Cat Among the Pigeons
Death in the Clouds

Dumb Witness
The Clocks
Third Girl
Three Act Tragedy
Sad Cypress
Appointment with Death
Evil Under the Sun
Hickory Dickory Dock
The Mysterious Affair at Styles
The Mystery of the Blue Train
Peril at End House
Murder in the Mews
Hercule Poirot's Christmas
The Labors of Hercules
Mrs. McGinty's Dead
The Under Dog and Other Stories

Tommy and Tuppence Mystery Series:
The Secret Adversary
N or M?
By the Pricking of My Thumbs
Partners in Crime
Postern of Fate

Center Point Large Print
600 Brooks Road / PO Box 1
Thorndike ME 04986-0001 USA

(207) 568-3717

US & Canada:
1 800 929-9108
www.centerpointlargeprint.com